Joanna Buckley is an author based in Melbourne. She has a background in creating short stories, poetry, social media content and educational materials, and has also worked as a copywriter and editor. Joanna is a mother of three and a part-time careers counsellor, and *Lily Harford's Last Request* is her first novel.

Lily Harford's Last Request

JOANNA BUCKLEY

FICTION

First Published 2022
First Australian Paperback Edition 2022
ISBN 9781867232469

LILY HARFORD'S LAST REQUEST
© 2022 Joanna Buckley
Australian Copyright 2022
New Zealand Copyright 2022

Published by
HQ Fiction
An imprint of Harlequin Enterprises (Australia) Pty Limited (ABN 47 001 180 918),
a subsidiary of HarperCollins Publishers Australia Pty Limited (ABN 36 009 913 517)
Level 13, 201 Elizabeth St
SYDNEY NSW 2000
AUSTRALIA

A catalogue record for this book is available from the National Library of Australia
www.librariesaustralia.nla.gov.au

Printed and bound in Australia by McPherson's Printing Group

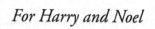

For Harry and Noel

NEW YEAR'S DAY 2008

Lily

I should have been expecting it, but then there'd never
been any particular time frame. Probably best that way, as
it would be too much to anticipate my own death all of the
time.

Normally I'd have another half hour of sleep before waking to the first blushes of dawn across Finn Bay, heralded
by the squawks of lorikeets in the garden outside my room.
Even then, I'd resist full consciousness, aware of my body
nestled into the slight dip of the mattress. The sun's rays
would begin to push into my room through a gap between
the heavy night drapes and for a while would strike at just
the right angle, allowing me to focus on the warmth delivered to the paper-thin and rucked skin of my right side.
This sensation and the birdsong afford me two of life's few

remaining pleasures. In the still-subdued light I'd let myself drift in and out, fully aware of my aged body's tender pressure points, but too dozy to let myself care.

But it's still dark, and I don't hear the sound of my door swinging on its hinges. The first indication I'm not alone is when a shock of cool, silky material is contoured around my nose, cheeks and mouth, jolting me from my stupor. I know from the overpowering smell of lavender that the fabric belongs to a cushion, a Christmas gift designed to help me sleep. How fitting.

My eyelids shoot open but the cushion blocks the face of my assailant. I don't need my eyes, though, to tell me whose weight is being used to smother me, who has been kind and brave enough to agree to perform this ultimate, unselfish act of love. My memory might be rotting away but I've known this moment was coming, and I welcome it.

For a short time I don't move, or try to breathe. I feel a humbling gratitude to my saviour for having the courage to bestow on me the gift of death. I want to cry for the sweet relief that will soon be granted to me. I will, as promised by our pact, be spared dementia's heartless progression. The pressure on my face builds, and it hurts. But I don't mind the pain. I'm counting on the fact that my collaborator wants this to be over quickly, before their resolve turns to dust. As if from a vast distance, I hear their grunts of effort and, like a pinprick of light in a black tunnel, something about the sound catches my attention. It's not right, not expected …

Like an absurd, macabre duet, my own groan, a visceral but muffled whimper, rises from somewhere in the depths of my being. The stench of lavender fills my nostrils, burning my throat, saturating my lungs. I feel a rising panic, a desperate need to inhale. Fighting with everything I have, I kick out with adrenaline-fuelled violence. My bladder releases its warm contents. My spindly legs struggle against the sheet, now a cruel straitjacket. I try to wriggle sideways while scrabbling and clawing at the cushion but the material is slippery and, as my left arm is still without strength, I can't grasp it. Please, whoever you are, let me die now, or let me breathe. I never imagined this terror. Have mercy on me.

I'm fading, black turning to white as a sense of peace washes through me. I let go, surrendering once again to the prospect, the relief, of death. My core, in its original and pure form, will soon be free. Using every ounce of strength I whisper, the words of my request floating along on the river of what I pray will be my last exhalation. *Please ... don't ... stop ...*

1999

The change room's heavy burgundy curtain traps us in a musty fug of dust-ridden carpet and stale sweat and, despite my best intentions, the first grumblings of impatience niggle my insides. I watch on with amusement though, as my daughter wrestles with a shiny, cross-strapped dress in custard yellow that is only part way over her head. The two of them seem to be in a stalemate.

This must surely be the twentieth outfit Pauline has tried on. Still, I'm delighted the two of us continue to share this kind of activity together.

'Mum, I think I'm stuck.'

I can't help but smile at Pauline's muffled plea for help. She really has got herself into a tangle of shoulder straps and arm- and neck-holes.

'Here, let me help,' I offer, and, as we attempt to determine which bit of dress is supposed to go where, my daughter's laughter is infectious. 'I think you need to take it back up over your head and start again,' I suggest, just as her face and hands burst through the garment in triumph.

'I thought I'd be stuck in there forever,' she says, looking flushed but highly entertained. She turns to examine herself in the mirror, smoothing the dress's material over her thighs as her expression falls into a mix of bemusement and analysis. 'I quite like the colour on me, but there should be a danger warning on the label: *Beware. This garment is not for the faint-hearted.*' She twists to inspect the rear view. 'Seriously, though, what do you think?' she asks, striking a flamenco-like pose. 'Have we finally nailed it with this one?'

Pauline's always appreciated honesty over platitudes so I don't feel I have to tiptoe around her. 'After all that effort, I hate to say it but I think you can do better. The shape is nothing special on you. And in this humidity a synthetic fabric isn't the best choice.'

Pauline flips up the hem in search of a label. 'You're right. Ninety-five per cent rayon. I'd be sweating up a storm.'

'Maybe we should just get in the car and drive to Rorook,' I suggest. 'Most of the shops there are open until five-thirty.'

'I'd love to, Mum, but I've got a hair appointment at two and Rachel's bringing her new boyfriend over this afternoon to meet me and Sam. She's made a fancy cake and everything. She might really like this one. Christos, I think his name is.'

'My granddaughter's been baking? In this weather?'

Pauline rolls her eyes with a small smile. 'Yeah, well, young love,' she says before raising her arms above her head. 'Back into battle, then?'

I laugh and help her navigate her way free of the dress. 'Remember when you were little, how you used to get all manner of ingredients out of the pantry and invent your own recipes? There was always a hell of a mess but it was nothing if not entertaining.'

'Oh god. You were so patient with me.' Pauline deftly flips the garment right side out and gives it a solid flick. 'You still are. Even now, you're happy to come along and do this,' she adds, gesturing with the polyester number towards the other dresses fighting for space on the *No* hook. 'And I really value your input.'

A familiar current of maternal love drenches my body. I place my hand on Pauline's shoulder. 'Even at seventy-nine?' I fish.

'Yes, so don't you go getting old on me,' Pauline says with uncharacteristic solemnity. 'I need you for a few good years yet.'

I raise my eyebrows. 'You do realise I'm already pretty ancient, don't you?'

'On paper, maybe, but honestly I don't think of you that way, Mum.'

'Thanks, darling. And touch wood my good health keeps going.' I reach for the timber frame of the change room's mirror, even though I don't believe in that superstitious nonsense.

In the end my daughter settles on a conservative knee-length black skirt with a floral halter-neck top that shows off her square shoulders and athletic figure.

'Let me pay,' I offer as we approach the counter. 'As a reward.'

Pauline hands the items over to the cashier. 'Reward?' she asks, smiling at me through a frown. 'What for?'

'Maybe "reward" isn't the right term. As a congratulations then. For your promotion to principal. You deserve it after two decades of service to Glenmore. That's quite an achievement.' I know I've laden Pauline, especially as an only child, with the burden of expectation that she will have the same ambition and work ethic as me. She could well have rebelled against that. Instead, she has always risen to challenges, from the day she could crawl. But I'm so proud that her capability and drive haven't come at the cost of a beautiful heart. 'So, let me buy these for you.'

'Are you sure?'

I reply by handing over my credit card and she doesn't protest.

We emerge into blue-sky brightness flooding the main street. Pauline reaches for her sunglasses before looking at her watch. 'What do you have on for the rest of the day?'

I used to worry, before I retired, that I'd dread being asked that question. That I'd feel lost without the daily invigoration and stimulation of clients and conferences and work colleagues. But it turns out that in the decade and a half since I hung up my accounting boots I've never been bored. And certainly not dispirited. Without having to go out of my way to keep busy, I find each day seems to present necessary tasks to undertake, or unforeseen opportunities to grasp, or simply quiet moments to surrender to, just as and when I need them.

I do a quick run over my mental checklist. 'I need to pop into the greengrocer for a few things and then thought I might drive out to the nursery for some mulch. Other than that, just a bit of house-cleaning and bill-paying.'

Pauline looks across the road to the bay, sparkling under a determined summer sun, and I follow suit. Between us and the water, the esplanade's casuarinas provide fine slivers of shade and a handsome green curtain against the blue of the Pacific. Half a kilometre away to our right the headland stands with modest majesty, and about the same distance to our left the almost-black rocky platforms defining the bay's northern end are today playing host to a handful of fishermen.

I hear Pauline fill her lungs and I know what my girl is thinking before she even speaks.

'After a lifetime of this in my backyard, I never get sick of it,' she says, spreading her arms as if inviting the view for a hug. 'It's like a tonic. How did we get so lucky as to live in Finn Bay?'

I sigh my agreement as we continue to stare out to the ocean. Three cars in succession drive past, their pace languid as, after all, it takes only twenty seconds to get from one end of the main street to the other.

The sun bites at my skin, breaking the reverie. I reach for Pauline's hand and give it a light squeeze. 'Well, you'd better get going. Have a wonderful time tonight and don't let the students get up to too much mischief on their big night.' I kiss her on the cheek and we embrace.

'Thanks for your help, and for the outfit,' she says before mumbling more quietly in my ear, 'You're my rock, Mum.'

And despite the heat doing its best to get the better of us, we shuffle even closer, and being in her arms is like finding home.

MONDAY 5 JUNE 2006

Pauline

From her vantage point on the stage and flanked by fellow senior staff, Pauline stared out over the mass of beautiful, uninterested young people in a sea of Glenmore College blazers. The smell of wet wool permeated the hall as steady rain drummed on its tin roof with gentle persistence.

The school captain stood at the microphone, delivering the week's notices in a way that indicated bored confidence. From behind her, Pauline observed the shortness of the girl's skirt, the way her upper thighs were almost fully exposed. The hem length was, she knew, a nod to unfurling sexuality and independence, a statement of rebellion from someone who was, to be fair, almost an adult.

Still, any shorter and ...

As if to highlight the contrast, Pauline sat ramrod straight, shins pressed snugly together and legs crossed just so at the ankles. Her knee-length linen dress, bought on a whim, scratched uncomfortably on the backs of her legs and she was regretting having pulled her hair into a too-tight pony-tail she was sure would soon give her a headache.

The students muttered and shifted, their restlessness no doubt exacerbated by the equally unsettled weather. Dragged down by a level of weariness unfamiliar to her and certainly out of place this early in the school year, Pauline sighed, the heavy exhalation involuntarily rounding her shoulders.

'You okay?' Janet leaned in, her whisper heavy with concern.

Inwardly cursing at having let her guard down, Pauline delivered her deputy and long-time friend a grateful nod. She would pull herself together, of course, as she always did. But she felt a mounting dread at the thought of visiting her mother later in the day to bring up the topic of a care home.

The school captain's words slid in and out of focus as Pauline's thoughts shifted to ones of her mother at the age Pauline was now. In her mid fifties, Lily had well and truly reached her full professional stride. A femininely handsome woman, she had always been a living embodiment of the traits she'd espoused to Pauline from a young age – strength and capability, confidence and willpower, optimism and control. Solid at every turn. And in recent years a long-retired great-grandmother, still so vibrant, so *hard wearing*. Not like now.

Pauline's attention landed back in the auditorium with an internal thud as she felt the upward pressure of Janet's palm under her elbow. Registering the animated babble as pupils began to pour out of the hall's side and back doors, Pauline blinked then stood.

'Do you have a class today?' Janet asked as the two of them made their own exit.

Pauline glanced skyward. The rain had eased into a barely noticeable misty drizzle. 'Just my Year 12s.' They turned towards their offices in the administration block.

'No-one expects you to take on a history class every year. You don't need to keep proving yourself, you know.'

Pauline kept her eyes forward. 'You know as well as I do that that's not true.'

'I don't know any such thing,' Janet said firmly. 'It's you that puts such ridiculous pressure on yourself.'

Pauline stopped at the base of the administration building's wide entrance steps and looked up. Soaring rectangular windows symmetrically interrupted tangerine-coloured bricks, the structure's Art Deco facade reminding her proudly of the college's rich history. She turned to her deputy and smiled, aware her face was relaxing, her furrowed brow releasing for the first time since she'd woken up. 'Jan, it's in my DNA,' she said, bumping her shoulder good-naturedly into Janet's. 'But thank you for caring. You're a good friend.'

Janet blushed. 'Do you want to go over the board meeting agenda now?' she asked as they climbed the steps. 'I'm not teaching until third period.'

'Yes, it needs to go out before lunch. I've had the chairman emailing me – you know how he gets. Let's start the day on the front foot.' Pauline could hear her voice as they passed through the school's reception area but it seemed to belong to someone else, someone in control.

Floor-to-ceiling bookshelves covered one wall of Pauline's office, while on either side of the opposite window framed portraits of past principals in academic gowns kept tabs on their old headquarters and its current occupant. Janet sat across from Pauline at the oversized timber desk positioned in the room's centre, and looked sideways at the row of portraits. 'Their expressions range from compassion to downright disapproval, don't they? But I bet the old buggers all had amazing wives taking care of everything else for them.'

Pauline threw a glance towards her predecessors, only managing a not-quite-smile. 'Well, Sam helped a lot with Rachel over the years. As did Mum.'

'True. How's your mum doing these days?'

Pauline flinched. Janet wasn't to know this subject was a touchy one of late, a bruise that hurt when prodded, even gently. She hadn't told Janet about her mother's recent memory lapses. How she'd left the gas stove on multiple times. How she'd lost her way when driving to Glenmore College for her monthly lunch with Pauline, having to ask a passing man for directions. Fuelled by worry about that incident, Rachel had got stuck into her grandmother. 'Nana-Lily, this is serious. Mum was beside herself. What if you'd driven the wrong way and got lost heaven knows where? What if that guy had been, you know, a total creep?'

Unable to bring herself to talk about her mother's mental deterioration, to give it life, Pauline decided instead to take the easier angle. The half-truth. She shifted a little in her seat. 'Mum's hip's not the best and she's actually got pretty bad arthritis. You'd be shocked if you saw her fingers, especially on her left hand. They're bowed and twisted like she's permanently about to grab an apple out of a bowl,' she said, demonstrating the claw-like effect. 'On top of dealing with the constant pain, her rheumatologist has said she should seriously consider giving up driving.'

'Oh, that's awful for her. I had no idea.' Janet frowned. 'So without her own wheels, does that mean you'll be the one mostly transporting her around?'

'Probably. I already go over to King Street several times a week, pick up her laundry, drop over frozen meals, run the vacuum over. Being her taxi on top of that, and this job, as well as trying to spend some time with Rachel and the little ones …' Pauline trailed off, blinking the self-pity away.

'It's hard when everything falls on you.'

'Oh, look, I honestly don't mind. Life is busy but that's the way I like it. And Mum won't let this setback stop her from enjoying life. It's just that I think she'll have to move.'

Pauline experienced a quick, tiny quiver in her chest at the thought, akin to zipping shrapnel clipping her heart. 'Sam and I have been looking at a nearby facility for her, ideally Blue Vista – you know, the care home on Finn Bay's headland? It has fabulous views and doesn't seem, well, as extreme a step as a full-on nursing home.'

'It's always a massive adjustment to leave your own home.' Janet reached over the desk and rested her hand on Pauline's forearm. 'But at least she would still be close by to you.'

Pauline nodded. 'I'm just praying she'll at least see the sense in selling up and moving to somewhere she'll be looked after properly. King Street is a beautiful old home but just not suitable any more. Too big. Too much garden. Too many steps to even just get up to the front door. I'm heading there after work to talk with her about it.'

'Is there anything I can do?'

Tears perilously close to the surface, Pauline withdrew her arm. She needed to pull herself together and shift her focus. Wallowing would achieve nothing. That's what her mother would expect of her, after all – to dust herself off and just get on with things.

'Oh … I'm all right. Exhausted from adding a few extra k's to my runs this week, but nothing a good night's sleep won't fix.'

Janet looked at Pauline with kindly scepticism. 'I didn't realise how much strain you've been under, Leeny.'

The affectionate nickname threw Pauline, softening her, and for a moment something in her begged for permission to purge. She looked towards the window, sensing she had to tread carefully or risk the floodgates bursting open. 'Mum getting old is a bit depressing, that's all. And it's not just that. It's the constant worry that anything could go pear-shaped out there,' she said, pointing with her thumb towards the window. 'You know, that one of the teaching staff might seriously snap from the stress, or a parent will sue us for any number of things, or,' she added, dropping her voice, 'that there'll be another tragedy like Tom. I don't know – I can do the right thing ninety-nine per cent of the time but I can't control everything. It's scary.'

'But that's always been the case, and you've never let it get to you before. You're a perfectionist, but you're not usually a worry wart.'

Pauline's eyes widened before Janet continued. 'Don't look at me like that. You *do* set high standards. But I guess if you're dealing with things on the home front, it's under-standable stuff at work will get under your skin more than it normally would. You're only human.'

Pauline experienced a sudden urgent need to be on her own, to retreat once more beneath the safety of her usual reliable armour. The conversation with Janet was stirring up thoughts and weaknesses she'd rather remained well below the surface. 'Come on,' she said, putting her best game face on. 'I'm being silly and melodramatic. Let's get that agenda finalised ...'

Afterwards, as Pauline sat alone, she recalled the shocking incident just two years ago when Tom Beresford, a middle-school student, had hanged himself after the school had failed to pick up on low-level but persistent bullying. Her customary positivity had been shaken to its core. Tom's distraught, grey-faced father had spat at Pauline at the funeral. Wiping the back of his hand across his mouth he'd hissed, 'You negligent bitch. You might as well have killed Tommy yourself.' No litigation had ensued but she was still haunted by the image of young Tom, with his freckles and an expression always seeming somehow apologetic, passing her office window every Tuesday afternoon on his way to the music rooms. She felt an almost physical need to reach out for his ghost, to pull him in to her and whisper her regrets.

And now her strength was again being tested, this time by her mother's recent decline.

Reading over her punishing calendar for the week, Pauline knew that, somehow, she had to push herself through the rest of the day, present a veneer of normality and put her mind to the jobs needing attention. After all, they were nothing compared to the heartbreaking task she was due to carry out later that afternoon.

Lily

I haven't travelled as much as I'd like, but Finn Bay must surely be one of the earth's most triumphant jewels. Its bay's gentle waves, the water clear as glass, a perfect arc of soft, white beach spooned at its southern end by an almost untouched jungle of thick vegetation home to all manner of lizards, butterflies and birds. The town has been an idyllic place in which to grow up and grow old, a tight-knit community where people know each other and look out for their neighbour, and until recently I felt safe. It was an unconscious thing, of course. I suppose it would be more accurate to say that I didn't feel unsafe. Life was in equilibrium. But now? I'm teetering on less certain ground.

It's a Monday afternoon and Pauline, having dropped in on her way home from work, leans against the kitchen sink, her body turned sideways to me, her arms crossed as she watches the kettle coming to the boil. I sit at the kitchen table, trying to read her mood. We've agreed to talk about my living arrangements today and I'm hoping she'll be open to my thoughts.

'You're looking smart in pink. Is that dress new?'

Pauline turns to face me. 'Fairly. It's a bit uncomfortable, though. I should have sought your opinion first – you would have warned me against linen this scratchy.'

'Well, I like the cut of it. It looks very professional,' I say with pride.

'Well, I learned from the best.'

The compliment warms me. 'Thanks, darling. It's just a shame the body underneath my clothes has fallen victim to time,' I say, sighing. 'About all I recognise in the mirror these days are my green eyes.'

Pauline lifts the whistling kettle off the stove. 'You know what else hasn't changed one bit? Your voice. It's still got such oomph.'

'It's funny you should say that – and I wouldn't admit this to anyone else – but sometimes I close my eyes and say something, just to allow myself the momentary fantasy that it's a youthful me uttering the words. I know that sounds stupid and foolish but in lots of ways, *inside*, I don't feel all that different to when I was young.'

'It's not silly at all, Mum. You're still the same you, regardless of a few wrinkles. Nothing can change that.'

The optimism of her words hangs in the air for too long before she breaks the silence. 'How have you been doing the last few days?' She's focusing on dipping tea bags in both cups simultaneously.

'Oh, not too bad. Usual aches and pains, especially these bloody hands,' I reply, presenting them as evidence. 'But old age was never going to be a walk in the park, I suppose.'

As Pauline sets down two steaming cups on the table-cloth, I notice how drained and pale she looks. I'm keen to mull over my living situation with her but feel Pauline's pallor needs attention first. 'Is everything all right at work?' I ask, prising a biscuit from the packet of digestives lying open in front of me.

She turns towards the fridge and extracts an open milk carton. After sniffing its contents, the action offensive in its implication, she slops a little into both cups and sits herself down. 'Oh, I suppose so. Business as usual, I guess.'

I examine the face I know so well. Framed by dark hair inherited from a father about whom she knew almost nothing, it's bird-like and can easily appear harsh and judging, but behind the dark eyes there's a caring and more brittle persona than most people realise. She's hiding something, and she knows that I know and that I won't be satisfied until she coughs up.

'Being principal's a fantastic job, Mum, don't get me wrong. But the role seems to grow every year. More compliance, more unpredictability, more appointments, more legal crap … the scope of the job has become so huge. One day I'm meeting with a psychiatrist to get a report on a student with serious mental health issues, but whose parents are in complete bloody denial. The next, I'm having to fight tooth and nail with the board to get the funds for something that's so overdue for replacement or repair that it's not funny. I always seem to be fighting fires. Last year I didn't achieve half of my goals, and I can't see it being any better this year.'

Pauline's voice has been rising and she is jiggling her knee in a way that tells me she's very wound up. I want to embrace her but know it's best to just let her keep venting.

'Between staff meetings, information nights, concerts and plays – it's all part of the role and I don't mind the hours, it's diverse and challenging – I even had a parent threaten me with racial discrimination the other day because his son wasn't picked as next year's swimming captain. Can you believe it?'

Her voice catches and she finally takes a breath. While I calculate how best to placate my overwrought daughter, I sip my tea. It's still scorching but I like it that way.

More softly she adds, 'Sometimes I just wish I could retire and leave someone else to deal with it all.'

'I think the world in general is getting more hectic. I don't know how you keep up with all the changes. I could never have done what you do. Such a big responsibility, all those students and teachers and support staff ...'

'You can talk, Mum. You ran your own company, for heaven's sake.'

I give a little nod of appreciation for the recognition. 'Well, it was just a small concern, really. At its peak I still only employed half a dozen people. And that was a long time ago. Things were so much simpler then.' For a moment I'm back inside Harford Accounting Services. I blink and focus my thoughts back onto my daughter. 'But you're only fifty-five, Pauline. Anyway, could you afford to stop work right now?'

'You know I couldn't. We're still scraping our way back from Sam's idiotic business venture.' Her eyes flick to the ceiling and back in disgust.

I won't take the bait on the topic of my son-in-law or their financial situation. 'Can't you cut back a bit then? You work such long hours. Sam says you're in there every second Saturday and three nights a week. It's great for the school but it can't be good for your marriage.'

My daughter exhales noisily, bordering on a snort. 'Those hours go with the job, so no. And it's not so much that anyway. It's more that even with all the best policies and procedures in place, there's such a huge, I don't know, human factor. I'm dealing with kids, parents, teachers; and people are so fickle and unpredictable. It's unnerving.'

Pauline picks up her teacup and cradles it in both hands as if to leach the heat into her body as a salve. She stares at the vapour still rising from the brew. What can I say to restore a sense of calm in her? I might be the one increasingly needing help these days, but right now I need to be the one caring for her.

'There are some things you can't control,' I say. 'You do what you can, my darling, so don't be so hard on yourself.'

This seems to have no placating effect. Pauline lifts her head and looks at me, her eyebrows rising to a significant curve. 'You're the second person to say that to me today. But it's a bit rich coming from you, isn't it?'

I flinch. This is a stab I didn't see coming. 'I only ever wanted you to do your best, Pauline. Hard work pays off. I don't think that's such a bad tenet to instil in your child, is it?'

My girl finally takes a sip of her drink, wincing at its temperature. I've already drunk a third of mine. I lean forward and tenderly alight my crooked fingers onto my daughter's. She seems so delicate, so in need of gentle handling, like a twitchy colt. She puts her cup down and briefly places her other hand on top of mine. Picking up her tea again she blows, sending ripples across its surface. It seems to release some tension.

'And it doesn't help that I'm worried about you,' she says.

Ah. So work isn't the only thing eating at her. I should have known. She's never been one to let her career get the better of her. But I'm sure my proposal will allay her concerns about me.

'I know you are. And I've been doing a lot of thinking on this matter. It would be ridiculous to pretend that living here, alone, can continue for much longer.'

Pauline's shoulders visibly drop as if she'd braced herself for a physical fight that never materialised. Colour returns to her face. Whether it's the tea warming her or a reaction to my declaration, I can't tell. She takes a biscuit and dunks it into her cup. It hovers in the air as a surge of words barrels out.

'That's great, Mum. I can't believe you're being so sensible about this, considering the whole driving thing, trying to maintain the garden, and your hip. The family is worried you might fall, not just getting up and down the front steps but in general, and a broken hip can be the beginning of the end. And we – I – want you around as long as possible.'

She smiles with affection before a different expression settles on her face. I recognise it immediately. It's the same one she used on me when she was nineteen, just before she broke the news that she was moving away to study, warning me I wasn't going to like what I was about to hear.

'Sam and I are happy to do the research and come up with a short list of facilities, and in the meantime you could sort through your things and do a bit of decluttering in preparation. I admit I've wanted to raise this with you for a while. This house is wonderful, but it's showing its age. It needs repainting outside and in, and some proper aircon installed, and with so many front steps ... it's really not right for you any more.'

My pulse skyrockets. I hold my breath mid-inhalation. Her plans and mine are, it's immediately clear, poles apart. I've conceded I can no longer fully look after or transport myself, but I just wanted to get some hired help in. Moving out of King Street, this old but proud Queenslander home I've single-handedly raised her in, into a bloody retirement village, or worse? Not on your nelly. My smile retracts like a touched anemone.

'I hope you're joking,' I snap, spilling the remaining contents of my cup as I unceremoniously slam it onto the table.

Pauline looks bewildered. 'But, Mum, it's not just those things. Maybe you don't realise how muddled you've been recently. I just thought, *we* just thought ...'

'What, that because my memory's not as sharp as it used to be, you lot want to dump me in a nursing home?' Pauline visibly recoils, but I won't let her win this one. 'I will not be degraded like that, Pauline.'

'Mum, this is my childhood home and I'll miss it as much as you will. You know we'd have you move in with us, but the stairs would be too difficult; and we'd build a granny flat if our block was flatter. So I'm sorry, but I think you need to consider other options.'

Her exasperation is all too evident. She's actually serious about me selling this house, the home that sheltered and watched over her as she grew up. The place where she sent well-meaning notes out into the air, her six-year-old fingers barely stretching across four piano keys. Where she drew squiggles on an A-frame blackboard set up on the back verandah, pretending to be the teacher in an imaginary class-room. Where she paraded around the living room singing a unique rendition of 'I Want to Hold Your Hand'. She'd used a spatula as a microphone and had me in stitches of laughter before I'd joined in and performed my own best John Lennon impersonation.

My jaw clenches. Just like in business, though, I need to remain calm and level-headed. I draw a long, sluggish breath, despite my mind whirring. I admit my memory's been having fun of late, teasing me mercilessly. Words, names and recent events sometimes tiptoe in towards me, then, when they're close enough to grasp, cruelly leap away again to a hidey-hole in the back of my brain. Just the other day I'd got a bit confused in the main street and old Jim Parker's boy had pointed me in the right direction, bless him. Jim was a client of mine who ran a boat yard back in the seventies. Knew everything there is to know about boats but absolutely nothing about accounting.

There's a sinking, heavy feeling in my stomach as real-ity hits me. Maybe I'm worse than I realised. My daughter certainly thinks I'm losing my marbles. What if she's right? As individual, unrelated incidents my memory lapses could easily mean nothing. Banded together, however, maybe to those around me they are like pieces of a larger jigsaw, a picture of a woman in mental decline.

I shudder as I stare at Pauline, dark thoughts niggling. I'm scared and embarrassed. I've seen this insidious afflic-tion of memory firsthand. It starts as something irritating but manageable, even at times a little bit amusing perhaps, but ends with the person disappearing, replaced by a husk that looks and breathes like a human but recognises no-one, not even itself.

Frantically, I search for a viable compromise. 'All right, I concede this house has become too much for me to manage alone and that "other options", as you say, are needed. So what about those villa units they're building overlooking the foreshore?' That strong voice of mine is holding true but inside I'm crumbling.

I can see Pauline reworking what she'd been about to say, so take the opportunity to press on, aware I'm trying to convince myself as much as her. 'If I can get a unit with a small courtyard garden I could still have my carnations and put in annuals. But I'll need a big enough dining area to still be able to have you all around for lunch. I won't compromise on that. We'll have to take a look at the architect's designs. You can save a lot buying off the plan ...'

Interrupting me before I can finish, my daughter pushes her chair back. Its feet scrape on the floorboards, the sound grating. Without asking if I'd like to drink the rest of my tea, she sweeps up the two cups and transports them to the sink before returning for the biscuits, placing them back in the pantry cupboard. I stubbornly resume talking to Pauline's back as she busily washes the cups in silence.

'I wouldn't expect you to run around after me. I want to still be a bit independent and I know how much you have on your plate these days. Someone from the council could be arranged to drop by each day to look in on me, perhaps do some cleaning; even cook me a meal now and then. I've got more than enough savings. Maybe Sam knows a contact there. Meals on Wheels, perhaps. And those units are so close to everything that I wouldn't need a car.'

The more I imagine this set-up, trying it on in my mind to see how it fits, the more it seems plausible. In fact, good god, I need to get a grip. This could even be a little bit exciting. Even if my memory is deteriorating, surely the need for a nursing home is years off. It would certainly be a wrench to sell King Street but I could make a newer, more compact place look nice. It might actually feel cosier than this rambling old house. And I've been meaning to go through all my accounting papers since I retired, and this would force me to. And to be just across from the esplanade, so close to the water – well, what could be better?

I straighten my back, content with my returned confidence and optimism.

Pauline turns stiffly, dries her hands on a tea towel and hangs it back on its hook by the sink. There's an aura of detachment about her. 'All right, well, that was a nice cuppa, Mum. We obviously need to talk about this a lot more but I have to get going. I need to prepare for a meeting first thing tomorrow.'

She comes over to me and for the briefest moment we lock eyes, hers showing softness and strength engaged in a battle, as if her heart and her head can't agree. After a quick peck on my cheek she delivers a brief goodbye over her shoulder as she heads for the hallway. I hear the front door close, her key turn and the clack of heels down the front steps.

I push myself up out of the chair and grimace as shots of pain rocket through both hands. Taking a moment to gain my balance, I go to the sink and lean on the bench to look out over the rear garden. My hip is more uncomfortable than usual and I prop most of my weight on my right side to accommodate. Between the carnation beds, the garden's looking embarrassingly overgrown. I turn the idea of a villa unit over some more, contemplating its suitability. There's a lot at stake but, after decades of managing companies' and people's finances, I'm used to being thorough and considering all details and angles.

Something catches my eye on the bench next to the sink and I pick up the glossy brochure. Pauline must have left it. A glamorous couple, whose salt-and-pepper hair is supposed to make them representatives of the elderly but who are clearly mere babies in their sixties, beam at the camera. *How wondrous!* their eyes sparkle. *How exciting!* their skins glow. Blue Vista. The place was built on the southern headland in the nineties. I was at the protests. When the old cottage up there was sold, the substantial land should have been purchased for public use. Instead, our arguments and submissions were ignored. I flip the brochure over. Smaller photos adorn the back, to make you think the facility is a hip, bridge-playing, cocktail-swirling community of retirees ducking out every other day to play eighteen holes. No mention of walking aids, the reek of boiled chicken, or locked doors designed to prevent the really gaga inhabitants from wandering away and off the cliff edge in their pyjamas.

Is this really what Pauline wants for me? In other cultures the elderly are revered, kept close to the family fold, their wisdom actively sought, their presence valued and appreciated. I don't want outsiders to handle the burden of my decline, where I'm shunted off to an artificial world, a final whistle-stop where people don't so much live as wait to die.

No wonder Pauline went quiet and couldn't get out of here fast enough.

Well, even if my brain and body are on the way to buggery, I'm not going to let them go downhill without a fight. And I'm not going to make things easy for Pauline. Why should I? I'll leave this stupid brochure where I've found it, as a hint. I believe the modern term for my approach is 'passive aggressive' but I don't give a damn. Surely my daughter knows the woman she's dealing with.

I can't remember: did I hear her lock the front door?

1982

'What did you think of him, Mrs Harford? Wasn't he a giant? Did you notice he had to duck down to enter your office?'

'I had a good feeling about him,' I say to my secretary after seeing the candidate out. I peer out of the tall, narrow window beside the entrance and watch as the young man strides away across the street, his tie blowing sideways in the wind. I knew he was buttering me up, of course, with his line about me being 'a highly trusted financial adviser in the wider region' or some such comment. But he had good eye contact during the interview and I liked that. Confident but not cocky. He called me Lily, which I found a bit forward, but I've become pretty adept at sizing people up after over thirty years of running this business, and overall I think he would be an asset to us.

I catch my reflection in the glass. My hair is auburn but not without the help of chemical intervention any more. I've thought about cutting it short, maybe even perming it, but

I admit I feel more youthful keeping my hair long, even if I do wear it in a bun most of the time.

'He was checking a few things with me before you called him in, you know – about our services,' Gretel says from behind her desk. 'He seemed very keen to get the position.'

As I'd sat listening to the applicant display his knowledge of what we do, it made me proud of the company I've created and of how far I've come. The days of combing through bank statements, cheque butts, deposit books, purchase invoices, and inventory and sale records are well behind me. I'm happy to delegate that grunt work to my employees, leaving me free to concentrate on tax advice and estate planning for our long-standing clients in Finn Bay and the wider area, who've come to trust me implicitly.

'Yes, he'd clearly done his homework. And he said he's a whiz with the Paxus, which will be very useful to us. Seems we'll be throwing out all our pencils and pens soon.'

'Computers are making a difference but I can't see that ever happening, Mrs Harford. Surely we'll always need paper.'

'You're probably right. Speaking of which, can you please type up a letter of offer for him? Usual conditions of employment, start date the sixteenth. Oh, and did you remember to send off the fax to confirm I'm happy to speak at the ASA's conference in Sydney?'

'Yes and yes.'

I return to my office feeling weary. It's no secret I plan to retire in the next two or three years, as by my mid-sixties I'll be ready to relinquish the reins to someone else entirely. I want to have more time for the Women's Auxiliary, and to play tennis, tend to my garden and, most importantly, help Pauline by taking a more active part in little Rachel's life. I know how hard it is to feel you're split in two between career and family. At least my daughter has a man by her side. There's nothing Sam wouldn't do for her.

Gretel knocks and enters, looking somewhat sheepish.

'I hope you don't mind me doing this, but I meant to give these to you yesterday.'

A small pile of travel booklets is passed to me. I scan their covers. *Walking Trails of the Grand Canyon, The West Coast of America, Colorado's Hidden Treasures.*

'You've been talking about your retirement plans and I was in the travel agency booking flights for the honeymoon and thought I'd grab some information for you about places you've mentioned.'

'Thank you, Gretel. That was very kind of you.' I've toyed with the idea of trekking, but I'm not getting any younger so maybe I'll just end up on an organised tour of some sort. Pauline thinks that would provide an opportunity to meet someone, but there'll never be another Robert. 'I'm heading out to Jim's boat yard in a minute and the meeting could take a while. The stupid man just isn't getting how deep in financial trouble he is and what he needs to do to turn things around. And he doesn't seem to like taking advice from a woman.'

'He doesn't realise who he's dealing with, Mrs Harford. I'm sure you'll get him on side. You always do.'

I trust she's referring to my business acumen, although I admit I do usually get my way. With no-one else to depend on, I've had no choice but to stand up for myself – in my work life and as an unmarried mother – and to push for what's right. But I won't apologise for that. I'm proud of my strength. It's given me the freedom to live life the way I want to live it.

I steel myself for what will probably be a difficult meeting, a quick flutter brushing against my insides. I smooth down my skirt, straighten my jacket and place the auditing papers I need into my briefcase, the clip giving a satisfying snap as it shuts.

Pauline

Dispirited from the moment she'd closed her mother's front door, Pauline arrived home to mellow jazz oozing from the speakers in the living room and the delectable aroma of onions frying. Walking straight through to the kitchen, she perched on one of the wooden bar stools and propped her elbows on the burnt-orange laminate bench.

'Oh, I'm glad today's over.' She inhaled deeply, watching her husband top up his glass of red from where he stood on the other side. 'Dinner smells fantastic. What's on the menu?'

'Stroganoff.' Sam leaned across for a kiss. His breath smelled of garlic and wine. 'You're home earlier than I thought you might be. Is that a good or a bad sign?'

'Your upper lip is sweaty,' Pauline said ungenerously, pulling away and wiping her mouth then immediately disliking herself for it.

'Nice to see you too.'

Pauline frowned and looked down, resting her forehead on her hand. Sam deserved better. 'Sorry.'

He offered up his glass. 'Here, you look like you could do with a drink.'

Pauline took in Sam's smiling brown eyes and not for the first time admired his perfectly proportioned mouth and chin. At sixty-one, her husband was still, she thought, a very handsome man by any measure.

'I opened the bottle for the strog so we might as well finish it,' he added.

Sam's sleeves were rolled up and his tie sat loose over several undone shirt buttons, revealing the mass of silver and caramel on his chest. Taking the wine, Pauline experienced a strong desire to bury her face in the hair like a fragile child might do in search of reassurance. With sheer determination she'd pushed through menopause, so she knew this sense that her reserves, her resilience, were thinning wasn't hormone related.

'Busy at work?' Sam opened a cupboard under the bench to extract another glass.

'Let's just say if I had my way I'd retire tomorrow,' Pauline replied, her tone sullen.

'Hmm.' Sam poured himself a generous portion of wine. 'So, how was Lily? How did she take the idea of a retirement home?' He had always been good at changing the topic, especially from one that had come to give him the shits.

'I couldn't believe it. Before I had a chance to, she was the one who brought up the need for a change.'

'Seriously? That's fantastic. So you needn't have worried after all.'

Pauline took a sip of her drink. 'Well, I wouldn't say that. She has it in her head to downsize into a villa unit; she started to talk about buying off the plan. I couldn't bring myself to burst her bubble.'

Sam turned to the stove and began stirring the contents of the saucepan. 'Well, a small villa unit mightn't be such a bad option. It would certainly be better for her than staying in King Street.'

Pauline willed him to look back so he'd be forced to register her level of incredulity, but he was taking his time with the saucepan so she had no choice but to talk to his back, annoyance mounting. 'For how long? Sam, she's a danger to herself. She can't live alone any more. She needs professional care.'

'You're right, a unit would only be a stop-gap. A care home is the best option, especially given she's eighty-six and getting more frail, not to mention forgetful,' Sam said, still stirring. 'But, love, I can understand her not thinking along the lines of a facility yet. She's been so independent for so long. This is Lily Harford we're talking about.' He tapped the wooden spoon on the edge of the saucepan before settling the lid back on and returning to face his wife.

'You think I don't know my own mother?' Pauline felt her throat constrict and heard the strain and bite in her own voice. 'Look, I hate the idea of her moving into an institution, even a quality one like Blue Vista – *if* we can get her in there. But I know that's the logical next step for her. I'm just feeling ...' Pauline struggled to find the right word.

'What – guilty? You're going to have to stop feeling that, and she'll have to be more realistic.' Sam cocked his head to one side and screwed up his eyes a little, as if measuring up his wife's reaction. 'Look, she knows how much you love her,' he continued in a gentler tone, 'and that you've always had her best interests at heart in everything you do. I don't think we should rush her though. Let's just let the idea of leaving King Street sink in first.'

Pauline wasn't sure guilty was the only adjective she'd been looking for. She nodded and swallowed a second, greedier mouthful of wine then proceeded to drain the glass. She didn't normally drink at home but needed something to take the edge off, to dampen her tension. Alcohol always went to her thigh muscles first, followed by her head, and she could feel its soothing effect already.

'You look tired, love. Maybe give the running a rest in the morning, eh?'

Feeling frustratingly out of sorts, she shrugged her shoulders, her throat refusing to loosen despite the wine. 'I might head upstairs for a shower before we eat, if that's all right.'

What Pauline couldn't confess was that the effort and motivation required to pull on her runners every morning, her eyes sleepy and dry, was driven by knowing that only physical fitness was keeping her on an even keel. She was sure her husband simply saw fatigue and disgruntlement, when what she was experiencing was a mental frailty she'd never known – and couldn't reconcile within herself.

'Want a refill before you go?'

Although tempted, she shook her head.

Donna

As Donna worked the remote in search of something halfway decent for the residents to watch, she couldn't resist snatching glimpses of the couple. She guessed they were in their mid-twenties. Pressed together from hip to knee, the two had dragged a sofa to sit opposite the young man's grandmother, Mrs Selbourne. The armchair enfolded the old lady's feeble and shrunken frame and resembled a leather-skinned monster slowly devouring her.

Of all the spaces in Blue Vista, the residents' lounge was Donna's least favourite. Whereas the gardens provided the therapy of a breathtaking view, and the dining area the ready opportunity for dialogue (even if it was largely to complain about the food), the lounge could be just plain depressing, a regular reminder of the lack of visitors. In many cases, the residents had no family, or loved ones weren't close by. For

others it was a sad case of out of sight, out of mind – adult
children too caught up in their own important lives. Donna
did what she could to provide companionship, but nothing
could evoke the same look of pure delight as when a caring
sister, grandchild or nephew dropped by.

Mrs Selbourne was muttering away to her guests but it
was clear the minds of her grandson and his girlfriend were
more focused on the contact of their fused bodies than on
her monologue.

Wonder if they'll last. We certainly didn't.

Donna briefly treated herself to the memory of Derek's
torso pushed hard against hers when she was their age. It
was almost fifteen years ago but she still remembered how
he would croon over her long, thick hair as he ran his fingers
through it on their way down, grazing her nipples and stomach, to strum them expertly and exquisitely between her
legs. Under his lustful attentiveness she had felt so unques-
tionably beautiful back then, even though it had turned out
to be a temporary glow.

These days Donna didn't particularly care about her
looks, one way or the other. She'd been told once that her
flaxen hair, now kept at shoulder length, set off her unusual
eyes of hazel surrounded by an outer band the colour of
straw. Referring to her compact figure as 'unremarkable',
she accepted she was never going to be glamorous, whatever that entailed. She had certainly given up on ever feeling
desirable again, and had settled instead with feeling content.

Having found a worthy BBC documentary, she checked
the volume level then her watch, relieved to see it was close
to knock-off time. Although she loved her job, after eight
hours on her feet she was ready to relax. After glancing once

more in the direction of Mrs Selbourne she headed back through reception – its raised countertop decorated simply with a fern-filled terrarium, visitors' book and round silver bell – to the nurses' station situated behind it, collected up her things then marched out through the building's main entrance to make her way home.

Although it was winter and overcast, the afternoon was pleasant enough, with no sign of the persistent rain from earlier in the day. After exiting Blue Vista's front gates, Donna began the walk down the headland's spiralling road, thankful as always for the support and comfort of her sensible nursing shoes. She could hear the surf of the Pacific way below, slapping the rocks at the cliff's base, while gulls cawed overhead.

Flicking open her mobile to check for messages she noticed a missed call from Vedya, a professional dog walker Donna had befriended in the local hardware store only a few weeks after she'd moved to the coast from Brisbane five years earlier. Vedya had been in the middle of redecorating her own flat at the time, so that she could rent out the second bedroom for extra cash. Her business had grown surprisingly well since then though, and Vedya had wasted no time evicting the tenant ('His feet stank and he was a total loser') and was on the brink of expanding Wild Side into a mini empire.

'Hi, Ved. Sorry I missed your call. I've been on day shift and only just checked my phone.'

'That's cool. I only rang to say hi. Nothing particular to report. How was work? And what *is* that noise?'

Donna looked skyward. 'Oh, just seagulls squawking over something. I'm a bit tired but I think it's because I was on afternoon shift yesterday, and today I did a lot of lifting and cleaning. I don't mind – it's all part of the gig – but, god, I'm ready to sit down.'

A Lycra-clad cyclist came into view from around the bend, puffing as he headed up the slope towards her in low gear, legs working furiously. It was common to see bike riders here, struggling up or flying down. Not a fan of exercise herself, she supposed it was a conquering thing, the view from the top offering a reward for all that lactic acid pain. As Donna expected, he passed her without so much as a sideways glance.

'Tell me about it! I must have walked over thirty k's this week. I like that part though. It's just the poop scooping I'm not so crazy about.'

Vedya giggled but Donna couldn't conjure her own laugh. 'You know, sometimes when I'm helping with toileting I wonder if I should have become a real estate agent or an interior decorator or something.'

'Yeah, right. You are in exactly the right job, Donna Charleston. What you do for the oldies is fantastic. Don't underestimate providing a shoulder or an ear when they need it. They all adore you there.'

'You shouldn't call them oldies, Ved ... But thanks for the compliment.'

'Hey, you sound really flat. Are you sure you're just tired?'

'I guess I am feeling a bit blah. I was watching this couple just before that were visiting his grandma and it reminded me of when Derek and I were together. They couldn't keep their paws off each other. Actually, it was totally disrespectful and kind of gross, but still, it made me a little, I don't know, nostalgic.' Donna paused for a moment to look towards the ocean, choppy and grey-green today. A slight on-shore breeze caressed her face.

'But you said Derek was a twerp of epic proportions.'

Donna grinned and continued down the hill as Vedya continued. 'I obviously never met the guy, but didn't you tell me he went from being your Prince Charming to being all withdrawn and uncommunicative?'

'Well, yes, things didn't turn out quite how I'd hoped. The way he just kind of switched off from our marriage, and never explained why – the silence killed me.'

Derek, a telecommunications whiz, had been introduced to her by mutual friends. She'd fallen hard and fast, the whole romance a whirlwind cliché. Drugged by their formidable chemistry and similarly dry sense of humour, she'd glowed in the aura of coupledom, something she'd craved since she could remember. It was a state of being that formed the basis of a newfound self-belief, sitting under her skin like an invisible cloak of strength. For the first time, at twenty-four and with a partner in her corner, she was backing her own thoughts and opinions, even as her sister and two brothers did their best to pull her down with jokes about punching above her weight.

It had all been smoke and mirrors though. She had navigated a difficult, belittling road through childhood only to find herself further wounded, this time by the shards of a splintering marriage. After only four years Derek had, for whatever reason, retreated to an emotional island and she had tried and tried to swim out to him but he'd clammed up, seemingly unprepared to fling out the life raft and pull her in to his shore. She suspected he'd met someone else, but if so he never scraped together the backbone to admit the truth.

For a short time, when things were starting to fall apart, she'd made extra efforts in the bedroom in an attempt to bridge the widening gap. But it had only served to create a sickening mess of emotions, and the emptiness between them deepened. In the end, even the physical part of their relationship, the superglue that had held fast from the beginning, came unstuck. That was over seven years ago but it still hurt, that was clear now.

The road had led away from the water now and she could only vaguely hear the gulls and the ocean over her own footsteps.

'Well, there you go,' said Vedya. 'A *quitter* is how you described him. You've regained your confidence, especially since you've been working here. You said your relationship with Derek ended up making you question yourself, which is an awful way to live.'

Donna absorbed her friend's uncomfortable reminder. 'I'm amazed how much you remember of our talks about him.'

'Well, I'm just fascinated by relationships, so that sort of thing sticks in my brain.'

Donna reached flat ground, passing the old Commercial Hotel where the esplanade adjoined the base of the headland. All was quiet at the dingy pub, just a grimy, white Ford Territory parked out the front. The other pub servicing the town was Nobody's Inn, the hip crowd's venue of choice, situated on the road leading out to the larger town of Rorook. Another hour though, and the fishermen and farmers would pull up to the Commercial in their well-worn four-wheel drives and utes to stake a place at the bar, not seeming to care about its gloomy wallpaper and beer-marinated carpet.

There had been a time back in Brisbane, towards the end of Donna's marriage, when alcohol had provided a welcome escape and she would have struggled to resist even the Commercial. Drinking had been a gradual hook, imperceptibly reeling her in. Initially it was an occasional quick fix when she felt despondent over an argument, or when loneliness had her physically yearning for Derek's touch or even just his attention. Losing herself in drink quickly became a protective crutch. A regular salve of comfort and escape, it offered a feeling akin to being underwater where the truth of their marriage, her increasingly flimsy self-worth, and her colossal resentment of Derek's emotional withdrawal were pleasantly muffled. But it had also inflamed their problems. Eventually, Donna had found herself as a drunken, single woman in her early thirties while he found for himself a sober, single woman in her early twenties.

Cradle snatcher.

'You know, he once shouted at me that being shit-faced was like telling a joke only I understood,' said Donna, checking for cars before crossing the esplanade and heading west towards the town's residential area behind the main street. 'And that he was sick of trying to get the gag. So no wonder it didn't work out. After always telling myself I'd marry a man who knew how to be in a loving relationship, I went ahead and married someone just like my dysfunctional father. I only have myself to blame.'

'Yadda yadda yadda. I don't buy any of that garbage. It takes two to wreck a marriage. Or, in your case, him to set it alight and you to eventually give up trying to rescue it.'

'Thanks, Ved,' replied Donna.

'For what?'

'For talking sense into me.'

'Any time. Look, I have to fly now, but let's catch up soon, huh?'

When Donna walked into the driveway of her block five minutes later, she was aware of a lightness in her step. Rows of palms down either side of the street added to a holiday atmosphere in a coastal area increasingly attracting the tourist dollar, but Donna was happy to claim picturesque Finn Bay as home, no longer seeing herself as a newcomer.

The flat she rented was a modest but clean ground-floor apartment in a two-storey block of eight. Being a mid-century building there was no shortage of improvements to be made in her unit but the owners were more than happy for Donna to undertake any cosmetic changes she wanted, to add her own touches. She'd painted the walls white, erected shelves for her books and knick-knacks, even changed over the bathroom and kitchen taps to a more modern style. She enjoyed that sort of thing. Her father might have his emotional failings but he wasn't too shabby with a tool and she'd picked up some handyman know-how.

As Donna unlocked her front door and crossed into the sanctuary of her nest, she was also reminded of how glad she was to be single. She had no desire to risk a relationship again. She had all she needed – a worthy job, a small, sufficient circle of friends, her own space. It was a thoroughly satisfying existence she had carved out for herself in gorgeous Finn Bay, and she couldn't foresee what could possibly disturb it.

SATURDAY 6 JANUARY 2007

Pauline

'Can we please not have that discussion again? You don't
know when to leave it alone, do you?' Sam asked before
ingesting the last piece of his toast.

'What, so I'm not allowed to answer your question?'
Pauline's resentment curled its way over to her husband
and appeared to sit on him like an unwelcome smell. It had
taken six months for them to persuade Lily to move and
to secure a place at Blue Vista. Pauline was therefore prepared for today's declutter and packing up of King Street
in a practical sense, but not emotionally. After all, it wasn't
every day you forced your mother to sort through a lifetime
of possessions, almost certainly crushing her spirit in the
process.

Having gathered most of the bits and pieces they'd
need – masking tape, textas, stickers, lists – Pauline tossed
them into a small wicker basket on the kitchen bench.
'You asked me how I am, and all I'm saying is that I'm hot
and tired and stretched thin, and really, Sam, all I'd like
is to have the time to help Rachel by being a more present grandma to Luke and Rosie, especially while they're so
little. But we can't afford for me to retire for a very long
time, so that's that.' Pauline crossed her arms and stared at
the basket, pondering what else needed to go in it.

'I know, love. I'd like you to be able to do that too,' Sam
said with his mouth still full, 'but how long are you going
to pile the bloody guilt trip on me?'

Pauline grunted. The whole issue of finances had been
festering between them for several years, following two
separate but equally aggravating decisions on Sam's part.
She knew she should let the topic of money go but it still
rankled, perhaps now more than ever, when she was desperate to at least know she wouldn't have to keep working until
well into her sixties.

Over thirty years ago, just after they'd married, the global
price of oil had jumped and the crash in manufacturing
had extended its tendrils to Newcastle's steelworks. Sam's
junior engineering position hadn't escaped the broad sweep
of redundancies so he and Pauline had made the decision
to put down roots back in her hometown. Sam had, fortu-
nately, secured work with the local shire's water treatment
works, and the whole move to Finn Bay was enthusiasti-
cally supported by Pauline's mother. But his income had
remained lacklustre so when he'd turned down the offer of
a role in the shire's management team not long after her

Lily Harford's Last Request

own promotion to principal, Pauline had been shocked and unapologetically pissed off, to say the least. She'd tried to persuade him to reconsider.

'But the time is right for us, while you're still in your fifties,' she'd argued. 'You haven't tried it before. With your expertise, you might like it,' she'd added, the slightest hint of hope infecting her voice.

'But I'd be a total fish out of bloody water, dealing with all that office politics and HR crap. You know that.'

'I can't believe you're being so selfish!'

'And I can't believe you'd ask me to do something that would make me so unhappy!' Sam had stared at his wife as if he didn't know her.

So here he was, having decided to remain upwardly immobile within the shire council in essentially the same engineering job he'd been doing since he started. It was the only area in which Pauline regarded her husband with an air of disenchantment, and her soul ached as a result because he was a supportive and wonderful partner in every other way.

That was beside the point, she thought now as she hunted with impatience through the top kitchen drawer for a pair of scissors. Especially after his badly considered attempt to make up for his stagnant income a few years earlier. Without discussing it with his wife, he had invested in an ill-fated housing scheme in a development a short way up the coast. Luckily they had put most of their savings into her superannuation fund, but a significant chunk had still gone down the drain, setting their finances back by years and nearly costing them their marriage in the process.

'I'm not piling on any guilt trip. I'm just telling it like it is,' Pauline said, glad of something else to focus on but cursing under her breath as her knuckle made contact with the blade of a peeler. 'Why are the scissors never where they're supposed to be? Who used them la— never mind. Found them.'

The afternoon would only go smoothly if she ran it like clockwork. The last thing she wanted was to draw out the whole sorry process any longer than needed. She understood with painful sympathy how difficult today was going to be for her mother. Adding the scissors to the other items, Pauline picked up the basket, and carried it out to her car where she threw it on the back seat, the boot already crammed full of flattened boxes. Unsettled and on edge, she slammed the car door as she looked back towards the house and remembered the day she and Sam had first laid eyes on it.

They'd known as soon as they drove up the snaking gravel driveway that House on the Hill was *the one*; the split-level red-brick home around which they would build a future together. Sitting on an elevated bushy block, it gave them expansive views over the hinterlands of Finn Bay, with its rolling hills of cattle pasture and smallholdings of macadamia farms. Inside, its exposed brick walls and cream shag-pile carpet were now considered unfashionable and the bathrooms and kitchen needed facelifts, but she couldn't contemplate the emotional upheaval of ever having to leave it behind.

A dull ache sprang up behind her left eye and she pushed the heel of her palm against her brow as she walked back inside, where she found Sam struggling with another stack of boxes. In less than an hour they were due at King Street. She sensed her irritability with him was a symptom of obvious stresses as well as other frustratingly intangible forces eating away at her. But, at least on the surface, facts were facts and there was no getting around the situation: right now she just had to focus on getting the day over with, for everyone's sake. She couldn't let emotion get in the way of what had to be done.

Lily

In a few days I move into Blue View or Vista or whatever the hell the holding pen's called. It will be a shrinking down of my life, like a wool jumper that's accidentally been put through the wrong wash cycle. I admit I've been moping and I'm sure my recent weight loss was the final straw. Pauline and Sam pounced when a room came up. I can just picture them falling over themselves to fill in the requisite paperwork.

It's a stinking hot day and the old wall air conditioner is struggling. I suppose the next owners will need to get it replaced. My son-in-law looks like he's just been for a swim, his T-shirt clinging to his back, beads of sweat dotting his forehead. But even in the heat my daughter appears cool and calm, a picture of organisation. Rachel and her

Christos, in what look like matching khaki shorts, sit on my couch but keep a gap of air between them, every bit of evaporation treasured. Now and then one of them tilts left or right, trying to unstick the backs of their thighs from the leather, making me glad to be adhesion-free on the corduroy armchair. Where my granddaughter's husband is what you might describe as 'swarthy', she is blonde-haired and soft-featured, in total contrast to her mother. Her apple didn't fall far from Sam's tree, not only in looks but in nature. Rachel is as quietly spoken and even-tempered as her father – and similarly a little lacking in ambition, I have to say. How she thinks she's going to make a living from her pottery, I've no idea. Luckily her Christos seems to make a decent crust.

'Should we bring the pedestal fan in from the garage?' I ask.

'I think we're good, Nana-Lily, as long as you are. Anyway, isn't it out there because it's broken?'

'Oh. Yes. Perhaps you could look at it sometime, Christos? After all, what's the point of having an electrician in the family if you can't get those sorts of things fixed?'

'Er, unless your drains are blocked I'm probably not much use to you.' Christos is smiling sheepishly but I catch the frown on my granddaughter's forehead before she and Sam exchange a look. Do they think I don't notice?

In their singlets and shorts, Rachel's little ones, Rosie and Luke, don't seem to notice the heat. Completely oblivious to the significance of today's proceedings, they are nicely distracted on the floor by a set of wooden blocks, their concentration focused on making a tower that won't tumble. I keep a tub of such toys and books especially for their visits, just as I did for their mother when she was their age. I doubt there'll be enough room for my great-grandchildren to play on the floor of my new room, though. I wonder if they'll still want me to read stories to them once I'm there. No doubt the place will smell of talcum powder and menthol (or is it eucalyptus?) and old peoples' stale, fusty clothes, and chicken soup. Perhaps they will prefer to stay away. I wouldn't blame them.

Pauline and Sam are the only ones moving about. Sam periodically disappears from the lounge, coming back with item after item – a pot plant, a bedspread, a hat rack, a table lamp – collected from one or other room in the house. Pauline crosses it off one of her lists, and everyone contemplates it and talks about it, then looks to me. If I indicate I want to keep it, the article will hopefully be relocated with me. A shake of my head, and it becomes fair game to the family or, if they don't want it, to charity or the bin. The entire contents of King Street, my whole history, sifted through like a trash and treasure. I have to hand it to Pauline; she's mighty efficient.

'Lily, anything you can't bear to part with, we can keep at our place,' Sam offers.

'And Nana-Lily, some things can be donated to Rosie's kinder for their fete. It's coming up in March.'

I nod but can't find my words. Painstakingly, we make our way through everything I own. Every piece of furniture and trinket carries its own story or ritual or meaning. Inherited silverware put on display with pride for dinner guests, books received for birthdays, kitchen bowls playing their part in the countless chocolate cakes or all manner of desserts ... these objects are a reflection of me. I'd like to be anywhere but here right now. This is cruel.

'I'd like to take that with me,' I say, pointing towards the sideboard.

'Mum, there's no way that piece will fit in your room. You have to be sensible.'

I sigh, frustration and annoyance now scraping at my insides. 'I am being sensible. I just thought it would be a good way of storing some of my things.'

'I get that, but there really won't be the space, especially as you have one wall mostly taken up with the glass doors.'

I try to visualise the reality of living in a single room too miserly to fit one of my most treasured belongings. I'm aware of my pulse racing. What am I doing? Why did I agree to this? After I refused to even acknowledge *that* brochure, Pauline and Sam doggedly provided every argument as to why a villa unit would be a short-sighted solution to a longer-term problem. Selling then buying, moving, then selling and moving again; it would make no economic sense, they argued. They cleverly tapped into my accounting instinct, knowing full well I couldn't ignore the financial logic. Then, with precision, the final thrust of the dagger. It was better, they said, to secure a room in a purpose-built care home while a place was available and I was still doing well, than to have the upheaval of another shift – possibly into a less desirable institution (though they were careful not to use that word) – should I break my hip or become chronically ill.

'I'd prefer to walk under a bus,' I'd said.

Although on one level I accepted the rational arguments, I refused to go down that path quietly. It was embarrassing to admit to myself but I got a certain satisfaction from being a thorn in their sides. They eventually wore me down though, Pauline's stubbornness even more robust than mine. The reality is there's been a role reversal: in growing old I have, in all practical matters, become the child and they the parents.

Having disappeared briefly, Sam lumbers back into the room, carrying my bulky old typewriter. I'm not sure where he found it but the sight of the machine instantly takes me back to my twenties. With a heavy nostalgia I see my smooth, unblemished hands dashing over its keys like two elegant spiders dancing a jive. The action would be more of a leisurely waltz these days.

'I have no use for it but it's not to go to charity. Do you understand me?' I look Sam squarely in the eye.

'Loud and clear, Lily. We'll keep it at ours.' Sam places it carefully in the corner with the other items earmarked for House on the Hill.

'The kids will enjoy playing on it when they visit,' adds Christos, while Pauline and Rachel remain engrossed in discussion over my silverware. Sam stands in the middle of the room looking ready to combust, the red flush on his face extending to his neck and the hair framing his face now clumped by sweat into damp waves. He appears to be at a loss, no doubt waiting for instructions from my daughter. I actually feel sorry for him and decide to make conversation.

'Sammy, this room I'm going into. Why is it the only one with external doors?'

He looks relieved at having a task, albeit merely answering a simple question. He comes closer and my nose wrinkles as I suffer a whiff of his underarms.

'Apparently it was part of what used to be a small visitors' lounge for the southern wing residents that didn't get used much, so it was converted into two bedrooms. We're just lucky – you're lucky – that it happens to be the room that's become available.'

Curfews, cafeteria-quality food and the awkwardness of being the newcomer attempting to break into established social circles? Add to that facing one's imminent mortality, and 'lucky' isn't quite the term I'd use.

'Yes, indeed.' My mouth makes an enormous effort to curve upwards despite my whole being feeling yanked in the opposite direction. On a tour I was shown the room I'm to move into, and the facilities, but I don't think I took much in. What I most recall is having my solicitor go through the fine print before signing the contracts, because, I have to say, the fees were a shock.

I blink a few times and purse my lips to stop the wobble. 'Will you all still come to see me?' Silence descends on the room as my daughter and hers turn to face me.

'Of course, Mum. I'll visit you just as much as I do now. I promise. And take you out shopping and whatnot.'

'So will I, Nana-Lily. And I'll bring the kids in whenever I can,' says Rachel. 'You're moving to Blue Vista, not another country,' she adds with a reassuring smile.

I picture my family saying goodbye after the care home's visiting hours are over. They'll wave at me with phony beaming faces but there will be a hint of pity and relief in their eyes as they leave to go back into the world of the living, to cook up a family meal or head to the pub or get in their car on a whim to drive wherever they like, no questions asked. They'll quietly thank their lucky stars they're not me, the one staying behind, bound by rules and timetables and restrictions – not yet, at least. Keep that particular wolf at bay for as long as possible, they'll think.

'What about this rug?' Pauline is pointing to the floor beneath my feet in an obvious attempt to change the topic.

'Gosh, is it Persian silk, Nana-Lily? It's beautiful, isn't it, Christos? If you don't need it we could put it to good use in our family room, couldn't we, honey?'

Before he can answer I clear my throat in the hope my voice won't betray me. 'I'm not sure. I think there'll be room for it beside my bed.' I look to my daughter, who's already marking a name on her list: Rachel's, I suspect.

'I don't think so, Mum. And my bet is that they regard mats and rugs as a trip hazard. Anyway, the room has carpet so you won't need it.'

'Oh.'

So that's that, then, is it? Each piece, large and small. Pass, fail, this is worthy of transporting, that doesn't make the grade, space for this, no requirement for that. My coveted Wedgwood serving platter, twin silver candlesticks (a wedding gift from Ma and Pa they couldn't afford), my mother's pale blue napkin rings, two handtowels embroidered with cream ribbon, red high-heeled shoes now too narrow to accommodate the bunions on my feet, silk scarves in colours of the sea, boxes of cut crystal wine glasses, the Victorian oak dining table that has eavesdropped on many a family conversation. My life is being offered up, judged, valued and dispensed.

I tighten my jaw like it's the weir stopping a brewing fury from escaping. I sit, as straight-backed as I can, willing my emotions to follow suit as the animated discussion and pointing and measuring and nodding and stickering happens around me. I'm expecting a rage to rip me apart any minute. I try to tell myself the move will be all for the best, that they have my interests at heart. But all I want to do is bellow: 'Put everything back and get out of my house! I've changed my bloody mind – you can take the *For Sale* sign down and stick it where the sun don't shine!' But as befits a great-grandmother, I portray the grace expected of me and hold my tongue. Besides, I just don't have the strength to fight them any more.

When the only items remaining on Pauline's lists are my clothes, Rachel and Christos make noises about leaving. Luke and Rosie are rewarded for their patience with icy poles dug out of the chest freezer on the back verandah, and told they can lick them in the car. This seems foolhardy to me in this heat but I suppose it's not my problem. I savour a precious hug and peck on the cheek from them, their velvet skin so delectable on mine, before they and their odds and ends are rounded up. After we wave goodbye to Rachel and her little family from my front porch, the house is pleasingly quiet.

My back is stiff from sitting too long and I'd like to run a bath to soak my weary bones, but there's still one task remaining. Sam tidies up and stacks boxes while Pauline and I walk slowly towards my bedroom, arms locked, my girl's other hand stroking mine with tender affection. It's a silent, shared intimacy that has been sorely lacking all day.

I see she's already laid out most of my wardrobe on the bed. Despite the whirring blades of the ceiling fan, it's stiflingly humid in this room and as we sort through dresses, shoes and coats we both become more and more exasperated, with the task and each other.

'Mum, just how many white business shirts do you think you'll need, for goodness sake? And a couple of lightweight jackets should be enough. Why don't you just hold on to the navy and black ones? They go with everything. It will be easier getting dressed each day if you only have a few pieces to choose from. Less decision-making. And the cupboard space there is limited, remember.'

I grunt, now hungry as well as hot and tired. We're almost done when Sam pops his head in. 'How's it going in here, ladies? It's way past dinnertime.' He ventures further in and hands me a sheet of paper. 'I thought you might find this handy, Lily. It's a list of what will be going with you, in case you forget.' He looks about to apologise for the assumption, but I nod at him and his relief is obvious. 'Can I at least get you both a glass of water?' he asks.

'Yes, please,' replies my daughter, not trying to disguise her exhaustion. 'And I think we can soon call it a day.'

'A water would be marvellous, Sam,' I say, hiding my dismay that I'm able to look over the items far too quickly.

Wedding photo
6 x other photos in frames
Walnut bureau
Armchair
Black suitcase of clothes and toiletries
Finn Bay watercolour
Oil painting of Glasshouse Mountains
Silver trinket box w jewellery
Medium size crystal vase

Ceramic fruit bowl made by Rachel
Selection (9) of novels, plus books to read to the kids
Ebony elephant bookends
Lemon yellow notepaper/matching envelopes
Foldable umbrella
Bedside lamp
Clock radio
Red and grey mohair knee rug
Scrabble, pack of cards, pen
Sexy at 70 mug

Is this really happening? I wish I could somehow have lassoed time when I was younger, hauled it in and slowed it down. When I was a girl looking into the future, life seemed a corridor with no end, or a huge stockpile of money in your bank account that you couldn't ever believe you'd spend. Yet looking back in the opposite direction I'm left a little dazed and wondering how the decades have roared past in the blink of an eye.

It takes another hour before Pauline and Sam finally take their lists and leftover stickers and, I notice, a few pieces of the more expensive tableware. Perhaps I agreed to that earlier and just can't remember. Resentment glues to me though, ugly and uncomfortable. I see them to their car. Sam gets in on the driver's side but Pauline doesn't open her door straight away, instead leaning her back against it, squinting into the setting sun.

'I know how hard today has been for you,' she says. It's the first time since she arrived that her voice has been gentle. I take a moment, then step forward and into Pauline's open arms.

'Thank you,' I murmur.

I understand that in her mind she's helping me and I'm taking the most sensible course. But sensible can be over-rated. Stripped and bruised, I watch their car disappear down the street, the rear red lights making me think of devils' eyes. I want to leave as well, to walk and keep on walking, through town to the sea, into the sea, and let it take me. There are worse ways to go. They say drowning is peaceful, and then I wouldn't have to endure all this. I could quit while I was ahead.

It feels like the calm before a storm because in only a few days my life will be turned on its head. I climb my front steps and return inside, detecting as I enter the hallway a subtle difference in the sound of my footsteps. With pieces of furniture shifted around, some items gone and all these cartons, it's altered King Street's familiar echo. The house seems to understand and to have infused my grief into its foundations, taking on a forlorn persona in sympathy and comradeship. It's lost its usual warmth and familiarity. But still, I can't imagine being anywhere else.

I have an overpowering need to go into every part of my home to say my goodbyes, to carefully gather into myself one strong and enduring memory for each room. Limping my tired and bowed frame, I weave my way through piles of boxes, each marked with *Charity, Pauline* or *R&C* in thick black texta. I walk first into the bathroom and there's Pauline, spotty from head to toe with chickenpox sores, marinating in a mix of water and baking soda to help relieve the itches. She looks up at me and says with such positivity, 'At least they're pink, Mummy – I do love pink.' To Pauline's old room next, where she rushes in, exclaiming, 'Mum, guess what? I won the

History prize!' and we bounce together on her bed, laughing and whooping. To the kitchen, where my parents visit. Pauline is still a baby. Pa sits at the table, a soldering iron in one hand as he fixes my radio, displaying his usual patience. With loving instruction, Ma shows me how to make meringue, her strength of purpose and motherly guidance buoying me at a time when I'm so full of uncertainties as a single mother. She expertly measures, beats and spoons as I keep one ear open for the grumbles that will let me know Pauline's nap is over.

In the dining room it's twenty years ago. My cedar sideboard has just been delivered, its richly patterned grain so lovely. Who'd have thought a Haversham Road girl who grew up in second-hand clothes in a house with peeling paint and a rust-ridden, leaking roof could have risen to afford a home like this, with furniture as handsome as that? Finally, across the hall to my bedroom. Although he never knew this room or this house, Robert tries to appear but I block him and retreat. The recollections of the two of us entwined are too soaked with pain.

It's still light outside, but only just. Memories harvested and bundled tight, I return to the front door to check it's locked. Placing the flat of my hand on its upper panel in a kind of salute I close my eyes and lean in, resting my forehead on its faithful timber. 'Forgive me for abandoning you,' I breathe into it.

For a long time I can't sleep, having realised with dismay that I forgot to collect a memory from the back garden. How I will miss having my own plot of soil and the satisfaction it has brought me over the decades – planting and pruning, tilling and feeding, watering and simply watching its pretty displays grow and wither over the seasons. I toss around with an agitation I haven't experienced since the period after Robert passed, when our bed in Rorook became as vast and cold and lonely as the Antarctic.

I finally drift off but only by imagining that the whoosh of the fan is the sound of the bay's wind and waves as I let the water swallow me.

1967

'Mum. Mu-um!'

'I'm out the back, sweetheart.'

The carnations are particularly beautiful this season, living up to their botanical name: *Dianthus*, Greek for 'heavenly flower'. Especially my Peach Delights, their delicate pink blooms drenching the garden with colour and fragrance. My gloved hands in the soil, I look up to see my daughter framed by the back door. She appears tall from this angle, too tall for a little girl. But she's not really little any more, is she?

'Can I borrow a lipstick for tonight, the pink Revlon one?'

Pauline is going to her first formal dance, a joint event put on by the local secondary schools.

'I suppose so, but are you old enough to be wearing make-up?'

'I'm sixteen, Mum. Is it in the bathroom drawer?'

She's going to be a head-turner with those penetrating dark eyes and infectious energy. Not a hint of my reddish-brown locks or fair skin. Thank goodness she's accepted a father's absence from our lives. I have been, it seems, enough for her.

'Yes, I think so. Do you want me to help you get ready; do your hair for you?'

'Thanks, but I'll manage. I've been practising with Sue and Jill.' She turns with a flick of her hair and disappears back inside.

From the day she was born our bond has been powerful and instinctive, fattened even more by being a crew of just two. But now we're entering a new era, one where my importance is gradually diminishing in favour of her peers. Once my helpless infant, my toddler in search of beach flotsam ('Quick, pick up the treasure before those dastardly pirates sail into Finn Bay and claim it!'), my pigtailed girl executing perfect cartwheels on the sand, she no longer reaches for my hand, tells me everything, or habitually asks me for my counsel. I'm having to reinvent myself into an unfamiliar role, with a whole new set of terms and conditions. My mind will never stop turning to her welfare and happiness, but I have to prepare myself to eventually let go. No matter the pain, it's what we have to do for those we most love, isn't it?

I yank out a few more unwanted plants, but my thoughts are elsewhere. I gather up the trowel and bag of weeds, peel off the gloves and place everything on a shelf on the back verandah. I can hear Pauline rummaging through bathroom drawers. She's singing, a sure sign of a good mood. She can be very serious and I have sometimes found it easy to misinterpret her earnest nature as boredom, disapproval or discontent, worrying (in the middle of the night, during a business meeting, as I iron clothes, as I drive) about my ability as a mother. Have I failed her by working such long hours? I've run myself ragged trying to juggle Harford Accounting with commitments at her school – commitments, it seems to me, that every mother in Christendom apart from me is able to attend. At times the self-reproach crushes. But Pauline is emerging from childhood unscathed for all intents and purposes, so perhaps all that guilt and remorse at not being there at every fete or athletics day has been wasted energy. Who knows? I do my best.

I enter the bathroom and fight a carnal need to throw my arms around her. 'Do you want a hand to find the one you're after?'

She spins around on one heel. 'Yes, please. Thanks, Mum.' Our eyes meet and my heart lurches with pleasure. I still hold back from an embrace though, nervous of taking the moment too far and ruining it. Searching for the lipstick provides a handy diversion.

'Here, I think this is the one you want: Luminous Pink.'

She accepts the shining gold cylinder from me and removes its lid before rotating the end to reveal the pretty, waxy stick.

'Yes, that's the one I like. Can I take it with me tonight? Please? I promise to look after it.'

'Of course.' Her happiness is infectious but in the absence of a hug, I trawl for reassurance. 'Darling, does it bother you I've always worked instead of staying at home?'

Pauline looks bewildered, a quizzical expression on her face. 'No way. My friends think you're the hippest mum ever because you have an actual job and are an actual boss.'

I should give my daughter more credit. I couldn't love her more if I tried. I stroke her long dark hair and she doesn't pull away. I'm replete.

'How about this Avon eye shadow as well?' I ask, reaching again into the drawer. 'That could set off the colour of your dress really nicely. If we're going to do this, let's do it properly.'

Donna

'Hey, the new resident arrives next week.'

Donna accepted the paperwork from Molly to see the details for herself.

'Local woman, Mrs Lily Harford, eighty-six, some minor memory issues but otherwise fairly healthy. Hip dodgy. Bit of arthritis.'

'Dodgy?' asked Donna. 'That's highly technical.'

'Well, I'm paraphrasing.'

Donna smiled. Her co-worker's heavy black eyeliner and tersely cut fringe of bleached platinum-blonde hair left Molly looking like she'd be more at home on a catwalk than in the dowdy uniform of a nursing assistant. Her shift was finished and Donna's had just begun. Handover from the charge nurse had covered the usual ground, including which medications had been reordered, whose lesions had been dressed, and an accident report detailing that one of the residents had slipped in her shower and been transported to Rorook Mercy General for x-rays. Other than that, all was in order and according to routine.

'She's taking over a good room,' said Molly as she logged off from the nursing station's shared computer. 'The best, really. Sad about Mrs S, though.'

Donna thought with regret of the resident whose place this Mrs Harford would be taking. She had even bought a new black dress for Mrs Selbourne's funeral. At least the grandson and his girlfriend had managed to keep their hands to themselves during the service. Donna had made a point of watching. 'Yeah, Mrs Selbourne was a lovely lady. They all are, really.'

Molly lowered her voice and glanced over her shoulder to make sure the charge nurse wasn't within earshot. 'Are you kidding me? Look, I'd probably lose my job if you quote me, but honestly, sometimes I'd love to tell a few of the bitchy biddies in here what I really think of them. C'mon, Donna, I'm sure you know which ones I'm talking about.'

Donna placed the admittance papers on the desk, wanting to take the time to read them more thoroughly later. 'Okay, some of them can get a bit much. But being old can't be fun, let's face it. I reckon I'd be grumpy if I had to deal with even half their issues.'

'Hmm. I reckon if Cruella de Vil herself was a resident, you'd find something nice to say about her.'

Donna let the deadpan comment slide, unable to tell if it reflected admiration or derision. Being teased was nothing new. Her family had certainly provided her with enough experience, although their comments had been more of the toxic variety. Anyone visiting 68 Furness Drive in one of Brisbane's most resolutely middle-class suburbs would have thought it a den of fun and games but there was a flip side; the atmosphere in the Charleston household was thick with banter but it usually degraded to sarcastic or callous jokes and thinly veiled jibes. Baring any kind of vulnerability wasn't an option, unless you enjoyed the resultant teasing. It was as if a show of sympathy, affection or thoughtfulness indicated weakness, her family's approach being that, while nice, kindness ultimately gets you nowhere, *sucker*. Donna had learned from an early age that she'd need to look outside her kin for any morsels of appreciation. More than once in recent years she had, in moments of self-reflection, wondered if her pleasure in putting other people first, then receiving the resultant thanks and gratitude, was connected to an unhealthy and pathetic need for external validation.

'I just try to give all the residents here a sense of dignity. It's what everyone craves, isn't it?' she asked, extracting her name tag from a desk drawer and pinning it to her uniform.

'You're a good sort, Donna. Makes me feel inadequate, if I'm honest.' Molly flicked her wrist around to read her watch. 'So, I should get moving. Before netball I'm off to buy some new togs. The elastic on my old ones has completely gone around the bum and it's not the hottest look. Have a good shift,' she said while waving her fingers. 'See you later in the week.'

Donna felt a wave of humid, hot air brush past her as the heavy sliding entrance doors next to reception closed behind Molly. She sighed quietly as she watched her colleague's hips swinging noticeably and with unapologetic self-assurance, even under such a sexless uniform. Molly was the sort of girl to whom the teenage Donna had habitually and unfavourably compared herself in appearance and social status, having firmly categorised herself by that age as uninteresting and unworthy. Even now, at nearly forty, she prickled with an old longing to be that inherently confident.

Pursing her lips, Donna forced out an exaggerated puff of air to blow away such cobwebs, directing her mind instead to the tasks of the afternoon and evening ahead. Day shifts largely involved helping residents to dress, shower and toilet, as well as assistance at mealtimes. Nights involved a good deal of toileting and gently turning the less mobile patients to avoid the onset of bedsores. For Donna it was also the chance to get extra little jobs done, especially ones that helped brighten the place. Most of her efforts went unnoticed, but occasionally another staffer or resident would say: 'Don't the indoor plants in the rec room look shiny – did someone wipe over their leaves?' or 'Who added the nice border to the *What's on This Week* notice?'

She sometimes watched on with interest as a registered nurse attended to a wound or dispensed medication, but all in all Donna was content working at the grassroots level of care. To break up the more humdrum tasks, she occasionally helped conduct an outing or a craft class, or simply sat with the residents when a guest speaker or entertainer was brought in. Plumping a cushion, adjusting a hearing aid, setting hair in curlers and colouring nails, or just being available to hold a shaky hand – Donna usually finished her shifts wrapped in the warm glow of knowing she'd helped make the lives of others more bearable and even, in scattered moments, enjoyable.

She'd reinvented herself as a gainfully employed, together person. Sure, she knew her confidence still needed work, but moving into aged-care assistance had turned out to be the best decision Donna had ever made, giving her the mechanism to once again feel robust, wanted and worthy. She'd given up drinking the day her divorce from Derek went through, substituting the buzz of booze with the highs of self-reliance and altruism. Certainly it felt to her as if the chemicals in her brain were responding in the same way. Her job at Blue Vista seemed secure, she successfully and actively avoided the pitfalls and risks of romance, and she engaged in as little contact with her family as possible.

Still, when Donna was tired and let her mind contemplate such things, she was aware even a slight tilt in this tenuous equilibrium could send all of the pieces tumbling.

SUNDAY 15 JULY 2007

Donna

Although she still missed Mrs Selbourne, if there was one resident Donna most looked forward to seeing it was Lily Harford, who'd taken up residence in South Wing's coveted Room 18 at the start of the year. Knocking on the door, she paused for acknowledgement before walking in, past the en suite to her left and around Lily's bed to the double glass doors, throwing open the night curtains. Light drenched the room, causing Lily to narrow her eyes as they adjusted.

'Morning, Lily. A sunny but coolish day today, I think.'

'Good morning. How are you, my dear?'

Donna warmed with a pleasant rush at the term of endearment. 'Not too bad, thanks. I think your son-in-law is visiting you later today. That'll be nice. He seems a really decent bloke.'

'Oh. Sam. Yes, of course. Do you mind bringing my dressing gown closer to me?'

'Not a problem.' Donna moved back around the bed and dislodged the bathrobe from its hook just inside Lily's cupboard. 'Did you sleep well?'

'I'm still adjusting to a single bed but yes, I think I slept all right.'

Donna placed the gown on the end of the bed. 'It's only been five or so months. Everything takes a bit of getting used to.'

'What do you honestly think of it here, Donna? My daughter feels it's the best of its kind, but what do you think, in your experience?'

Donna appreciated the deference. 'I reckon it's up there with the best. It's less than ten years old, as you know. The facilities here are a lot better than some I saw in my training, that's for sure. Your daughter did her homework, I'd say. And of course its position is hard to beat,' Donna said, twisting to take in the spectacular view through the glass doors. A mix of white and brooding grey clouds had gathered on the horizon above the sea beyond the lawns, as if the day couldn't decide whether or not it intended to deliver some winter rain.

'I can't argue with that,' said Lily, following Donna's gaze before slowly pushing back the sheet and swinging her reedy legs over the side of the bed, the effort noticeable. 'Although before it went up I nearly spent a night in a police cell for threatening to whack an excavator driver with a placard. I was highly opposed to the building of this place, you know.'

Donna splutter-laughed as she aided her charge into an upright position and discreetly pulled Lily's nightie down over her thighs. 'Are you for real? I'd like to say I can't picture you holding a placard, or hitting someone with one, but in fact I can,' she said as Lily stood up. 'Here, slowly does it. I can help you get into the shower as well, if you like.'

'I think I can manage on my own, but thank you. Anyway, I'm in no rush. I actually don't know how you nurses cope, you know, changing dirty sheets and showering people's old, sagging bodies. Give me a balance sheet over a bed sheet any day. Doesn't it ever make you want to run for the hills?'

As a nanny for many years, Donna had been accustomed to bathing and feeding fresh-skinned, bright-eyed babies and toddlers. How would she feel dealing with dentures and adult nappies, she'd wondered in the first few weeks of her TAFE course. Would she find the elderly tiresome, uninteresting or even repulsive? As it turned out, false teeth and incontinence hadn't bothered her in the slightest. After all, it was hardly their fault. They couldn't help what their bodies were doing. They'd been fresh skinned and bright eyed once, like her and everyone else.

'Don't be silly. And I should remind you I'm not a qualified nurse, just a personal care assistant. Cleaning peoples' bits and pieces is part of my job.'

'Donna, I think you should consider getting your full nursing qualification one day. You could go a long way in this profession. You've got what it takes. In fact, you remind me of myself when I was starting out.'

Donna couldn't help emitting a small scoff as she passed the bathrobe to Lily. This was the last thing she had expected to hear. It seemed a huge compliment and not one she felt able to take seriously, but she appreciated that Lily saw such potential in her.

'I started off doing secretarial work,' Lily continued, 'but took myself off to university to get a degree at a time when very few women were doing so, and ended up creating and running Harford Accounting. I'm not saying it's for everyone, but I suspect your mind, like mine did, might enjoy the challenge of further study. Am I wrong?' Lily raised her eyebrows before piloting her arms into the dressing gown.

'I guess not. I'll think about it, I promise. I really do love what I do now, though.'

Lily scoffed. 'Surely there must be *something* about your job you dislike. I couldn't stand, for example, people who would spend an entire appointment moaning about paying lots of tax. Didn't occur to them to be grateful that it was only because they were making a lot of money in the first place.'

Donna grinned, imagining Lily giving short shrift to a whingeing client. There were only two really negative aspects to her job. The first was confronting the reality of death. She'd never forgotten the moment she'd seen her first corpse. It had been hard to reconcile the cadaver with the man who had, only the day before, joked proudly about the healthy and robust nature of his burps. The second was advanced dementia. Every person with the condition presented differently, in the degree and range of their symptoms. Some became agitated when their routine was disrupted. Some became aggressive, others paranoid or infantile and wanton in their behaviour. One man in Donna's care last year had regressed so far that he delighted in playing with his faeces, flinging them on the walls of his bathroom. It had distressed Donna greatly, knowing how mortified his healthy self would have been to see it.

But of course she wasn't about to relay any of this to Lily.

'Well, I suppose I'm not mad keen on the paperwork.'

'No, most people would agree with you there.'

Lily had been trying without success to gather her bathrobe's ties into a bow, so Donna gently moved in to take over.

'How did you get into this field of work, anyway?' Lily asked, relinquishing the task.

'I was thirty-one, single – divorced, actually – and needed a qualification. I'd been looking after children up to that point but it didn't pay very well and was unreliable and clunky, moving from one family to the next as each household's kids grew up. Not exactly a career as such.'

'I'm sure you were an excellent nanny.'

Donna didn't normally talk at work about her private life or past but there was something encouraging and accepting about Lily that made Donna feel comfortable opening up. 'Thanks. I suppose I was reasonable at it,' she said, supporting Lily who had started to sway a little as she took a step towards the cupboard. 'I like kids, even though I don't want any of my own. It started out as a source of pocket money in my last couple of years of school. Then one of my regular families asked if I'd consider becoming their full-time nanny because the mum had been promoted to a high-powered job that didn't lend itself to part-time hours. I was kind of tired of studying after finishing school so I made the call to put off university for a year. I wanted to get some cash behind me and have a bit of independence. A year turned into two and eventually into thirteen.'

'But why choose to work in aged care? Surely something exciting would have been more tempting,' Lily said, rummaging through the clothes in her cupboard drawers.

Donna set about making the bed. 'I felt I could build on my experience but apply it to a totally different age bracket. I'd researched the job prospects and aged care stood out as a no-brainer.'

'No-brainer? What do you mean by that?'

'Oh, sorry. An easy decision. An obvious choice.'

Donna noticed Lily had stopped what she was doing, as if she wasn't sure why she was standing there.

'Oh, I see. Well, I'm glad you did because otherwise we might never have met.'

The kind words felt akin to an embrace and, like compliments, were something Donna wasn't used to receiving. 'Here, let me help you put together some clothes for today.'

'Was it easy to get a position here?' Lily asked as Donna placed the selected clothes on the back of the armchair that lived by the end of her bed.

Donna thought back to when she had first enrolled in the certificate course, only a few months after her split with Derek. She'd assumed she would stay and find work in her home city. It never crossed her mind to spread her wings further than the boundaries of suburban Brisbane.

'A tutor suggested I could do my final semester at a regional campus so I decided on Rorook Tech because of its reputation in aged care. It turned out that a change of scene was just what I needed. And after returning to Brisbane for my final assessments, the contrast made it even more clear that I wanted a job away from a big city.'

'And that job turned out to be at Blue Vista?'

Donna returned to straightening Lily's sheets and blankets. 'Yes. I found out about a vacancy here through the Rorook campus. I submitted my resume, not really expecting anything to come of it, but they offered me a position. I was shocked, to be honest, but ecstatic.'

'So you packed up your life and moved to Finn Bay, and now here you are, years later, looking after me.'

Bed coverings and pillows in place, Donna faced Lily and smiled. 'It seems fate brought us together. Now, are you sure you don't want me to help you into the shower?'

'No, I'm certain you have others who need you more. Though perhaps when you have time you could find me a good book. Non-fiction if possible.'

Donna experienced a tiny sting of rejection before chastising herself for being so daft. Lily was right. She should get on with her rounds and see who else might need her help, or just a bit of company to start their day. Like poor Betty Klein. She and Jack Manningham, both outgoing and possessing wonderfully wicked senses of humour, were the first residents Donna had got to know at Blue Vista, and it was largely due to them that she had first gained a true ease and connection with the elderly. Jack's back was so rounded he walked with the crown of his head facing forward. His jokes would make a wharfie blush and no topic was off limits; he had once provided Donna with agonising detail about his prolific ear wax.

Betty also never held back in saying what she thought, whether that was about the world of politics or in the vacuous arena of celebrity gossip, and right or wrong her strong convictions couldn't easily be ignored. She often had Donna in stitches of laughter at her insights and the way she referred to the residents as 'inmates'. Betty's face, toasted and corrugated from a life of sun worship, was unfailingly decorated with red lipstick and topped with purple-rinsed hair. However, the clown-like bright colours belied a melancholy loneliness. Betty had only the occasional caller, generally one of her three sons, none of whom disguised their resentment at having to drag themselves away from something terribly important in Brisbane or Sydney in order to visit their mother.

Walking into the library in search of an interesting biography for Lily, Donna almost stepped on a beetle, its black carapace shimmering in a beam of morning light. She crouched down and was about to grasp the insect when three fingers closed round her wrist with a gentle firmness. Startled but immediately recognising whose hand was on hers by its missing digits, Donna looked up to see another South Wing resident, Frank Dartnell, his sapphire eyes twinkling.

Tall and remarkably straight-backed for his age, Frank had features that reminded Donna of Prince Philip, but without the Greek nose. He kept to himself a lot more than many of the others, so Donna had only developed a friendly association with him rather than anything more substantial.

'Oh, hi, Mr Dartnell. I didn't hear you come in.'

'If you try to pull her up you'll hurt her. Her legs are caught in the thread of the carpet, see?'

Donna, turning back to the creature, leaned down further to get a better look. 'Oh, so they are. Poor thing,' she said with concern.

'Here, let me.' With a delicacy and tenderness belying his large hands and the absence of two fingers, Frank prised the beetle from its fibre shackles before carrying it outside to live another day. He returned just as Donna was plucking a book from a shelf.

'That for Lily Harford?'

'How did you know?' Donna replied in surprise.

'Oh, just a lucky guess.'

Donna fixed her eyes on Frank before he added, 'A smart woman, isn't she? You have a soft spot for her, I'd reckon.'

Donna couldn't argue. The truth was she had, in fact, come to regard Lily somewhat like a grandmother. She'd asked herself more than once what it was that particularly drew her to Lily, unsure if it was the occasional twinkle in her eyes or the stories she'd told Donna about her youth. For whatever reason, there was something indefinable about the woman. Donna appreciated Lily not just as someone in her eighties but as someone comprised of all the ages she'd passed through in order to get there. It was as if she saw into Lily, to the layers underneath, the strata of younger women Lily used to be but who were now encased, like Russian dolls, in a body crumbling around them.

'Yes, I suppose I do. I'm fond of everyone at Blue Vista though,' Donna added.

'Well, don't get too attached, lassie,' Frank said, the kindness in his eyes softening the blow. 'None of us residents is here for too long.'

Pauline

Ignoring the morning light and the raucous screech of a cockatoo, Pauline tried to ward off the switch from sleep to wakefulness as the pleasant dream slithered away, taking with it an unidentifiable location in which she was identifiably single and definitely happy. But it was no good and she tensed, ashamed, as Sam placed his arm across her middle and sidled closer, his hand alighting tenderly on her breast.

'What are you doing?' she muttered, aware of a slight pitch in her gut at her frostiness. When she didn't meet him halfway he spooned firmly into her back, as if seeking the reassuring familiarity of her body.

The school year was only midway through but already Pauline felt pinched and strained, akin to the steady but sure onset of a heavy head cold. When she thought about it, the almost chronic mental lethargy she was battling had begun in summer, in the lead-up to Lily's move to Blue Vista. The whole sorting exercise at King Street had been horrendous, Pauline able to see right through her mother's brave front. Hiding her own misgivings, she'd tried with reluctant resignation to focus instead on getting the job done, but as she and Sam had driven away in silent contemplation the atmosphere had been heavy. The day had nearly broken her. Since then, it seemed to Pauline that only running, increasingly further and faster, could go any way towards countering her mental tiredness.

Acquiring a room at Blue Vista, especially one at the end of a wing, had been both fortunate and timely. Its glass doors facing the lawns and ocean beyond, as well as a garden-facing window on the adjacent wall, provided an abundance of light and views, and Pauline was confident the facility, five minutes' drive from House on the Hill, was delivering the promised excellent care of her mother. But the deliberate despatching of responsibility and a sense of having abandoned and failed her mother clung to Pauline. Worry over Lily's safety had simply been replaced by a profound remorse. The stress and strain of Lily's worsening condition hadn't, as she'd hoped, been eased by a change in location but had simply been traded for the weight of sorrow. Why had she thought the move would be a panacea? An institution, no matter how lovely its aspect, facilities and staff, was no substitute for a family home and its happy, rich lattice of memories.

To assuage her guilt, Pauline had taken on as many peripheral care tasks as possible given her long work hours, driving Lily to medical appointments or the shops. Some days she simply took her mother out of Blue Vista for a stroll along the esplanade or just chatted with her in Lily's room or within the facility's pretty, low-walled garden. And she arranged (and supervised with fervency) a roster of visits from the family, so that Lily had no chance to feel abandoned or forgotten. Pauline was almost as busy with her mother as she had been before the move but she was determined not to complain. After all, she'd been the one pushing for it.

'I'm snuggling in. Is that a crime? Would you prefer I didn't?' Sam asked, his voice sleepy but tinted with irritation. He shuffled back slightly, keeping his arm around her waist. 'Please don't tell me you're still cross after last night.'

Pauline pushed her backside into the concave of her husband's torso by way, she hoped, of a white flag. There'd been times in the last few months when she'd known she was being mean-spirited, using Sam as an emotional punching bag by falling back on the topic of their finances as an easy justification for her behaviour. She experienced a pang of guilt each time she bad-mouthed Sam but it was like scratching an itch and she couldn't seem to find her way through to act otherwise. Although she loved him and her snitchy barbs embarrassed her, the criticisms slithered greasily out of her mouth, even as she watched her husband's face close over in battle-worn surrender.

When she'd brought it up with renewed venom during last night's row, he'd exclaimed in frustration, 'For fuck's sake, Pauline, not that old chestnut. Surely there has to come a point where my financial sins can be relegated to water under the marital bridge.'

Lately, she had seen her resentment at Sam's financial naivety and ineptitude begin to scrape at his masculinity.

So perhaps she could at least accept his touch, she thought now, letting herself relax and allowing Sam's hand to caress her hip. Maybe intimacy was just what she and they needed. But instead of making any further moves, Sam simply kissed her shoulder.

'Go back to sleep, love. You could do with the shut-eye. All you have to do today is take the littlies to that pirates and princesses party. But that's not until midday.'

'Oh, I'd actually forgotten. Want to come with me?'

'I can't. I'm seeing your mum then, remember?' he said, planting a prolonged kiss on her upper arm. 'Much as I'd love, of course, to see all those preschoolers eating fairy bread and drippy watermelon, surrounded by parrots, swords, tiaras and tantrums.'

'Ha ha,' Pauline replied, smiling as she rolled onto her back, her eyes still shut. 'I'm tempted by the sleep-in but I still want to get in a quick run.'

She could sense Sam looking at her, and with something on his mind. He always took in a breath and held it before raising an important topic. 'What?' she asked.

'What do you mean, what?'

'What are you thinking?'

'What are *you* thinking?'

'I asked first.'

'Okay, if you must know, I was thinking that you look so relaxed right now. I know you say you dream a lot, but you look peaceful and ... dare I say it, almost contented when you're asleep.'

'That's because in my dreams I'm retired and on holiday somewhere exotic,' she retorted a little too loudly, trying to sound flippant but knowing it probably still came across as having a dig. 'Sorry', she went on, trying to deflect the direction in which their discussion could easily head again if she weren't careful.

Sam's elbow nearly knocked Pauline on the temple as he moved onto his back, transferring his hands to behind his head. 'I know I disappoint you,' he said. 'I regret not pursuing a different path when I had the chance, before being over sixty was career-change suicide.' He paused, staring up at the ceiling. 'I was selfish not taking that promotion. I should've thought more about how my decision would affect you. And then the investment debacle ... I'm sorry I've let you down. Twice.'

Pauline hadn't seen this coming, this earnest confession and vindication. It threw her. She reached down to finger the thick mass of curls on his lower belly. 'Please, let's not talk about this now. You don't disappoint me.'

As a whole orchestra of squawking cockatoos flew over the house, the two of them lay in stillness, Pauline chewing over both of their conciliations and wondering if they'd been said in complete honesty. She doubted Sam was being truthful about wishing he'd moved into a paper-pushing managerial role, but she adored him in that moment for saying otherwise; and for his apology.

Sam tilted his body towards his wife and stroked her forehead, pushing away a stray strand of her hair. 'And I hope you realise you're a fantastic principal, a wonderful wife, a great mother and grandma, and one of the strongest people I know. And you're tireless in taking care of Lily. Your mother's a huge drain on your time and energy. I do get it, you know, and I'm sorry our money situation doesn't help.'

It wasn't often that Sam expressed his feelings like this and Pauline turned her head to look deeply into his eyes, knowing she didn't need to say anything in return.

'I know it can't be easy to watch her become so frail and forgetful. Her memory's become a bit like Swiss cheese, hasn't it?' he continued. 'She's always been so vibrant and self-reliant – funny, reminds me of someone I know – but in the last year she's taken such a dive.'

Pauline yawned and rolled away from Sam so he could no longer read her face, docking her back once again into the sturdy, warm curve of him. As he pulled her in tighter it reminded Pauline of their early years when they couldn't nuzzle close enough, get too much skin contact, no matter how fervently their bodies pressed together. And in that one affectionate moment Pauline forgave him for his financial stupidity. Forgave him for his reliance on practicality over expressed emotion. And forgave herself for smearing the grime of her own sorrow and sense of failure all over her marriage until she could no longer see its shine and true value.

'I can't presume to know how hard it must be for you,' Sam mumbled into her neck. 'I know you feel guilty and sad that she's moved to Blue Vista, but we did the right thing, okay?'

Pauline felt like a tortoise. One minute curled up in her shell, holding everything in for self-protection as if her life depended on it, the next finding a terrifying temptation to open up and bare all. The tears came knocking but Pauline breathed through the urge purposefully and slowly. She didn't like to show vulnerability. It wasn't in her personality description. It wasn't, she thought, the package Sam had signed up for when they married. Nurtured by the comfort of her husband's embrace, she fell back asleep.

It wasn't until several hours later that she was woken by fierce daylight swamping the bedroom as Sam whisked opened the curtains.

'Wakey-wakey.'

Blinking to force her eyes to adjust and focus, Pauline croaked, 'God, I didn't even feel you leave the bed. I must have been sound asleep.' A welcome aroma of coffee beans hit her as Sam placed a steaming mug on her bedside table.

'Dead to the world, love. I didn't have the heart to wake you until now but I have to get going. Anything else I can bring you before I head to the Vista?'

'Um, no thanks,' Pauline replied, propping herself on her elbows. 'What time is it anyway?'

'After eleven. So you should probably be thinking about getting up if you don't want to be late to Rachel's.'

After the front door closed and Sam's car tyres crunched on the driveway's gravel, Pauline lay back down. Kicking off the blanket but keeping the sheet over her, more for emotional than physical comfort, she moved onto her side, curling into a foetal position. Tears stung her drowsy eyes and tickled her cheek as they rolled down and onto her pillow. By the time she stopped weeping, the coffee was stone cold.

Lily

I watch Sam walk into the residents' lounge, his eyes scanning the room for me. I've always had a lot of time for my son-in-law. There've been many occasions over the years when I've wanted to tell him to pull his finger out, but his soul's in the right place. I wave at him and he smiles as he approaches, before bending down to kiss me on the cheek.

'Your hair looks nice,' he comments as he sits next to me.

I touch the grey bun and tuck in a few stray hairs. 'Thank you, Sammy. Donna did it yesterday. She always does a good job, I think. Is Pauline not coming today?'

As soon as the words are out I sense we've already had this conversation. There are times my brain feels more like it's composed of vapour than solid matter. But it's hard when I'm distracted by the mindless drivel of a game show blaring on the television nearby.

'She's taken Luke and Rosie to a children's party, so that Rach and Christos can have an afternoon to themselves without the rug rats,' he says before sandwiching my hand in both of his. 'How's the arthritis? Giving you gip?'

'It's not too bad. In this cooler weather they seem to hurt a bit more, but perhaps it's just getting worse anyway. The only time it's a real nuisance is when we use those slippery packs.'

'Packs? Oh, yes. Pauline said you've joined the cards group.'

'I've been told I should also join the music appreciation group, but we'll see. That might be taking things too far.'

Sam laughs as he releases me. 'Want a coffee?' he asks, pointing to the refreshments trolley only a few metres away. He stands up.

'Yes, please.' I watch him select two white mugs and spoon coffee into each from a large Nescafé tin.

'So,' he says, as he concentrates on filling the cups from the urn, 'how are you, Lily? Be honest.'

I smile at his consideration. 'I'm fine. Obviously I'd prefer to still be in my own home but it is what it is, eh? I have to say, though, that I really dislike the demotion to a single bed. It's not that I need to stretch myself out that much, but I feel a bit patronised and – what's the word – oh, what *is* that word – demeaned, yes, demeaned, going back to a child-sized bed. I still haven't got used to it. It's like I'm being put in my place, like being a child.' A streak of embarrassment warms my face.

Sam looks across and down at me, a tower from this angle. I feel so small.

'I totally get it. I could see if we could have a double bed brought in if you like.' Sam passes me a cup and sits down again.

'Thank you, but I think that would be frowned upon. And I don't think it would fit anyway.'

'I suppose everything has been such an adjustment.'

I bend forward and give his forearm a little pat, grateful he isn't trying to sweep the topic under the carpet. 'I suppose I also need to let go of the notion that having fewer possessions makes me somehow less accomplished or ... important. Does that sound vain?'

'Not at all, Lily.'

'But I do at least feel safe and well cared for. In fact, being here has made me realise that at King Street I depended too heavily on Pauline for help *and* for company. Now I'm here I try not to add to her workload but she still insists on running errands that I'm sure the nursing staff could easily arrange for me, like taking me to the doctor in town when there's a perfectly good one who visits.'

'She never minded. She'd do anything for you. We both would.'

There's a pause as we sip our coffees and silently acknowledge the sweet truth of that.

'You've also finally put some weight back on, which is good,' Sam adds. 'I'm really glad you seem to have settled in well here. Pauline's been almost sick with worry about you, feeling guilty.'

I hate to think of my daughter being as upset as that. She must work hard to hide it from me. 'Please reassure Pauline that although I miss King Street I'm mucking along all right, all things considered. I've made friends and renewed a couple of old ones, and by and large everyone gets along and seems to look out for each other.' I point to the other side of the room and lower my voice. 'See the woman snoozing over there, with the bright red lips? Betty, her name is. We used to play tennis against each other.'

'She looks a bit scary, even when she's out of it,' Sam replies with equal precaution.

'You know, she wore that amount of make-up even on the court.'

We chuckle in a mood of conspiracy.

'She's quite a nice person though. We sit at the same table for meals. And so is Frank Dartnell. He's probably tucked away in his room. He's very shy, I think, but from what I can tell he has a caring and honest nature. Much more refined, anyway, than that Jack – I can't remember his surname, but he's over in the corner, see?' I indicate to the furthest arm-chair. 'I hate to think how many times he probably had his mouth washed out with soap as a child.'

Sam is smiling at me, his eyes wide and shining. 'Since when did a crude joke bother you, Lily Harford?'

I try to keep a straight face, putting a forefinger to my lips. 'Shh, you'll spoil my reputation. Yes, they're funny but I can't laugh out loud or else I'll be seen as completely unladylike.'

'Never change, okay?' My son-in-law looks wistful, then grins again, and it's catching.

'I'll do my best, Sammy. Even if people only see me as a crusty old apron, I still have my memories and know what's gone into making me the person I am. And it's nice you see that too.'

We finish our hot drinks and chat for a while longer, about the weather and Labor's chances of getting into power. Eventually my son-in-law stands up and takes both empty cups back to the trolley. 'We could debate that all day but I should probably get on home.'

'All right. Thank you for coming,' I say, looking up at him. 'And tell Pauline not to worry so much about me, and that she really doesn't have to do so much. I'm paying enough for this place – she should let the staff here do all those jobs.'

'But that's your daughter for you, Lily, a whirlwind of energy and capability,' he replies, a certain pride in his voice. 'Now, before I go, is there anything I can get you?'

'If I had a bigger room I'd suggest a double bed. The single is so demeaning. It makes me feel like a child.'

I've come to know what the look on his face means. 'Have I already mentioned that?' The hesitation in my voice gives away my embarrassment.

'Yes, but that's okay.' Sam leans in and down to encircle me with sturdy arms, just as Lexie appears and reminds me I'm rostered on to feed Roast, Blue Vista's pet duck. Lexie's a sweet young girl, blonde and petite and still learning the ropes of her job, I think. I get the sense she struggles to handle the more challenging parts of aged care. Not just the heavy lifting but the troubling aspects too. Old age ain't all a bed of roses.

My body's particularly stiff today so I take my time heading outside to the central garden, a pretty space edged and reasonably well sheltered by its low sandstone walls. I clean out then refill Roast's water and food bowls before letting him out of his enclosure for a waddle and forage. I watch him with envy as he happily searches for tasty treats in the grass. He has it all sorted. Just living in the moment, unaware of his mortality. Forage, drink, splash, dry wings in the sun, rest, sleep, forage again. That's the extent of his repertoire. It's all about the immediate, unburdened with the anticipation of what might be around the corner.

I stare beyond the garden to the lawned, sloping grounds behind, past the smattering of million-dollar homes sitting smugly on the clifftop to the expansive panorama of Finn Bay. Relishing the touch of a light sea breeze, I feast my eyes on the water of the bay and the vast and glorious Pacific Ocean into which it melds. On clear days like this the sea glistens but sometimes, when a gale rears up, it paces like a wild beast. Either way, I'm always mesmerised.

I take a seat on a nearby bench. The rays of a mellow winter sun feel marvellous on my face and arms, and I picture myself down on the beach. To know it's so close by gives me such solace. I close my eyes and I'm with little Pauline as we search for shells, her toddler feet leaving tiny imprints on the damp sand. Even as a one-year-old she would stand at the water's edge, her sweet little hand in mine, watching the waves' antics and shrieking with delight.

The sound is as sharp and delicious a memory as any from those early years.

1952

I called my daughter Pauline, as the name straddles both femininity and strength. At nearly twelve months old, her skin is still so perfect and pink and fleshy and she makes the sweetest humming noise as she looks up at me and suckles, her tongue thrusting, the pull rhythmical and exquisite. Her eyelids get rosier and heavier, the milk gradually weaving its soporific magic. At the beginning, feeding felt like tiny razorblades slicing into my nipples, but my baby and I soon got the hang of it and now I feel almost guilty at the physical pleasure as she draws milk through the ducts and into her perfect rosebud mouth. When her tummy is full, her lips gradually lose their hold on me until her body goes limp. I bend down to her, inhaling her milk-breath and the smell of her skin and the soft, downy hair gracing her scalp. It will be such a wrench to wean her but I know that day is coming soon, especially as she's now got her first tooth.

Each time she'd fall asleep in the first few weeks after her birth, I was too afraid to move for fear of disturbing her. Sometimes the two of us would sit on the couch for hours, my arm going numb under her head as I joined her in slumber. The randomness and unpredictability of sleep was torturous on my body, but even in my dog-tired state it felt like our own little paradise in the cosy nest of our King Street home. Those early days passed in a mist of feeding, dozing and nappy changes. I did my best in between to put something together by way of a meal, but often just found myself staring at her chubby little forearms or tiny fingers that kneaded my breast as she fed. As soon as I got her down for the night, I would begin checking letters, ledgers, tax returns or reports from work, dropped in to me by Fred every couple of days. Sometimes I typed my own correspondence, the click-clack of the keys a handy way, as it turned out, to settle Pauline in her cot.

I stayed at home with her for six months, entrusting young Fred to take charge of the business in my absence. He proved himself to be a star employee, phoning me on anything that was beyond his experience and generally keeping Harford Accounting Services ticking over. But since then I've been easing myself back into the office, spending the mornings there. Ma helps on days when she isn't too busy with her sewing business, and the rest of the time I reluctantly leave my girl with a nanny who comes highly recommended by the district health nurse. Although the pull of Pauline is momentous, once I stop breastfeeding her I'll return to work Monday to Friday, maybe even Saturdays again. The firm is coasting along all right but I can already see we've lost two valuable clients due to my absence. I know I'll need to take the reins fully again before coasting turns into slipping. I can't afford to go backwards, not after everything I've built up.

The company has only been in operation for four years but I'm already in a higher income bracket than I'd ever dreamed I'd be. Sometimes I pinch myself that I'm a business owner and employer. I know it takes me away from Pauline, but I'm determined my child will never have to count pennies like my parents do. She will grow up without a father (and when she's old enough I will tell her what she needs to know about him) but I am determined she will have the opportunities to pursue any dreams she conjures for herself.

I blink now as Pauline's mouth slides off my nipple. Did I just drop off to sleep? My baby certainly has. Groggily, I cover my exposed breast and hold Pauline in one arm then stand, using my free hand to push down against the armrest for leverage. I'm bushed but the fierce instinct to protect and provide for my daughter keeps me putting one foot in front of the other. She remains dead to the world as I place her with care in the cot. I watch her ribcage rise and fall for several moments and release the breath I've been holding, as if afraid that exhaling might have woken her. How odd that one day this small creature will be talking, walking, making important decisions, going to school, falling in love, I hope holding down a satisfying job, probably marrying. How strange to think a time will come when she'll be old, older than I am now. Pauline in her forties, or her fifties. I'll be in my eighties then. Good god, imagine that.

Pauline

After taking Luke and Rosie to the pirate party, Pauline was physically tired but riding a high from precious time spent with her grandchildren. The afternoon had turned out to be highly entertaining, especially when one little girl had tried to kiss Luke, only to have Rosie push herself between him and Cinderella and declare, while brandishing a star-topped wand: 'No! You can't have him! He's my brother and *I* love him!' Pauline had instinctively spun around to share the laughter with Sam, only to remember he was dutifully visiting his mother-in-law.

Recalling this moment, as well as Sam's understanding and tenderness that morning, Pauline sought him out with a passionate kiss as soon as she returned home. Her intention was to drag him upstairs but before she got a chance he was undressing her, their hands groping each other with fervency. It felt wonderful to want him again so impulsively and instinctively.

Completely carried away as they fell onto the couch, they didn't hear the click of the front door. Having never shaken the habit of treating House on the Hill as if it was hers to come and go as she pleased, Rachel walked in. With Luke balanced on one hip and her house keys dangling in her other hand, she had no choice but to absorb the sight of her father's head buried and bobbing, accompanied by Pauline's groans. Rachel's mouth fell open as she emitted an involuntary moan of her own and almost dropped her toddler in surprise. In the time it took for her eye-patched little boy to ask, 'What Pa-Pa doing?', she had made a fast retreat.

As the front door slammed shut, a grinning Sam clambered to his feet, wiping his mouth with his knuckle. Pauline rooted around the couch and floor for her underwear, cringing in excruciating embarrassment, unable to shake the scene that her daughter must have beheld. There was no point trying to resurrect any carnal enthusiasm. That horse had well and truly bolted.

'That girl needs to learn some boundaries,' she hissed as she fought the clasp of her bra back into place. 'I just left their place. Why on earth was she here? The one time we actually get carried away, our daughter walks in on us. We shouldn't have been so careless.'

'It's our house,' Sam pointed out calmly. 'We can do what we want, love.'

As Pauline straightened the cushions there was a soft tapping on the door and a piece of paper came skimming under it. Sam walked over and picked up the note.

'What is it?'

'It's from Rachel,' Sam replied, frowning momentarily before smiling again. 'Seems we made a bit of an impression.'

'No shit, Sherlock. But what does it say?'

'Just came over with your purse because you'd left it at ours. I've popped it under the doormat and my key is in it. I sometimes forget you and Dad aren't just parents. Sorry.'

'Perhaps we should keep with tradition and restrict all future activity to the bedroom,' Pauline said, peering over Sam's shoulder to read the note for herself.

Sam turned and looked hopefully at his wife, one eyebrow raised. 'Does that mean there will be more *activity*, then?'

Her annoyance subjugated by her husband's chuckle, Pauline replied, 'Of course. But I think I've had all the excitement I can take in one day.'

If the bricks of their relationship had always been genuine affection, shared history and a similar sense of humour, sex had been the cement, prioritised and regular. Sam had been a skilled lover from the first time they'd explored each other's bodies, subconsciously able to read her mood and movements and fine tune his accordingly in order to bring maximum pleasure to them both. But even with his intimate knowledge of the way her mind worked between the sheets, more often than not over the past year Pauline had found herself just wanting the whole thing over as soon as possible, unable to corral the required energy and enthusiasm. Instead of focusing on the physical sensations, her mind would be off in another world, filled instead with her relentless to-do list. Her thoughts would race with anything from what medical appointments her mother needed taking to that week to how on earth the school was going to raise the funds needed for updating its computers. She felt like a wound-up spring ready to uncoil – not in sexual ecstasy but in an explosion of stress and sadness. So she didn't want today's misfire to serve as a convenient excuse to avoid any future attempts, in the bedroom or elsewhere.

She and Sam passed the evening watching a movie but, as the film played out, the warm glow of the day faded within Pauline. A dense pressure filled her head as she once again entered the gloomy tunnel in which she seemed to exist most days. When the credits rolled she went up to bed before her husband, who wanted to get a bit of work done and reply to some emails.

With an achingly heavy tiredness, Pauline lay on her back, the bedside light casting shadows on the ceiling, and sank further into her sorrow. Swelling and mounting, her dark emotions were like waves surging towards each other and a collision she feared could change everything.

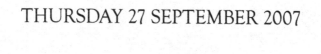
THURSDAY 27 SEPTEMBER 2007

Pauline

'Hi, Mum. Is this a good time or are you busy?'

Pauline stared out of her office window as she held the phone to her ear, marvelling at how her daughter's voice always had the power to warm and brighten. The call was a lovely distraction, a timely lift from the low frame of mind she still seemed unable to shake.

'No, no, it's fine to talk. I'm just in the middle of going through some enrolment data, so I'm more than happy to take a break. How are you? How's Lukie this morning? Has he come down with something, do you think?'

'Not sure yet. He was still a bit sniffly yesterday and he's definitely not his usual self but there's no temperature, so fingers crossed.'

Pauline's assistant poked her head in and flashed all ten fingers up in the air twice. Pauline nodded. Twenty minutes before some prospective parents were due to arrive for an enrolment interview.

'Kids pick up everything that's going around. You seemed to catch a cold every few months at that age, if I remember.'

'Well, I sent him to day care this morning, rightly or wrongly. I thought about keeping him home in case, but I'd promised to visit Nana-Lily and didn't want to risk him passing something on to her, so I chose the lesser of two evils.'

Pauline nodded to herself, appreciating her daughter's thoughtfulness. 'How was Mum yesterday?'

'That's why I'm calling, actually.'

Pauline's stomach clenched. She thought it unlikely to be something good. 'Oh? What happened?'

'She was fine at first and we were chatting as usual about things on the news, like that awful hurricane in the US, and the juicy scandal that cabinet minister is trying to wheedle his way out of. You know, the Kings Cross thing.' Rachel paused as if waiting for her mother to confirm she was following. When Pauline remained silent, Rachel continued. 'Anyway, she was particularly interested in that gossip. Then we started a game of Scrabble but we'd only had a couple of turns when she literally swept her letter tiles off their rack. I think she said something like "Stupid game. What do you want to play this for?" or words to that effect.'

Pauline leaned back in her chair and exhaled slowly.

'And just before that, there'd been this long, massively uncomfortable wait during her turn. I mean, I'm talking ten minutes. She was really struggling to make a word with her letters. I think her anger was a front, Mum. You know, to cover her embarrassment.'

Pauline shook her head as if the action could somehow reject the facts. 'What did you do?'

'What could I do? I picked up her tiles and started talking about the kids to, you know, deflect from what had just happened, but she went totally silent. And when I asked if she'd prefer I left, she just kind of nodded and, well, I took that as a yes and said I'd see her soon. Mum, it was awful. I feel like I bailed on her, but the atmosphere was so weird in the room that I thought I should leave.'

Pauline mustered up her most reassuring voice. 'You didn't desert her and I'm sure she'd understand. She's been having more moments like that, when she's a bit mixed up. Remember the specialist told us it's to be expected. With confusion comes anxiety.' Pauline was bolstering Rachel but her own tummy felt like a free-falling elevator.

'I just feel so bad,' Rachel whispered.

'I'll try to see her today or tomorrow. So don't dwell on it, all right?'

'All right. Thanks, Mum. Well, I'll let you get back to work. Let me know how she is.'

Pauline paced her office. In the eight months since her mother had moved into Blue Vista she had settled in well and seemed happier overall, but there had been a steady mental decline the staff said had taken even them by surprise. Mostly, thank goodness, she was lucid and rational but at unpredictable times she'd stop mid-sentence, not just forgetting a word but also losing complete track of the topic, and occasionally had been muddled about the time of day, exclaiming 'My mind's a fuzz, Pauline' or 'Everything's so jumbled in here' while tapping impatiently on the side of her head.

Despite all of that, however, the recent, formal diagnosis of vascular dementia had been a shock to the family. It was no longer a case of thinking Lily was a little forgetful due to her age, and assuming she'd largely level out. Now there was the real possibility, probability even, that the disease would progress, perhaps even to the point where she could no longer recognise Pauline. And that was unthinkable.

At every visit Pauline was also seeing Lily's constant physical discomfort. Mostly this was the result of her worsening arthritis but with the recent onset of a urinary tract infection and, at varying times, indigestion and skin sores, her mother's old body was finally declaring its limits. Lily did her best to conceal these issues or make a joke of the pain but her face inevitably lost the battle, giving the game away. It was all very well to put on a brave front, but Pauline could see that sooner or later even courage couldn't win this kind of war.

Without thinking, she picked up her mobile again.

'It's me.' She could hear the drone of a machine in the background. 'Sounds like you're out at the pumping station.'

'It's not like you to call from work. Everything okay?'

Pauline paused. Having phoned Sam, she didn't know what she'd intended to say. All she knew was that she needed to hear his calm and encouraging voice.

'Pauline, love? Are you still there?'

'Rachel called. Mum's had another episode. Are you free to talk?'

'Of course. Let me just move away from the pumps ... So, what happened?'

Pauline waited for a few seconds until the noise had dulled. 'Mum and Rach were playing Scrabble and she got

confused and completely lost it.' Pauline's voice quivered.
'Sorry. I'm finding it hard.'

'Well, it's a hard situation. Everything's clearly becoming
a struggle for her.'

'And I hate that. *Hate* it.'

'I know you do. It's confronting that she's going downhill.
We're so used to a stronger Lily; the woman we've always
known.'

Pauline smiled pensively. 'Do you remember the time you
first met her, and how nervous you were standing outside
the front of King Street, especially when Mum opened the
door and greeted you in her favourite power suit?'

Lily was in her early fifties then. Underneath a veneer of
silver hair stubbornly woven through with auburn strands,
and a slight spread around her middle, there was still a visible
core of pride and youth and vibrancy. In fact, Pauline had
always thought her friends' middle-aged mothers seemed, in
comparison, somewhat dull and monochromatic.

'Yeah. And she gave me this man-strength handshake and
her eyes said: "I might be a woman but if you mess with my
daughter I'll come after you like a big-balled bulldog having
a really, really bad day."'

Pauline laughed. She hadn't told Sam at the time but
she'd been sure her mother had intentionally kept her work
outfit on that evening, the flared pantsuit and jumbo-
rollered hair purposefully used to advertise she was not to
be messed with. Despite this, one of the things that had
cemented Pauline's confidence in Sam was the rapport
he'd so quickly developed with her mother. His respect for
Lily and the warm attention he paid to her gave no suggestion of an attempt to falsely impress or slyly ingratiate, but

seemed to stem from true admiration and, quickly on its heels, genuine affection.

'Mum has always been so resilient and expected everyone around her to be the same. It's difficult to see her as weak now. It's as though all that light and colour are leaching away.'

'She's not weak, love, just vulnerable. There's a very big difference. Underneath, she's still strong in her own way.'

Pauline wanted so badly to see this, but it was proving too hard. She preferred to focus on the mother she'd always known. 'Remember how she never let us get away with anything? How she had a way of expressing displeasure without having to utter a single word?'

Sam chuckled this time. 'She still does. Her eyes narrow and she tilts her head to one side as if she's getting the measure of you, and then she sighs; this long, exaggerated exhalation that comes towards you with such palpable disapproval.'

Pauline put her head in her hand and smiled with recognition. 'Oh god, that's so spot on. She was always the queen of making you feel like you could be a better person. Well, me anyway.'

'Come on, you've admitted you use the same technique on your students from time to time.'

'But not nearly as effectively,' Pauline rebutted. 'I miss her, Sam.'

'I know you do.'

'It was just the two of us all those years ...'

'Until I joined the family.'

Pauline was whisked back to that cold, crisp spring day. Wearing her mother's cream satin swoop-backed wedding dress, her dark tresses unadorned by a veil but allowed instead to waterfall over her shoulders, Pauline had stood at the entrance to St Stephen's, her mother by her side. As the music began, Lily had rested her chin on her daughter's shoulder and whispered, 'You're far and away my greatest achievement, my darling. Sam's a fortunate man.'

'It's so strange to think I'm around the same age now – no, older – as Mum was when she walked me down the aisle. Remember when the minister asked who was giving me away and Mum said something like "Officially I am, but as men don't own women, I think Pauline is perfectly capable of devoting *herself* to Samuel, don't you?"'

There had been an audible murmur through the congregation, mixed with some stifled giggles. Pauline had darted her eyes to Sam, thinking he might be, if not shocked, embarrassed at this break from wedding convention. Instead, he'd taken up the thread and announced 'And I give myself to her' before beaming back at Pauline. In pure relief, Pauline's eyes had silently pronounced: *That's my mum – isn't she just fantastic?*

'Your mother was – is – something. A powerhouse, really.'

'She was driven, but only because she had to put food on the table for the two of us. It's not as if she could turn to her parents for money.'

'Her father ended up with dementia too, right?'

'Uh-huh. I was ten when Grandpa Ken died. I remember visiting him in an awful nursing home a few months before. He didn't know who I was, just sat pathetically in a chair staring at nothing. I remember thinking how sad it was, and how weird that someone you'd known all your life could look at you so vacantly, as if you'd never met.'

'Perhaps he was so deep in his own world by that stage that he wasn't suffering.'

'Maybe. But – and I only found this out much later – he apparently endured a pretty drawn out and horrific death in the end. Mum hid it all from me at the time but admitted when I was older that he was bed-bound, in a fetal position, unable to swallow, and basically died of starvation, or dehydration, I'm not sure which. Maybe both.'

'Hell. It's best to think of him before he got like that, then, eh?'

'Of course, and I do. I've told you how much I used to love visiting his hardware shop, with its shelves and shelves of stuff. There wasn't a spare inch of space.' Pauline smiled to herself as she remembered. It felt better, safer, to be focusing on something positive. 'He used to challenge me to find a spade or a jar of screws or an extension cord or a sieve, and time me. I'd run around Ferguson's poking my nose into every nook and cranny until I unearthed the object. The only rule was that I couldn't move anything in my search. Even though the place resembled chaos, he knew where every single item was, and didn't want his system messed up. I think by the time I was eight or nine I could have been put to use serving customers, I knew the store so well.'

'Sounds like your mum's work ethic came from him.'

'And from Grandma Jean. I'm sorry you didn't get to meet her either. Her death hit Mum hard. I'm sure she expected Grandma to be around for another ten years at least. She'd worked hard all her life, raising Mum and Uncle David and running the house and taking in sewing work to help make ends meet, and if it weren't for her hip operation she'd have been able to enjoy some kind of retirement.'

Pauline knew she was prattling on but it felt good to bring her grandparents back to life, even if just for a few moments. 'The house in Haversham Road was the centre of her universe – her kids, her husband, her sewing, her fruit trees. God, her fruit! That house was bursting with jars of plums and apricots. I wish she'd taught me how to pick and stew and preserve them. I can still remember the smell. It was fantastic. We should have kept Grandma's jars.'

'Well, now I know what to give you for Christmas.'

'You know, I think Mum admired Grandma Jean but at the same time didn't want to be defined by domesticity and motherhood. She strove to have an identity of her own, out in the world. And she had to, having no-one else bringing in an income.'

Pauline heard the bell mark the end of the first period. Aware of the length of their chat, she asked with reluctance, 'Do you need to get back to things?'

'Soon, but that's okay, love. You know, I had nothing but admiration and respect for my mother. She was a full-time home keeper who raised three kids with a ton of humour and patience. But Lily owning her own business, well, that was an amazing achievement, especially back then.'

'It doesn't make her better than your mum, just an achiever in a different way.' Pauline was surprised but touched at Sam's frank comparison. If she were honest, she'd have admitted she thought her mother unequalled, but she was never going to say so to Sam. Her mum had worked harder than most men in similar positions, simply to make sure no-one had reason to question her professional ability or credibility. She'd needed an ego to survive in the business world in a time when the passions and talents and dreams of women were forced to lurk apologetically in the shadows of men.

Now, in her mid-eighties, she was under another shadow, under a different threat.

'Listen, I guess I had better go,' Sam said. 'It's good you sound a bit more chipper, more like yourself. I'll see you tonight, okay?'

Her slightly racing pulse signalled to Pauline her disquiet, a simmering disappointment. Sam had quickly got her reminiscing about the past, perhaps to cheer her up but probably to avoid the possibility of awkward tears over the phone. It was clear he was most comfortable when she was 'more like herself'. She suddenly regretted that their easy conversation had tempted her to fully open up to him.

She sighed and checked her watch. The visitors were clearly running late or had decided not to come at all. She wanted to vent her disappointment, at them, at herself, at her mother, at Sam. He always seemed to draw a line in the sand, making it clear how far his comfort stretched in emotional territory, forcing her into the lonely situation of believing she must face her anxieties and insecurities on her own instead of sharing her innermost fears with those she most loved. But what if she didn't want to be strong? Would her husband or her mother love and admire her any less?

Locked into a life where she had to be so fucking capable and dependable and robust, it occurred to Pauline that all she wanted to do was scream.

Donna

The wall clock showed it was bang on ten, although Donna knew better than to rely on it. The large black-rimmed face alternated being slow with being accurate, depending on how long it had been since someone had bothered to reach up and correct its hands. Where management had sourced it was a mystery, but Donna suspected a charity shop, or someone's great-auntie looking for an easy disposal.

Blue Vista was undergoing minor renovations, mostly involving coats of paint but also carpet replacement in the common areas. It had caused some inconvenience but nothing that couldn't, the staff thought, be worked around. Most of the residents were showing patience, except Betty. She had been complaining daily about the fumes, while simultaneously admitting she used to try to get high on nail varnish. This morning the smell of solvent was so pungent and overpowering that, on her tea break, Donna decided to seek refuge outside.

Adjusting her eyes to the glare, Donna noted that, despite the slight south-easterly, the walled garden was cosily warm. The direction of the wind meant she could just make out the sounds of waves collapsing on the rocks at the base of the cliff. Although not interested in tending a garden of her own, Donna appreciated the spring colour from the assembly of carnations, kangaroo paw, daisies and nasturtiums.

A number of the residents obviously had the same desire for clean air. Talking, reading or simply enjoying the ambience, they sat on the timber benches scattered around the garden, some in dappled shade from the purple-draped jacaranda, others more exposed. Donna spied Lily sitting alone, her face directed upward to the brilliance of the sun, her eyes closed, her skin looking radiant despite its undulations.

'Hello, Lily. Beautiful morning, isn't it?'

When there was no reply Donna moved a step nearer, bending down a little. She wondered if Lily had perhaps not heard her, that maybe she was asleep. But Lily's eyes opened and on closer inspection Donna saw her cheeks weren't glowing or tinted by the sun; they were wet and reddened from crying.

'Lily? Are you okay? What is it? Tell me.' As soon as she said the words Donna knew it was a foolish question. Jesus, she already knew the answer.

When Lily had first arrived at Blue Vista, Donna had immediately observed hurt and pessimism. The newcomer had been thin and withdrawn, her eyes reflecting suspicion and resentment, her skin pale. She had done her best to help

Lily settle in and things initially appeared to go well. Lily had regained some weight, and colour had returned to her cheeks. As time went on, Donna even saw signs of contentment – subtle twitches of her mouth at first then gradually a more relaxed and easy smile. But in recent weeks there'd been a return to restlessness and agitation, coinciding with Lily's tragic diagnosis.

When the old woman finally spoke, her voice was weary and her eyes seemed to stare into a faraway, invisible place. 'I've always imagined, or maybe it was hoped, that I'd go quickly. I'd be alive, then bang, gone, with no opportunity to think about it. But to die slowly and knowingly like this …' She blinked and appeared to properly notice Donna for the first time. 'Oh, Donna, what will happen when I'm room-bound? When I can no longer be out in the sun, feeling its touch on my skin? When I won't know which flower is which, or know who my daughter is, or remember Robert? When my personality disappears? What will be the *point*?'

Lily's lips were trembling. Sitting beside her, Donna patted the old woman's thigh but it felt like an inadequate, pathetic consolation. Donna fought her own disconcerting urge to cry.

'You're getting way ahead of yourself. You're still mobile and with it. Let's cross that bridge if we come to it, okay?'

'I'm withering like those bloody carnations,' Lily growled.

Donna was acutely aware of how dismissive she'd just been and was ashamed. Yet she had an urgent need to steer away from this distressing territory.

'It's such a gorgeous spring day. I'm glad we picked this afternoon for our outing.'

Lily sniffed. 'Are you sure it won't be too much trouble?'

Donna had started to feel closer to Lily than to her own nutty mob back in Brisbane, and hoped an excursion would cheer up her elderly friend a little. It would, she trusted, help to ease both Lily's anxieties and her own shame at brushing them off.

'Lily, you're never any trouble. I love the beach and it's been a while since I got down there. I think the last time was when an old school friend from Brisbane visited me and brought her twin boys. They complained the whole time about the water being too chilly, then that they were hungry, then that they wanted to go home to Brisbane because they'd just got Nintendos or PlayStations or some such thing for their birthday and were bored on the beach and preferred to stare at a screen than make sandcastles. At least you'll appreciate the trip. Here, I have a clean tissue,' Donna added, extracting one from the skirt pocket of her pale blue uniform.

Lily discreetly blew her nose then produced a forced smile as she tucked the tissue into a sleeve of her blouse. Donna's eyes moved across to Frank and Jack, sitting on a bench just a few metres away. Jack was rabbiting on about something but Frank seemed to be only half listening. Not a surprise, as Jack could, at times, be just plain tiring.

A smell of coconut oil wafted towards them as Betty walked past. 'Seems we're not the only ones trying to avoid the fumes,' observed Donna. 'But Jack looks like he could do with a hat. Lily, will you be all right while I go in and fetch one for him? And can I get you a glass of water while I'm inside?'

'No, no, I'm fine. Just being a stupid old woman. You go and get Jack a cap before the back of his head sizzles. I'll probably come in too, in a minute. It's already getting rather warm.'

Stop brushing her off. Stay with her and let her talk. Face this monster with her.

Donna wavered before standing up, but on impulse and fuelled by remorse, bent down and, against usual protocol, gave Lily a hug. Feeling the old woman flinch from the contact, she stepped back.

'Oh my gosh, did I hurt you?'

'No, it's not your fault. My shoulder is a bit tender, that's all. No amount of cream seems to be fixing the sores.'

'I'm sorry. I should've been more careful. I'll take a look at your skin when you go inside, see if something more can be done.'

As she opened the door to return inside, Donna turned to look back. Lily's head had slumped forward and one hand was caressing the other in her lap, as though trying to ease discomfort in her fingers or perhaps rub away her worries. Donna couldn't be sure from this distance but she thought Lily's shoulders were jiggling up and down ever so slightly. She hesitated but decided that if that was the case she should give Lily space to cry in peace.

Excuses, excuses, Donna. Stop being an arse by making light of her fears. And stop being a goddam coward, going out of your way to avoid the ugly truth.

Lily

'Forgive me, Lily. I got caught up with something. Are you ready?'

I've been waiting for Donna in one of the straight-backed chairs in reception, my walker at the ready. I'm feeling chirpier now. In fact, I'm excited. 'It's perfectly fine, dear.'

'It's a nice spot here, isn't it, with the afternoon sun coming in on your back. Though a wind's come up. I hope we won't get blown over.'

'I'm not fussed about the weather. And I'm certainly not worried about a breeze. It will be invigorating.'

'Well, as long as you don't fly away. I might have a bit of trouble explaining that to management,' she says with a smile.

I rock forwards a couple of times in an attempt to stand up but manage only to fall back again. 'Are you sure about this? I don't want to be any trouble.'

Bless Donna. There are no airs and graces with her. She treats everyone at Blue Vista the same, no matter our backgrounds, idiosyncrasies or moods; just gets on with things in her own quiet way. Betty's brashness, Frank's diffidence, Jack's foul mouth – she cares for us all with unconditional warmth.

'You're never any trouble, Lily.'

This trip to the beach will be just what I need. I'd got myself worked up about my diagnosis; had a little sook over it in the garden this morning. I don't think Donna knew what to say. She would move heaven and earth for me, but not, I suspect, do what I plan to ask of her. You see, I've recently learned that my short-term memory lapses are not merely a random jumble of annoying, odd or embarrassing incidents, but a maleficent disease, snaking its way into my head. It's an official condition now, gift-wrapped up in a neat package and presented to me with a card saying: *Dear Lily, This is for you – your very own dementia. Best wishes, Old Age.*

Strangely, however, having it diagnosed and labelled might have helped because now it's a concrete, real enemy I can take on, not an invisible creature under the bed. I feel less like a victim and more like a commander-in-chief, intending to go fully armed into combat. In fact, I've had a sudden clarity, a parting of the clouds inside my head as to what to do.

Helping me up, Donna steadies me and makes sure I'm holding on to my walker's handles before we take the few steps to the building's entrance. She punches in the code and as the glass slides open a waft of jasmine swims in on the slipstream. The temperature outside is mild, warmer than in the building. As we walk to her car, Donna makes light conversation before negotiating me into the front seat.

'Excuse the mess. I don't clean my car very often because I don't actually use it very often. I should have cleared the rubbish out last night.'

A few discarded lolly wrappers and an empty styrofoam cup are all I see.

'Oh,' she adds upon spying a hairbrush choked with light brown strands and wedged between the passenger seat and door. 'I've been looking for that for ages.'

'For goodness' sake, don't worry. I'm sure you don't have much time in your busy life to worry about cleaning your car.'

The ride is short, just a minute of descending, winding road before we reach the car park at the southern end of the esplanade. She prises me from the car and I look up and to my right at the rocky bluff above us. I luxuriate for a moment in the fantasy that we will be returning to King Street after our time at the beach rather than ascending the headland's road again.

I sit on my walker and Donna pushes it along the first asphalt section of beach track, through a mini jungle of subtropical vegetation. The wind passes with tiptoe ease through the dainty needle-like casuarinas in groves either side of us but stirs the long doubled-over leaves of the pandanus, slapping against each other like they're applauding our presence. As a little girl my imagination always went wild on this path. The splayed, exposed roots of the pandanus were a forest of teepees in which fairies dwelled. Their job was to protect the gold treasure of the coastal wattle and banksia flowers, when they exploded in a heaven-sent splash of winter yellow, from the pirates who sailed the high seas beyond Finn Bay's horizon. And when the banksias withered and fell away, seedpods like black lollipops became equally valuable bounty.

Where the bitumen turns to sand, Donna cautiously hauls me into a standing position. She supports most of my weight, little as it is, and I waddle and limp as we slowly make our way down the rest of the track towards the shore. Thick bush makes way for grassy dunes and suddenly we emerge onto open beach. I've been here a thousand times but it has never failed to instantly draw any manner of tension from my body. It's as if I have an almost spiritual relationship with the bay. Sometimes the sea is grim and churned up by resolute winds, and on such days you can barely hear yourself think over the roar. At other times the waves approach the sand neatly and individually, each measured crash audible over the more subdued background static. Today, it's somewhere in between.

Donna helps me to remove my shoes and we head towards the water's edge, the sand becoming progressively cooler underfoot, its gritty grains executing a familiar massage between my toes. We finally stop a few metres from the sea where the beach is firm and more kind on old, unsteady legs. My breathing is laboured but the air swirls and caresses and refreshes, taking the heat off my aches and pains. We watch as some children play a little way along, gasping with surprised delight just out of reach of the snatching water's ebb and flow.

'You wait here,' Donna says. 'Will you be all right to keep standing for a moment on your own?'

Returning a few minutes later with my walker, she guides me onto its seat then flaps out a lightweight picnic rug. I watch the material descend to its place on the beach like a falling parachute, the breeze catching its corners, before Donna positions herself on the rug beside me. Snippets of sunshine stream down in gaps between the clouds, warming our skin comfortingly as we chat.

'It's not as windy as I'd thought down here, but look at him go,' says Donna, pointing at a windsurfer. 'He's whipping along out there.'

I follow Donna's line of sight to a black-and-orange sail tacking its way, zigzag-like, along the water out past the breakers. 'Or she. I'd like to have tried that when I was still capable, but windsurfing didn't exist then.'

'I guess a lot has changed in your lifetime, Lily.'

'It certainly has. But you know there's something so reassuring about the way this beach is exactly the same as when I was a lass, and that it will continue long after I'm gone. The waves will keep rolling in, the sand will keep shifting its shapes.'

'I suspect the bloody seagulls will still be arching their necks and carrying on long after *I'm* gone,' Donna says with a smile, pointing at some red-legged gulls pecking for tidbits along the shoreline, keeping their eyes on the dotterels, outnumbered but arrogantly unfazed.

I notice the high waterline. After the tide goes out there'll be a fresh pool of clear, shallow water trapped in wave-imprinted sand, and all manner of decorating flotsam – pebbles, shells, seaweed, bark, sticks or the white endoskeletons of cuttlefish – will have washed up to be examined or simply stepped around. 'The beach has never permitted me to be bored. Sometimes I think it's been the reason I've lived so richly.'

'I didn't know you came here as a girl. Did you holiday here?'

'Holiday? Good grief, no. I was born and grew up in Finn Bay. Apart from some time spent at university, I've lived here almost all my life. My husband Robert and I were in Rorook for a short time during the war but after he died I came back here and lived with my parents again in Haversham Road for a while before buying my own place in King Street. Finn Bay is my home.'

'Why have I never known that? Wow. No wonder you like the view from your room and love the smell of the sea air. It's in your blood.'

'I guess you could say that. Lots of memories. Lots of memories ...'

It occurs to me this might be my last time on this beach, and my gut clenches. I turn from looking out at the water and shoot a quick glance at Donna. She sits cross-legged, leaning back on her hands, but must sense my mood as she twists her neck around and up to meet my eyes.

'What is it? Can I get you anything? Are you warm enough?'

The first job of a commander is to recruit the best troops. 'Donna, if I get worse, when I get worse, will you help me?' My pulse is galloping.

'Of course. I'll always look after you.'

'I'm not sure you understand what I mean.' I hold her gaze as her hair blows across her face, the wind playing havoc with it. She tucks it behind one ear but some strands immediately come loose again, that little bit too short to get a good grip. Partly to relieve my neck and partly to muster courage, I return my stare to the ocean and the windsurfer, who is hauling himself back up onto his board after a fall. 'What I mean is, would you be able to give me a little push along?'

Although afraid she might be horrified by my words, I risk stealing another quick glimpse in Donna's direction. She's turned her body towards me and is holding her hair out of her face, her mouth hanging open slightly. *Appalled* is the expression that comes to mind.

'If you mean could I help you to die, of course not. I understand your fear, but assisting you to end your life would, well, it would land me in jail. And anyway, Lily, I just couldn't do it.'

'Even though all you'd need to do is access some pills for me?'

'I can't just help myself to drugs, especially in the quantities you'd be talking about. It's not that simple. For good reason.'

Donna's jaw is set tight but despite observing her discomfort I'm determined to push my point. 'I'm sorry, but I don't know who else to turn to. It would upset my Pauline too much to even mention such a thing.'

I see from her expression that I'm making no inroads and I can't say I'm surprised by her response. From the time I met Donna something in her demeanour told me she's had a difficult past, had the stuffing knocked out of her. I'm sure of it. So the poor girl probably doesn't have the strength to handle all this. I need her, but I shouldn't be adding to her troubles. She deserves better. 'I'm sorry. I shouldn't be asking you. It's unfair and selfish of me, I know.'

'No, no, it's quite okay.' Her tone carries gentle sincerity. 'I completely understand where you're coming from. But Lily, my job is to look after you, keep you comfortable and support you. It can't go beyond that. You do understand, don't you? Best just to think ahead positively. You never know what the future holds. And you still have a lot to live for, like your family.'

At her refusal a leaden dread seizes my chest, its weight almost painful. I'm being hauled by a rapid towards a waterfall, helpless in the face of an inevitable and frightening conclusion. But I nod and smile, because what choice do I have?

'Hey, look, the windsurfer's up again,' she says, and I'm glad to think about something else. 'I wish I had the confidence to do what he or she is doing. Goodness, look at him go. It must be really windy out on the water.'

I track the movement for a few seconds then close my eyes, feeling drained just watching all that vitality. I think about what Donna has said, about looking forward. I do try, every minute of the day, to be positive, to be thankful for life. But it's impossible to ignore the constant, nagging pain plaguing my body from dawn until dusk and back again, from my fingers to my feet. All I see waiting for me in the months or years ahead is myself as my father in the horror of his final pitiful days.

My only relief is to go in the opposite direction, to the past, where the fog clears and I'm free of ailments and dreads. It's such a comfort to retreat to one of my younger selves. Every age and stage still exists inside me. After all, they're part of me. They *are* me.

1951

'She's perfect, Lilykins. You did well. I'm so proud of you.' My mother caresses my sweat-soaked forehead before returning to smile and coo at her granddaughter, fast asleep in my arms. Fresh linen has been put on the bed and my baby and I have been cleaned up and covered up. The swaddling has settled her. Only her head, covered with a shock of black hair, is visible, an uncomfortable reminder of her heritage. The mattress is a little too hard under my back and bottom for my liking but its heavily starched sheets are reassuringly no-nonsense, providing a much-needed sense of order and regimen after the harrowing journey my body has just taken me on. I shake uncontrollably and feel chilled to the core.

'It's the shock, luvvie,' says the midwife, leaning over and around Ma to cover me in a light blanket.

My milk hasn't come in yet but still my baby's mouth instinctively searches for me to draw sustenance. I can't take my eyes off her wrinkled face, primal and scrunched up and so serious. An overpowering euphoria and protectiveness envelops me, and I begin to sob – because she's perfect, because the agony of childbirth is over, and because my life won't ever be the same.

For months, Pauline's father (and I use the term very lightly) was blissfully unaware of the havoc his afternoon delight had wreaked on my body. He actually came knocking on the door of Harford Accounting again two or three months ago, on his biannual visit to the district, no doubt hoping to get his carnal needs met again. But when I came out of my office and he took in my belly's bump, he must have quickly done the maths as he didn't stop in the building's entryway for long. In fact, he mumbled about the weather and asked me how the business was going and then whirled around and exited, quicker than a wildfire ripping through bone-dry grass. In the harsh light of reality his charm had disappeared and he'd taken on a sleazy appearance – his tie not straight and his shoes needing a polish. I hope none of the staff puts two and two together. I've not told anyone at work who the father is. After all, it's no-one's concern but mine.

Physically it wasn't too arduous a pregnancy, although I became so tired toward the end that I sometimes found myself nodding off in the doctor's waiting room or at home between making myself a cup of tea and actually drinking it. Luckily I took on Fred Larson two years ago to work under me to help with my growing list of clients, because now the baby is born I'm going to need someone to take the brunt of the work off my shoulders for a while. Fred is not only an asset to the business but also great company. Slim and short like a jockey, he has the cleverest ability to deliver a punchline. Although it's not strictly businesslike, I encourage him to try out his gags on me in the office before impressing his friends at the Commercial Hotel. That way, I usually get at least two belly laughs a week, and it was this kind of laughter that I'm sure brought on my labour yesterday morning. Coincidently, as it was the scene of the original crime, we were in the kitchenette at the back of the office eating fish

and chips (as I'd been craving salty food – that and anything with lemon, the tarter the better) when I'd felt a flow
of warm water down my legs. I'm not sure Fred wanted to
know what was happening but my labour wasn't going to go
away simply because we were both embarrassed.

'Fred, I think my baby's coming. Could you fetch me a
clean towel from the bathroom and perhaps call the doctor?'
I asked, trying to conceal my fear.

My words stirred, or frightened, him into action. After
some fussing around we decided it would be easiest if we just
got in my Vauxhall and, after calling my mother, we managed to get to the car in between contractions. We picked
up Ma and continued on to the hospital here in Rorook.
Although Fred was being careful over bumps and around
corners, each wave of cramps gripped my insides like a hot
merciless vice.

The next eighteen hours passed as if my child was determined to take all the time in the world to arrive, each exami-
nation by the midwife bringing mental relief that I'd dilated
more but frustration and misery at the paltry size of the
increments. When exhaustion and pain reduced me to my
most primordial self, Ma held my hands and spoke the firm
encouragement needed for that final push, and in a surge of
will my baby entered the world from between my thighs in
a single, messy, grunting effort. I groaned and whimpered
as my daughter was whisked away, howling her lungs out in
protest at the effrontery of being removed from her warm
and dark cocoon.

I'm too tired to speak, staring at this new life that has
taken shape in me and already suckles for nourishment from
me. I feel traumatised by the pure brutality of her birth

but in awe that my body was tough, clever and resilient enough to make and deliver this new and tiny human. I know already I would kill and die for this child, and I will never again do anything without first thinking about her and her needs. The intensity of emotion is at once pure bliss and absolute terror.

REMEMBRANCE DAY

SUNDAY 11 NOVEMBER 2007

Pauline

Not being idle or wasting daylight hours were some of the many expectations ingrained in Pauline from an early age so, summer or winter, jogging generally meant setting an alarm that nudged either side of 5.30 am. Although getting out of bed had been a struggle recently, once she was up the running was reassuring and comforting and pleasingly tight. The injection of endorphins, the repetition and certainty of her route, the solid feel and sound of her trainers thudding the tarmac, and the rhythmic pattern of regular breaths – *in for four steps, out for four steps* – cleared Pauline's mind of the maelstrom of negative thoughts otherwise plaguing her of late, and gave her the will to throw back the covers.

This morning, however, the exercise seemed to be having little effect, the GP's solemn and kindly delivered but surprising and embarrassing pronouncement from yesterday still on a loop in Pauline's head as she pounded along the foreshore boardwalk. The rotation of the earth was bringing Finn Bay into the sun's reach but the day felt unusually cool for November, and the path still glistened from overnight rain. The sky glowed pink where it met the sea and the air remained thick with dew. An occasional cockatoo shriek emanated from the casuarina grove between the esplanade and the sand. Other than that, the only signs of life were a handful of other runners or dog owners in the distance and an approaching jogger she didn't recognise. He smiled right at her as they got closer, holding his scrutiny, and she experienced a momentary but delicious zap between them.

'Nice morning for it,' he remarked, his voice deep and silky.

Pauline heard rather than saw him come to a stop behind her. She could have replied over her shoulder and kept running but after a few steps something made her stop too. It felt wrong to engage with him, and certainly not something she'd normally do. But then again, nothing about today felt normal.

Barely able to get her breath, she turned to him and managed to puff out a reply. 'Gorgeous. All those people still in bed don't know what they're missing.'

'Maybe they're perfectly happy where they are, doing what they're doing.' Hands on his hips, he had salt-and-pepper hair slicked back with sweat, and a wry smile slid onto his face.

Instead of distaste, a wicked rebelliousness alighted, uninvited, in Pauline's head and it was a shock that her thoughts were now wandering entirely inappropriately.

Her own smirk was forming, so subtle it seemed to exist within her face rather than on its surface. The last few years she'd felt the sting of invisibility that comes with middle age, even from men in her own age bracket, all ear hair and bulging bellies. She wanted to still be noticed and, more than that, physically admired, as she suspected was happening now. What could be a more welcome diversion from her lack of cheer than zeroing in on a strong hint of primal, uninhibited sexuality?

But as quickly as the thought had come, Pauline swiped it away, giving a nod to the good-looking stranger but resuming her run. Getting into her stride, she worked her legs even harder, the physical strain a pleasant outlet for pent-up nerves. Since her mother's diagnosis and with the school year in its typically busy last term, Pauline had been finding it impossible to relax. It was as if her body was operating on a low but steady drip of adrenaline, resulting in the subtle impression of butterflies occupying her chest and leaving her with a constant tension and unease. She was quick to react when things didn't go her way, in situations where she would usually display more patience and understanding.

It was akin to walking on a ledge, not knowing minute to minute whether she might lose her balance. On one bad day she'd plunged into an abyss of boiling anger, displaying spectacular road rage at the driver of a ute who had tried to cut in front of her one evening as she'd been returning home from Blue Vista. She'd spluttered with venom, 'You shithole – just wait your fucking turn, you fuck!' while giving him the finger, jolting it up and down furiously as she pictured shoving something acutely painful up his arrogant arse. Then the worst example, a week or so back, when she'd reprimanded a middle-school girl who'd made the mistake of directing a derogatory remark to a more junior overweight student within Pauline's earshot. She'd verbally come down on the offender with the force of a category five hurricane, prompting looks of distinct unease from two canteen staff standing nearby. Puffing herself up, she'd walked away, blood pumping in her ears, trying to look indignant and self-righteous when inside she'd just wanted to skulk back to her office and lock the door for the shame of having displayed such a highly unprofessional, unkind and inappropriate overreaction. It was as if the Pauline she'd known all her life had departed, like her spirit had taken leave of the corporeal, walking away and leaving behind this unrecognisable shell.

As long as she focused and kept busy she could almost pretend her life was normal. Yet she knew she was existing in a state of precarious self-deception, as overarching these sensations was a persistent melancholy, as had been officially, medically confirmed yesterday. After a brief chat, the doctor had given her a questionnaire to fill out. It seemed to have lots of words ending in *less*, like helpless, restless and worthless. She'd answered some standard follow-up questions about her ability to sleep and concentrate followed by alarming ones on self-harm and suicide. Finally, the GP asked her: 'How often do you feel that everything is an effort?' (*Most of the time*) 'How often do you feel hopeless?' (*Sometimes*) and 'On a scale of one to ten, how happy do you feel you are?' (*Two*). She'd scored a total of twenty-nine out of fifty, a high enough number, it turned out, to qualify her for a category. 'Pauline, all signs point to you having moderate depression'.

Moderate depression, she thought as she moved off the path and crossed the esplanade, her back temporarily to the bay and the sun, now broken free of the horizon. *Moderate depression*, as she passed the fish and chip shop and what used to be Ferguson's, her grandfather's hardware store. *Depression*, as she huffed past the newsagent, the only place with lights on at this hour. *How am I supposed to digest that?* She turned the corner into Longmire Street and braced herself for the gentle but extended climb up and away from the beach. *Moderate*, she tried to reassure herself, now breathing hard, her legs feeling the burn of the incline.

Relax, you're not about to be admitted. You're still capable of going to work, being admired, having friends, looking after those you love. God, if they knew, though. Imagine the sympathy. The doubts. I wouldn't just be Pauline. I'd be Pauline-with-Depression. Moderate or Severe or Only a Little Bit – it's still depression. Shit.

She reached the top of the hill and curved over, resting her hands on her knees. She wondered, as she tried to steady her breathing, why joy felt so far out of reach when she knew she had so much to be thankful for, before another thought came to her; a shameful, dirty, feeble one that stuck like disgusting gum to the bottom of a shoe. It was as if this diagnosis had granted her psyche approval to allow the thought in against her will.

I am struggling. And maybe it's all right to surrender. To be fragile. To let others take care of me for once.

In a strange way, it felt as if a burden was lifting.

Pauline straightened up, spun around and surveyed the view, filling her lungs. The bay was leaden, although its waters would soon take on the blue of the cloudless sky that had been forecast. She thought about how the sea could look so different, like it was two beings: one calm and unperturbed, and the other unsettled, uncertain and not a little unnerving. And now there were two versions of her: the Pauline she'd always known – capable, positive and in control – and this new interloper who had walked out of the doctor's suite, a version that was weak and labelled yet also quietly desperate to let go and allow herself to be fully exposed. How could these twin personas, she wondered, ever reconcile? Was it possible to be strong Pauline, the woman whose skin she had lived in for fifty-six years with comfort and pride, but also be at-crisis-point Pauline, who she didn't like or respect but whose existence she could no longer deny? Who she quietly welcomed because it provided her thoughts and reactions and behaviours with a context, an explanation, an *excuse*, and, when she thought about it, an official mechanism by which she could ultimately heal?

The doctor had gone on to talk about the next steps. Did Pauline want to look at antidepressants? Seeing a counsellor? Perhaps incorporate some yoga? The problem was, she couldn't envisage being that still and serene. And spilling her insides to a stranger? None of those options were steps Pauline felt ready or comfortable to take.

He'd written out a referral in case ('The good psychologists don't come cheap, unfortunately, but I can make some recommendations in the local area') and she was handed a sheet with 'websites that might be a good start'. He'd spoken with kindness.

And, Jesus, had he looked at me with pity?

After what had ended up being a double appointment, Pauline had exited the medical centre, using the chance to take stock as she walked to her car. She wasn't sure she'd be able to concentrate well enough to safely drive home but started the engine anyway. On the radio, a DJ droned on in an obsequious manner about an upcoming studio guest. Pauline slapped her palm against the volume knob to silence him, the gratification worth the sting on her skin, and accelerated more heavily than necessary, arriving home in record time. She'd occupied herself with housework and bill-paying and correcting student work, keeping on the move before going to bed early to avoid Sam getting a good look at her face in case it gave anything away.

A dog barked and Pauline was jolted into checking the time, realising she'd been standing at the top of Longmire Street for ten minutes. The sun had made its full, glorious appearance over the sea and she was forced to squint as she cast her eyes south-east toward the chocolate-brick buildings of Blue Vista, perched a kilometre away on their vantage point. She pictured her mother fast asleep at the end of the far wing. She knew now that she'd need to introduce Sam to her alter ego, Miss Pissy Pants, but her mother …?

Would she be understanding and empathic, or just plain disappointed?

If you hadn't lived through a war, buried a husband, raised a child on your own and built up a successful business in a man's world, did you have any right to be so self-indulgent as to be *moderately depressed*? She thought of the beautiful old Queenslander in King Street – timbers painted cream and white, its thirteen lucky steps leading up to the front porch – demolished over winter by its new owners to make way for a newer, fancier brick home. She still hadn't told her mother. What, after all, would be the point?

House on the Hill was in the opposite direction, reachable most quickly by cutting through the back streets of town and across a stretch of open grassland, usually taking a bit over a quarter of an hour on a good day. Having decided to ban all thoughts from her mind, Pauline set off and managed to focus instead on her lungs and legs, pushing herself hard all the way back. In fourteen minutes she walked in the front door, as Sam sleepily called out from upstairs, 'Is that you, love? How was your run?' She managed between breaths to reply, 'Great, feeling fantastic!', her spirits sinking at the lie. Not a white lie, but a big, fat, significant lie.

Once she let this new knowledge about herself out into the world, even within the confines of her marriage, it would make it real and capable of growing into something possibly too titanic to manage. It was like she'd gone out into a snowstorm without a coat and knew she needed help but refused to turn back for the shelter waiting right behind her. And anyway, would she feel relief to confess to Sam that she was barely managing to keep everything from imploding, or just self-disgust?

She showered and ate breakfast before her husband surfaced from their bed, and kept her distance by immersing herself in more housework until mid-morning. As Rachel, Christos and the children were away for the weekend, she and Sam had decided that Pauline would head to Blue Vista rather than having Lily over to lunch, freeing up Sam to do some work in the garden and finally get around to cleaning out the gutters. As soon as he'd gone up the ladder, Pauline wasted no time in heading to Blue Vista. Halfway up the headland road, though, anxiety seeped in like a dank mist. Only through trying to steady her breathing was she calm again by the time she punched the four-digit code into the entrance's keypad and the building's large sliding door floated open.

Lest We Forget badges sat crammed into an honesty box on the front counter, the irony not lost on Pauline. She signed in to the visitor's book then made her way to Room 18, turning right past the dining area and right again, then left down South Wing's corridor. New artwork graced its length, depicting street scenes from the town, presumably to bring the outside world in for the many residents who were largely immobile. Would that soon include her mother?

She stood just inside the entrance to Lily's room, casting her eyes around the condensed, sixteen-square-metre version of their old life. It reminded her of a doll's house. It made her feel so very sad. Lily was in her armchair and listening to music through an iPod, strumming her kinked old fingers and tapping her feet.

On noticing Pauline, she drew out one of the earbuds and beckoned her daughter over. 'These tiny headphones are wonderful. Here, listen to this.'

'You looked like you were in another world, Mum.' Pauline leaned down, positioning her head next to her mother's and placing the spare bud against her own ear.

Without a care as to who might be listening through thin walls, the singing came so naturally to the two of them as ABBA's 'Dancing Queen' played. After just a few bars Pauline helped Lily out of the chair and, as if it was the most natural and normal thing in the world, they slow-danced, a mellow jigging and rocking from side to side as they held hands, Pauline fully supporting her mother's insubstantial weight. Lily seemed to find a gentle energy she hadn't displayed for a very long time and Pauline felt almost lightheaded with delight. The idea of moderate depression seemed suddenly ridiculous.

When the song faded out she eased Lily back down, this time onto the bed.

'That was marvellous, just marvellous,' Lily said between heavy breaths. 'You know, my body isn't hurting, at least not as much as it usually does. Could singing really be such an anaesthetic?'

'It was a tonic for both of us, Mum. And you knew all the words. I'd forgotten what a wonderful singing voice you have.' Observing her mother's face glowing, Pauline added, 'Are you hot? Want me to open the window?'

'No need, darling. There's enough of a breeze coming in already.'

Pauline was surprised to see the external doors were slightly open. 'I thought they were supposed to be secured at all times,' she said with a frown.

'Don't use that teacher tone of voice on me or look at me like that. They're supposed to be locked but I prefer them open, especially now the weather's getting hotter.' Lily's voice was defiant. 'It makes me feel less closed in.' When Pauline's expression didn't change she added, 'But if you insist, go ahead. I don't want them to know that I know where the key is, so maybe it's best to shut them now before any of the nurses come along.'

'What do you mean? Please don't tell me *you* opened them?'

'Of course I did. I know where that tall Molly hides the key. She's not supposed to, but she opens the doors now and then to put a bug out or let some fresh air in for me. Of course she thinks I'm not looking when she gets the key down from the ledge, but I'm old, not blind.'

Pauline stared at her mother's conspiratorial expression with incredulity and took a mental measure of the architrave's height, comparing it to the stretch of which her mother was capable. It didn't compute and her heart rate went up a notch.

'How on earth do you reach it?'

'I use my walker.'

'Mum, you've got to be kidding me. You could fall—'

'Not if I'm careful.' Lily's sharp interruption, her forceful correction, transported Pauline straight back to her youth. 'I don't open them often, only when there's a nice sea breeze like this morning. I put the brake on. I'm careful. You always fuss, Pauline.'

Pauline smarted at the criticism but, overcome with protectiveness, inwardly shuddered at the image of her mother toppling off her walker. 'All right, enough, this is madness. I'm shutting it. And I'm taking the key.'

'Don't you dare!' Her mother's warning boomed through the room, belying her delicate physique. Their eyes fastened in a well-practised battle of stubbornness.

Pauline made a quick decision. 'All right, Mum. I'm sorry. I won't argue. But I'll close and lock it now, okay? I don't want you doing any more climbing either so I'll put the key in your bureau.' Pretending to place it in Lily's drawer, Pauline surreptitiously slipped the key into her pocket instead.

They spent the following hour playing gin rummy, Pauline filling her mother in on news of the family and work. After dreading coming today, the visit had turned out to be lovely. Her mother was in good spirits despite the key incident and there were no signs of a fuddled brain. In fact, Lily seemed sharp as a tack. It went a long way to balance out the many exasperating and disheartening visits that had dominated the last few months.

When an orderly knocked at the door wanting to collect Lily's dirty washing, Pauline used it as her cue and made moves to go. 'I think they'll be ringing the lunch bell soon. Oh, I nearly forgot. I brought you more of those toffees you like,' she said, fishing into her handbag. 'Well, see you on Tuesday, all right? I'll pop in after work. Maybe we can listen to "Dancing Queen" again.'

'You know, I was once seventeen. Hard to believe, isn't it?'

Pauline smiled at the image, not finding it difficult to imagine at all. 'Have a good rest this afternoon, Mum. I love you.'

Pauline intended returning the key to Molly or one of the other staff on her way out. But as she walked past the nurses' station she changed her mind, not confident the same situation wouldn't happen again. At home she took the key out of her pocket and placed it on the mantelpiece in a shallow clay dish – a sea-green creation from Rachel's early pottery attempts – where it would be easily seen and not forgotten. She felt a pang of guilt that her mother might go looking for it in the bureau and become confused and upset at its absence, but rationalised that this was the lesser of two evils.

She hated to think of Lily being able to simply walk out of her room onto the lawns and beyond, where she might wander too far and get lost, possibly putting herself in harm's way at the cliffs, whether accidentally or on purpose. Or, just as frightening, forgetting to secure it, and anyone being able to steal in through unlocked doors.

Donna

Donna clenched the steering wheel, her eyes focused with fervour on the road ahead. For the last five minutes she'd been driving through a wide valley of fertile farming land boasting rows and rows of sugar cane that fringed the highway on both sides. As white lines rushed past, Donna was grateful each segment of asphalt was putting more distance between her and the hurt and humiliation of the night before. It was the child inside feeling the most betrayed. Had she really thought they might have changed? That she'd gained their respect and admiration? Or that she had developed a strong enough sense of self to be immune to their snipes and barbs if thrown back into the atmosphere of her childhood?

She'd been deluded and naive.

Late yesterday she'd driven in the opposite direction, to Brisbane, the sun assaulting her eyes, to join her parents, sister Jocelyn and one of her two brothers at a party being held by their cousin Shelley. Donna's parents, for all their coldness, had been good to Shelley through her secondary school years, taking their Barbie-doll niece under their wing for weeks at a time when Shelley's parents had found their interstate or overseas journalism assignments coinciding. When Shelley had first begun staying over at the Charlestons', Donna was fifteen and had hoped she'd finally found an ally, somebody to step in and shield her from the family's dysfunctional dynamics. But Shelley had merely blended into the background, neither adding to Donna's social isolation nor protecting her from it. She hadn't rubbed the others up the wrong way, but neither had she impressed Donna's siblings with any positive traits other than her looks. So despite their other differences, all three siblings shared apathy towards her. Shelley was neutral, almost a bigger sin in the household than being nice. But she had gone on, through sheer determination and stubbornness as much as natural talent, to enjoy spectacular success in the media as a television producer for one of the major Brisbane networks. And despite her achievements she'd kept in touch with her aunt and uncle with the regularity and earnestness of one who feels the legacy, and possibly the burden, of gratitude.

The gathering was an opportunity for Shelley to flaunt the fruits of her success, not least of which was her new penthouse apartment with coveted city and river views. Donna had agonised over whether to go, having no intention of being sucked into the agony of mingling. Shelley's social circle was largely made up of extroverted, highly articulate types from the broadcasting world and Donna felt rather beige in comparison; a socially invisible outcast. But in the end she decided it might be a chance to present a more confident and prouder version of herself to her family.

When Donna had walked into the party, Jocelyn was already there, in the centre of the room, a black miniskirt and shimmering gold top rendering her visible at twenty paces. A darker and finer-faced version of Donna and two years her junior, Jocelyn imported jewellery from Morocco and sold it to local retailers for a fifty-fold profit. Standing next to her was Rick, born only fourteen months before Donna and looking the part of corporate lawyer in a charcoal-grey suit with a shirt of a blue almost as glacial as his eyes. Rick was a party animal when among his own friends but Donna thought he looked a little uncomfortable here. He'd probably leave as soon as the oysters ran out or he could pick up a girl. Whichever came first, she thought.

Accepting a lime and soda from a roaming waiter and in no great hurry to catch up with her siblings, Donna surreptitiously took up residence in a corner where she could observe the room rather than form part of it. Scanning for her parents, she spied her father first, balanced on the arm of a sprawling cream leather couch, looking amused as he in turn watched his wife standing by the fireplace and clearly flirting with a recently retired newsreader with exceptionally hairy arms.

Donna hadn't ever been able to work out her parents' relationship but figured its odd dynamic was a product of their own difficult childhoods. They showed no outward signs of physical affection towards each other but she would occasionally hear terms of endearment quietly exchanged, suggesting at least some intimacy operated within the marriage. They had provided for their family in the practical ways one would hope parents would do – education, extracurricular activities, thought-provoking debates around the Charleston dining table, family holidays – and for that Donna was grateful. It didn't come close though to making up for the complete lack of warmth.

Donna approached her father, soon joined by her mother, and they exchanged pleasantries. She enquired after them and the wider family but apart from passing on local Brisbane gossip and asking her about the weather in Finn Bay, her parents put no questions to Donna about her life there. The party gradually came into full swing, the room filling with the raucous laughter and chatter of guests while Beyoncé penetrated every corner of the apartment from strategically mounted speakers. Noticing Jocelyn and Rick had retreated to the terrace, where a small number of guests had likewise congregated, Donna decided to take a break from the noise – and her parents – and make contact with her brother and sister instead.

She stepped onto the balcony and allowed her eyes to adjust to the night sky. The space was smaller and less impressive than she'd expected it to be. And, unlike in Finn Bay, only a few insipid-looking stars were visible. But the lights of the city provided a pleasant enough consolation prize, and Donna took a moment to appreciate their attraction before looking towards her siblings.

Jocelyn, standing with two women at one end of the terrace, was dragging on a cigarette between sips of something bubbly. Rick was one of six guests gathered a few metres closer. As Donna made her way towards Jocelyn, Rick stuck his hand out like he was hailing a taxi he fully expected to pull over for him.

'Hey, Donna. Come and join in,' he beckoned, though as a demand more than with any enthusiasm.

Donna obliged her brother but no embrace ensued, to their mutual relief.

'Everyone, this is my sister Donna. We've all just been swapping work histories, sis. Why don't you tell everyone about *your* job?' Rick urged, legs splayed confidently, his hands now in his pockets. Donna felt the discomfort of scrutiny rise inside her, not unlike bile.

'Um, hi, everybody. Okay, well, I work in aged care,' she said, flicking her eyes between faces in an attempt to convey at least a modicum of confidence.

'Oh, that must be so depressing,' a forty-something woman in a black denim overalls and huge hoop earrings exclaimed.

Slightly offended but determined to stay positive about her work, Donna replied, 'I suppose you just have to keep a sense of humour.' An example immediately sprang to mind and her heart raced as she tossed up whether to relay the story. She knew it was a funny tale but telling it would extend her being the centre of attention. Still, she decided to be brave. 'Like, for example, a couple of years ago there was this married couple who occupied adjacent rooms but often crept into each other's bed to sleep together, which you can understand ...'

She glanced around the group again, gauging if she had anyone's interest so far. Rick rolled his eyes, and over her shoulder she heard Jocelyn give a loud snort. Donna wavered, feeling thirteen again, but took a big breath. 'Anyway, they'd been there for a few years and the husband had become quite affected by Alzheimer's, forgetting even the most basic stuff. We hadn't realised how bad he'd got until one evening when my supervisor and I were doing final rounds for the day and just finishing up in the husband's room. His wife came in in her nightie and went, as usual, to climb into his bed, when he said: "Thank you for the offer, darl, but my wife would kill me!" It was so sad but hilariously funny at the same time.'

Donna gave a pre-emptory smile and there were a few genuine laughs, but before anyone else spoke Rick declared with a look of guilty pleasure, not even looking at her, 'But Donna, I thought you told me that only proper nurses were allowed to do the night-time rounds. Aren't you only qualified to do cleaning and feeding, kind of like a zoo-keeper, right?' he'd added with a chuckle, elbowing her in the ribs, the action clearly designed as a false nicety to counter the cruelty. Although expecting nothing, Donna nevertheless looked sideways to her sister for a back-up retort but Jocelyn merely ground out her cigarette with the sole of her high heel on the balcony's expensive porcelain tiles and stepped over the threshold to return inside.

What did I ever do to her that she's such a bitch?

Rick continued on, his lawyer voice more and more smarmy as the words almost spilled over each other in his eagerness to ride this tide of superiority. 'Donna helps old-ies and I take my hat off to her for that, I really do. I sure couldn't hack it. She puts her everything into all the jobs the real nurses don't want to have to do. Handles the grunt work, don't you, Dons?' He placed his arm around her now, and his deodorant smelled of power and toxic

masculinity. 'It's good there are people like you who don't
have a husband, or kids to look after, so you can devote
your time to doing all the menial shit.'

To camouflage the put-down he laughed again, louder this
time. Donna pointedly removed herself from his embrace
and took a step back, but found herself mute. She glared at
her brother with the intensity of a laser, her heart pounding,
her skin, from forehead to neck, red hot. But in the end, the
only words she could conjure left her feeling entirely disappointed in herself.

'Jeez Louise, you know how to kill a good story.' She tried
to keep her tone light and carefree but Rick's words and
Jocelyn's indifference had stung. She knew she should have
stood up for herself, should have explained that her work
carried responsibilities and provided support to those most
vulnerable and helpless. She should have cut his words off
earlier, directing them into a side alley that went nowhere
instead of letting him truck on down this highway of poorly
disguised ridicule.

Rick's reluctant audience appeared decidedly uncomfortable, some staring attentively at the lights of the city and
others pointedly peering back indoors as if something fascinating was happening in there. There were a few mumbles
before, one by one, they made excuses to slip away. Whether
or not they'd agreed with the assessment of Donna and her
job, she at least sensed they'd seen right through Rick's fal-
sity. The two siblings were left alone in their own private
boxing ring, Donna stunned and bleeding against the ropes.

Just when she thought she couldn't be more degraded, her
brother delivered his private crowning glory but in a hiss,
his hot whiskey breath against her ear. 'I'm surprised you

didn't turn back to the bottle. I wouldn't have blamed you. I reckon anyone would in your job.' He'd landed the final punch and, leaning away, had taken an exaggerated swig from his glass as if to ram home his point. He was avoiding Donna's glare, perhaps knowing he'd delivered a particularly low blow, even for him.

Donna felt powerless and ridiculous. Her conviction that she had found a commendable purpose in life was, in that moment, totally eroded. Perhaps she *was* no more than a reformed drunk, an unlovable spinster and a full-time bore. Even more acutely painful was the sudden awareness that the one thing she'd thought made her worthy, despite everything else being contaminated with the brush of ordinariness or failure, might not be seen that way by others. The thought was as stinging as if she'd been stockwhipped across the face.

Her silent look of wrath and bewilderment may have prompted Rick to reconsider his behaviour, or maybe he simply wanted to avoid any more awkwardness, but he stepped forward and shook her shoulders in a casual don't-worry-about-it manner, as if jiggling her around would shake off the toxic aura between them. It didn't work, but Donna wasn't about to give him the satisfaction of knowing just how deeply he'd hurt her. She pulled herself together as best she could and squirmed out from his hold, spitting, 'What the hell, Rick. You're such a dickhead.'

Heading back inside, she gave a passing excuse to Shelley that she had a long drive the next morning and needed to get an early night. With a quick, obligatory hug of her parents, she extracted her handbag from the pile on Shelley's satin-draped king-size bed and escaped the whole scene as soon as she could. Half an hour later she'd pulled up to Furness Drive where she tossed and turned for most of the night in her girlhood room in her suburban street, feeling like an intruder. She'd outgrown the pink curtains and the floral pillowcase and the white-painted bookshelf looming over her in the dark, still crammed with rows of teen science fiction. Her whole history seemed like it belonged to someone else.

Now, in the light of day, as she sped towards the reassurance of Finn Bay, Donna's self-esteem was still in shreds. She'd lost the shimmer and shine of the single thing that had, until Shelley's party, been making her feel worthwhile. And it gnawed at her that she hadn't retaliated. She'd been weak, the victim, falling back into the well-worn pattern of her childhood. She reflected on all those years of digs gently but laughingly directed at her, teasing cloaked in humour, jokey scrutiny of her personality carried out with the precision of eye surgery. Picking and prodding and tormenting, these events were now all joining forces, moulding into one black tumour of self-doubt, infecting Donna in a way she feared might be incurable.

A road sign indicated there were still forty-five kilometres between her and the bay, most of it forested, gently winding sections of road punctuated by cuttings of giant basalt rockfaces dwarfing all those who passed through. A prime mover whooshed by in the opposite direction and, although bracing for it, Donna was still startled by the sideways thrust of air that rocked her little Toyota, making her feel even more insignificant and flimsy.

The car's interior was heating up and she was hungry, having skipped breakfast in her hurry to escape Brisbane.

She turned on the radio and cranked up the air conditioner, craving a dip in the ocean when she got home. The closer she got to Finn Bay, the more the lulling beauty of its waters beckoned her, not just to cool off but to wash away the grub of her family and the filth and grime of her own failings; everything she didn't like about herself. Not just over the party but at the way she'd been fobbing off Lily, a woman who deserved better, a woman ten times stronger than she would ever be. Donna hadn't seen the first request coming six weeks ago, but since that beach excursion Lily had been talking to her on a regular basis about assisted dying, and in recent days the penny had dropped that Lily was completely relying on Donna to come to her aid.

She finally arrived home, her legs stiff from the drive and, she realised, a tension that had probably been holding her whole body in a siege since yesterday. Getting out of the car, she inhaled a lungful of salty air. It was as if she could breathe properly again, and she couldn't wait to get to the beach. But, like Lady Macbeth, she couldn't imagine how even the pure, perfect waters of the bay could cleanse the stain of her own pathetic weakness.

Lily

Pauline has left, replaced by a man who has come to collect my dirty washing.

'Hello, Mrs Harford. Been enjoying the iPod Lexie lent you?' he asks.

I don't think I've met him before. He's quite pimply for his age and is chewing gum with his mouth open. I don't care for him much. Perhaps he's the one who's been stealing my toffees. But I'm not one to be rude.

'Yes, it's marvellous. I might buy one for myself. We had a lovely time, dancing and singing to ABBA. Do you know them?'

He begins transferring items from my dirty clothes basket to his trolley. 'Sure do. Music makes life worth living, I'd reckon.'

'I don't think it's quite as simple as that,' I reply. 'Music has the power to lift anyone's spirits but life's like a profit and loss statement, isn't it? It's about net value. You have to weigh up the debits with the credits. The assets versus the liabilities.'

I'm not sure he's following my analogy. He nods unconvincingly and makes his exit without so much as a goodbye. How rude. Donna would never do that.

I peer out of the glass doors towards the Pacific. It's almost summer and the room feels stuffy. I wish I could open them. Ah, but Pauline is probably right. She has a good soul, despite her father's genes. Not that he was a bad egg as such, more … dishonest and cowardly. So many details of the past have faded with time, the strata of life muddying the images, but I can still recall that sorry chapter like it was yesterday. I shouldn't label it like that, though, because if I hadn't succumbed to Lenny Smythe's charms, my Pauline wouldn't exist.

1950

'Ma, Pa. I have something to tell you.'

My parents are listening to Perry Como croon on the radio while Ma mends yet more of Pa's socks. She can't understand why he gets so many holes. She suspects he takes his shoes off in the shop, though he's never admitted it when questioned. A mouth-watering smell wafts in from the kitchen. Ma must have a casserole simmering. Typical of her to be undertaking more than one task at a time.

'You sound serious, Lily.' Ma looks up from her needle and thread with a slightly alarmed expression. 'Are you all right, lovey?'

Recently I've been unable to zip up my skirts, so I'm not only feeling pregnant but also beginning to look it and the news simply has to be broken to the grandparents-to-be. There's no way to cushion it, so before I lose my nerve I let the words come right out, even though they sound alien and fantastical.

'I'm pregnant.'

It's odd to think that if he hadn't passed away, Robert and I might well have managed to conceive a baby. It's a thought that brings almost unbearable pleasure, but I've been widowed for seven or eight years now and bearing his child wasn't to be. No, this baby is not the consequence of a loving union. Nor has my pregnancy come at the best time, to say the least. On some days I don't leave the office until after most people have had their dinner. I've even started to go in on Saturdays to keep up with the workload. So how in heck's name will I fit a baby into my schedule?

At thirty years of age, I am part of a new generation of women who have chosen an alternative path to the curse of domesticity. Instead of having dinner ready when a husband gets home from his tiring day at work, the house spick-and-span and make-up perfect as I offer to take off his shoes and let him talk first, I'm the owner of a business, financially independent and intellectually fulfilled. Bobby's passing during the war was the hardest thing I've ever been through, but without the sale of his veterinary practice I'd probably never have enrolled in an accounting degree, nor purchased a house of my own in King Street, only four blocks from Ma and Pa here in Haversham Road. And it's unlikely I would have set up Harford Accounting Services, a company that has expanded surprisingly quickly. A bit like my girth.

Pa stands and turns off the radio, and the room becomes expectantly and disconcertingly quiet. I suppose it's no surprise I have his full attention.

'Who's the father?' His voice, carrying a hint of the Scottish accent of his own father, is blunt but not accusing. It's a fair enough question, but this is the part of the discussion I haven't worked out. I falter. My mouth is dry and I feel dirty. I can't bear to make eye contact, shuffling my feet just so I can focus my concentration on something else.

'No-one you know, Pa. He's from out of town.' I can't tell my parents what happened. How would they judge me if they knew the sordid circumstances of that one occasion? There's nothing to be gained from pointing out that I remained celibate for all those years after Robert was killed. There were a number of men during the war who'd tried their luck, some romantic and others simply trying to blot out the horrors of combat, things witnessed but never anticipated. Lust was written all over their faces but I turned away every one of them. Then, throughout my university years, offers of a date came but were sparse, maybe because my career aspirations were intimidating or because I exuded an aura of disinterest, the loss of Robert sitting with me like a constant ache. I suppose some might say my romantic withdrawal was a waste of a fine body in its prime but I found contentment and distraction by throwing myself into my accounting studies and, later, my work.

'I see,' is all Pa says, still standing with one hand on the radio. I venture to meet his gaze but he is giving me no indication of how he's taking the news. Is he contemplating simply turning the music back on, unsure whether he wants to know any more?

'How far along are you?' I hear my mother ask.

'Four months,' I reply in shameful agony.

I think back to that day. As an accomplished and supposedly sensible woman, you'd think I wouldn't have gone against all my better instincts and been conned by the compliments and charisma of a man I barely knew. But the body can only go so long without the touch of another's hands, so I suppose I can't blame Lenny Smythe entirely for what happened. This pregnancy wasn't planned, it wasn't even vaguely anticipated, but it only takes one moment of weakness, one indiscretion, to make a baby.

Lenny, an inspector in the Brisbane branch of the Australian Taxation Office, had called me out of the blue to arrange a discussion about a client of mine. Mac Clements was, Lenny explained on the phone, suspected by the ATO of tax avoidance by fudging his maize crop accounts. (How Mac thought he could get away with it, I have no idea, and I'm cross beyond words that he could potentially have dragged me down with him, especially as I thought we had developed a friendship. He'll be finding himself a new accountant from now on.) Anyway, Lenny turned up at my office, walking in with the swagger of a man who knows the power of his charms, with his sleek moustache and matching slicked-back hair. He couldn't have been more different to Robert. Where my husband had worn clothes that spoke of outdoor endeavours and a down-to-earth manner, Lenny reminded me of a shop mannequin, all smooth and polished in his navy-blue pinstripe suit. As he shook my hand he held it a few unsettling seconds longer than customary. I was at once repulsed and electrified.

After the introductions, during which I found myself concentrating less on maize yields and more on my guest's physical attributes, I showed him the notes I had in Mac's file. To my relief I was reassured the ATO had evidence releasing me from any suspicion of wrongdoing. Hearing this, or perhaps because my visitor was so silver-tongued, I let my professional guard down, my usual caution disappearing like a shadow vanishing into a patch of shade.

'Mrs Harford, or may I call you Lily? Tell me more about your plans for business expansion – it sounds fascinating ...'

Lenny paid me the sort of attention, although I now realise it was disingenuous, that I hadn't enjoyed since Robert had first courted me. And he wasn't wearing a wedding band, and he was tall and swarthy, and, for the love of god, did I like the look of his masculine hands.

'May I bother you for a glass of water?' he eventually asked. As I walked toward the office's kitchenette in the rear of the building he followed me, and when I turned around the raw desire on each other's faces was all the green flag we needed. He pushed my willing body against the sink and together we fumbled my knickers to down around my ankles, my stockings falling with them. As I felt the first thrust inside me I groaned in anticipation of the build-up and release for which my body was now desperate. The act was frantic and abandoned, but just as I was wondering why I'd let myself go for so many years without its pleasure, Lenny shuddered and whimpered and it was all over. I was left like a wind-up doll, my lower belly enduring a lustful ache but quickly understanding it wasn't going to enjoy relief.

It only took two months before I twigged to the tender breasts, the nausea, an acute aversion to the smell of cooking meat and, the final tell-tale sign, a second missed bleed. Making an appointment with a local doctor, my worst fears were confirmed: the result of that unsatisfying and messy encounter was that I found myself with child in an era when single women would prefer to be caught picking their nose in public than having their lascivious ways on display for all to see.

Mulling over this, I almost jump when Ma sets her mending aside, stands up and strides towards me. Drawing me to her bosom she repeats over and over, 'My darling, my darling.' I'm unsure if her tone indicates compassion or happiness, but at least she isn't scolding me. I feel some of the tension drain from my body as she steps back and, mercifully, smiles at me, grasping both my wrists.

Now there's just my father's reaction to resolve. He moves as if to join us but stops short, his hands now dug into his pockets. It's still impossible to read his face. The wait is unbearable.

'I haven't heard from Lenny since our … our … liaison, so I've already figured that perhaps he isn't the settling-down type,' I blurt out, Ma still clinging.

For the first few weeks after the pregnancy was confirmed, the idealistic part of me put silly notions in my head of a white dress and a domestic life, albeit with a groom about whom I was ambivalent. I made excuses for his silence and absence. He's a busy man, he's tied to Brisbane, he's shy (although I didn't really buy that one), he's someone who doesn't like to rush things, he's recently been involved with a girl and is reticent to get emotionally tangled again so soon ... This inner romantic chatter did its best to convince me but it was against all good reason, logic and probability. I knew deep down that growing old as Mrs Smythe was unlikely, especially as time went on without so much as a word from him. And I couldn't say I was entirely disappointed.

'Why didn't you tell us earlier?' Ma finally releases me from her hold and casts her eyes down towards my tummy. I feel guilty and foolish for not confiding in her before now.

'I suppose I wanted to keep the news to myself until I'd worked out what it all meant for me, and to me, and how I'm going to manage everything.'

'I'm your mother, Lilykins. I could have helped you cope with the news.'

'I know, and I'm sorry. I should have come to you. It's just that I've been in such a confused state. And I didn't want to add to your worries.'

'Don't you think I'm strong enough to handle your problems as well as my own, Lily?' Ma is almost daring me to question her strength, the red hair that frames her face matching the fire behind her words.

'Of course I do, but before telling you about the baby I needed to sort out a few things, such as whether I wanted to consider adoption.'

Ma sucks in an abrupt breath and I realise my mistake. This confession must have shocked her far more than news of the pregnancy itself. My nerves go up a notch. I continue before she can cut me with her tongue. 'And once I'd decided to keep the baby I also needed to work out whether I should I tell the father. And if I told him, did I want our lives to merge in any way? After all, and I'm sorry to disappoint you by telling you this, he's someone I don't really know.'

Pa still hasn't said a word but at this comment his bushy eyebrows shoot to the ceiling. I'm positive the phrase 'Except in the biblical sense' is being withheld only through sheer willpower.

'So you're going to keep the baby?' Ma asks, nodding. I suspect she's looking for assurance that I never actually intended to do anything else.

'Yes. Because I know I'll probably not get another chance at being a mother, married or not.' I dart my eyes from Ma to Pa and back again. 'But I've decided to do it without him. Having my own business means I don't need his financial support.'

'Lily, your mother and I are not going to judge you for being seduced,' Pa says, finally walking over to me and putting a practiced, reassuring hand on my shoulder.

I'm giddy with relief. 'Thank you, Pa.'

'That was your decision, as is becoming a mother,' he goes on, 'and you're a smart lass who I'm sure can take care of herself. But Jean and I will certainly think ill of you if you can't see that you have a moral obligation to inform this man of his impending fatherhood.'

I'm at risk of feeling sorry for myself. 'But I don't think he wants to know. He hasn't been in contact with me since that day, so isn't that a clear enough message he wants nothing more to do with me?'

'Lily,' says Ma, 'he might think he's not interested in you now but that may well change if he knew you were in the family way.'

'But I wouldn't want him to stick around merely because of a baby! That's not enough of a basis for a marriage. Not for me, anyway.' I lift my chin without thinking, the action telling me how much I mean it.

Ma looks uncertain but Pa nods. 'I agree from his behaviour that he doesn't seem the marrying kind, or worthy of you, but at least promise me you'll tell him he's to have a bairn. As a man myself, I think he has the right to know, and I hope we've raised you well enough, Lily, that you can see that to be true.'

I walk the five minutes from Haversham Road to King Street unsettled and anxious. I know Pa is right but feel sick at the thought of having to track down Lenny and deliver the news. How will he react? Every scenario flashes through my mind, most of them unpleasant. I might have a moral obligation to tell him of the pregnancy but I'm positive he won't want to marry me, and I know now that I don't want to marry him after his disappearing act. The whole thing is such a mess. Nevertheless, I respect my parents' opinion on this.

The next morning I take his business card from my briefcase, pick up the telephone and dial. A girl with an annoyingly singsong voice answers.

'Good morning. Australian Taxation Office. How may I direct your call?'

My heart is hammering in my chest. 'Good afternoon. My name is Lily Harford. I'm calling from Harford Accounting Services in Finn Bay. May I speak with Mr Lenny Smythe? I have a critical follow-up question regarding one of my clients.' I'm sure I must sound unconvincing. 'It's a legal matter,' I add, hoping to convey credibility through urgency.

'I'm afraid Mr Smythe is on annual leave, Mrs Harford. May I take a message?'

I draw some quick breaths to steady my nerves. 'Could you please provide me with his home telephone number? It really is urgent that I speak with him.'

'I'm afraid it's government policy that I'm not at liberty to give out personal information, Mrs Harford. I'm sorry. Is there anyone else here who might be able to help you?'

'No, I definitely need to talk with him. When will he be back, do you think?'

'The week after next, I believe.' She sounds a little unsure and I hear her flicking through paper, perhaps the pages of a diary. 'I can't find anything written down but, oh, I remember now, it's definitely then. I'm sure he mentioned something about he and his wife having to be back in Brisbane before their children's school term resumes. I'm happy to pass on your details if you like and he can get back to you …'

As I place the phone down, fury replaces tension. It takes two to sin, but at least I didn't knowingly cause hurt to a third party. It makes my skin crawl to think of his adulterous hands on me. Being an unmarried mother will bring stigma – looks and rumours – but I'm not going to drop my head in shame. When my womb ripens I will refuse to let other people make me feel bad for something as wondrous and beautiful as a child growing inside me. I dial Ma and Pa's number. I feel remarkably calm. All decisions are made. That liar doesn't deserve the truth.

'Ma? It's me. I tried to contact the father but it seems he has a wife and children. Do you think Pa will now give me his blessing to do this on my own?'

I hear Ma call, 'Ken, it's Lily on the blower,' followed by whispers and then my father's strong and comforting voice comes on the line. Before I have a chance to repeat the question, he says, 'A man like that isn't good enough for you, Lily. I think through his own deceit, to you and his unfortunate wife, he's forfeited the right to your honesty. Whatever your mother and I can do to help, you know we're always here for you.'

I stammer my thanks, put the phone back on its receiver, and weep.

SATURDAY 8 DECEMBER 2007

Lily

The dining room is filling for lunch, the sound of clanging plates coming from the kitchen in a last-minute push to get our meals out. The stronger personalities gravitate to their usual cliques, leaning in to gossip into a keen ear as they take their place at a table, or to nod in collusion. It's no different here to a school playground: by making sure you're in the know, you're automatically not left in the outer. How juvenile. I'm glad not to be part of that. No, I'm usually at a table with Betty, Dora and ... the other one, with almost no hair ... Ugh, we should all be given name tags.

Names aside, I feel I'm having a good day. I'm *focused*. Unlike other times when I almost scream at the frustration of not being able to draw forward a name or idea or object from the black depths of my memory, to bring it somewhere in the light where I can take hold of it and speak it and swish it around in my mind like I would a pleasing taste in my mouth. That luxury, of not ever having to give a second thought to the instant and easy accessibility of language, has gone.

'Another day, another lunchtime, another stew.' Jack is sitting, hunched, at an adjacent table with Frank. Jack isn't the sharpest tool in the shed but I have to hand it to him – he comes up with good lines.

I pick up today's menu card. Beef casserole, chicken schnitzel or assorted sandwiches, with chocolate mousse or canned peaches for dessert. I consider what to select, but don't have much appetite, probably because of the heavy, aching sensation deep in my belly that I think has been troubling me all week. Perhaps I'll opt for a bread roll and a cup of tea. I look around the room to ask, and instead catch Jack looking at me.

'Would you like to join us? It's a bit lonely with just him and me.' Jack wiggles his finger between himself and Frank before leaning towards me and lowering his voice. 'Four-year anniversary of the poor bugger losing his wife to a particularly nasty cancer. So he's not the chattiest chap today.'

I should help to cheer up poor old Frank but it was such an effort to get seated and comfortable at my own table that I don't want to have to repeat the exercise. 'Thank you, but maybe another day,' I reply, grateful but staying put. Hopefully Betty and co will turn up soon.

There's a buzz of chatter and much fuss as several women organise themselves into chairs around another large table situated in the centre of the room. The more nimble are assisting the frailer, and carers help where needed, busily pushing a chair in here and picking up a dropped napkin there as everyone gets settled. I'm about to beckon Donna over about the bread roll when a warm wetness saturates my underwear followed immediately by a foul, fishy smell.

The blood drains from my face and I can't move, frozen in embarrassment. I don't know where to look. A thumping in my ears mutes the sounds of the dining room, but I hear Frank clear his throat with gusto as if he's choking on a piece of meat. My heart is thudding so powerfully I think I might pass out, and I begin to fall sideways. But Donna is right here, helping me up off my chair and calling for assistance. My legs collapse from under me and I almost drop back onto the urine-soaked seat before being guided instead into a wheelchair.

'Let's get you out of here,' Donna whispers as she cloaks me in a blanket and whisks me away.

I've disgraced myself, my dignity lost for all the world to see. Misery floods over and through me and I collapse into sobs, desperate to simply melt away. We reach my room and Donna speaks in rushed tones into the phone next to my bed then helps me into the shower to clean away my mortification. I can't speak, not even when she aids me into one of those pull-up napkins, lord help me. A fresh blouse and pants are produced from my wardrobe then my limbs are gently manipulated one after the other into sleeves and neck-holes and pant legs as if I'm a helpless toddler, the unfamiliar bulk of the nappy not helping.

'I'm so ashamed,' I eventually whimper through residual sniffles as I reach for a tissue. I sit on the edge of the bed and blow my nose then look up at Donna, my lower lip quivering.

'I'm sure no-one noticed,' she replies with a shake in her voice, and for the first time I see pity in her eyes.

'Thank you for helping me. You're a good girl.'

'Oh, my gosh, it's what I'm here for. But I wish you'd told someone about your symptoms a bit earlier. You know that a UTI can become quite serious if left untreated.'

'I'd think of it but then forget, I suppose. And I don't like to make a fuss.'

I watch through watery eyes as she bundles my soiled clothes into a large plastic bag.

'I don't like to think of you suffering unnecessarily, that's all,' she says.

There's a knock on the open door. From the bed, the corner of the en suite blocks my view of who is there, but a familiar voice asks, 'Hello? Is there anything we can do to help?'

I reply without hesitation or manners, but what do I care? Wretchedness has taken me beyond that now. 'Go away, Jack. I don't want to see anyone. I just want to go to sleep and never wake up.'

Donna puts the plastic bag down and goes to the door. 'We're fine. But thanks anyway, gentlemen,' she says.

'Righto, we'll leave you to it, then.'

Donna returns and sits next to me, taking my hand in hers. 'That was kind of Jack and Frank.' When I don't reply she asks, 'Do you feel up to any food? I can bring something to your room if you like.'

'No food. I don't care if I never eat again. I'm done. I mean it, Donna,' I say with as much conviction as I can muster, although my words sound feeble and insipid.

'Please don't talk like that. You've got lots to live for – your daughter, your granddaughter and those gorgeous great-grandkids. Your family adore you. Speaking of which, isn't Pauline coming to see you later today?'

I try to recall whether that's true, but I can't be sure. 'Yes, I think so. She doesn't visit often, but everyone's so busy with their lives.'

Still clasping my hand, Donna turns to look at me, her brow knotted. 'Lily, all year Pauline has been visiting you at least three times a week.'

Our eyes hold contact as I take in her words. How could I forget something as fundamental and precious as that? And how long will it be before I no longer *realise* just how bad things have got? Fear scrapes its nails down my spine. I need to take action before my life disintegrates to an inconceivable point.

I release her hold and our eye contact, staring instead at the carpet. 'You know, my own mother died at seventy-seven, never having ventured from Finn Bay and its surroundings. She tripped one day and snapped her hip. She went into hospital for an operation, but didn't wake up from the anaesthetic.'

'That's not a bad way to go,' Donna says, no doubt eased by the slight shift in subject matter but unaware of exactly where I'm going with this.

'Pa had died a decade earlier. They called it "senility" back then, in the early sixties, or "being off with the fairies". He'd always been the family's bedrock, but all of a sudden lost his ability to fix things or hold conversations. Once, he even forgot to put on his trousers. Went out the front gate and Ma had to chase him half a block down Haversham Road, calling "Ken!" and frantically waving his pants in the air, hoping the neighbours were none the wiser.'

I hear Donna give a little chortle at the image. Inside, I'm bawling for my father.

'We had to commit him to a dismal facility out past Rorook, an old converted convent. It doesn't exist any more, thank goodness. I remember driving out to visit him in those last few months, the trepidation worsening with every mile. I can't even imagine what it must have been like for my mother to watch him deteriorate. He got to the point where he couldn't do anything for himself and didn't recognise any of us, including Ma. The prospect of that happening to me ...' I shake my head. 'Anyway, after that his body shrank away, except for his stomach. It bloated. It was grotesque. I can still so clearly remember the disgusting smell of his breath, like a mix of rancid butter and ammonia. I have never rid myself of the memory of that smell, so potent even now. We were all put out of our misery when he died a month later from starvation.'

Donna grabs my hand again, giving it a gentle squeeze. 'I didn't realise you had a loved one go through this. But everyone tracks differently.'

'Maybe so. But there's a possibility, isn't there?' I turn to her. 'Donna, please, tell me. I've got worse, haven't I?'

'Oh, Lily, I know you must worry but like I said, you won't necessarily follow the same path as him.'

I try to smile, to acknowledge that Donna's understanding is providing me with a measure of support, but my face remains frozen as I continue to picture my father in his gruesome last days, all life and recognition gone from a vacant face.

'Please, I beg of you. Don't let me suffer like he did.'

Donna stares earnestly at me and a shadow passes over her expression, just for a moment. But instead of providing reassurance, she replies, 'I'll let you have a bit of a rest now, okay? But I'll pop in again later. Doctor Grieg will be here soon and she'll get some antibiotics into you that will make you feel a lot more comfortable.'

I don't answer. Instead, I lean back on the bed against pillows Donna has plumped and straightened for my ease. I feel so alone. And so miserably ill and achy. I should have said something earlier about my symptoms but I didn't want to make a fuss, and now I'm humiliated beyond belief.

I haven't felt such utter, black despair since my Robert left me. Why won't everyone just let me join him?

1943

I lie numb, coiled into a tight ball on our iron-framed bed, my knees tucked up to my chin. My throat burns from the howls, primal and raw. I whimper, begging in a silent, ridiculous prayer for time to wind back, knowing it's a fanciful indulgence, a destructive delusion. I reach for him, imagining running my fingers along the warm body I crave and imagine still sleeps next to mine.

'Bobby,' I whisper. 'Can you hear me?'

I wait for a reply, a croon in my ear, a sign he is in this room with me, loving me, wanting me, reassuring me. I hold my breath, fearful even the sound of my own breathing might mask his message. But I hear nothing, see nothing, sense nothing. Inhaling now with fierce determination, I close my eyes and the scent of his skin, still lingering cruelly and mercifully on our unwashed sheets, brings him home.

'Robert,' I plead this time. 'Don't leave me.'

I turn over to see us smiling back at me from our wedding photo. Steely grey clouds balloon behind us, as if to signal it's the first day of winter. Can it be only a year ago that, having exchanged our vows and declared utter devotion, we stood on the steps of St Stephen's, the same church in whose grounds he is now buried? A headstone is being arranged and I suppose when I can drag myself from this bed I will be expected to kneel, lay flowers and publicly expose my grief in front of his grave. I look at the bride in her figure-hugging lace-trimmed dress, a young woman anticipating a lifetime of experiences to be shared, children conceived. You can't see from the photograph but her dress has a low back, and her bouquet is made of dark red roses intertwined with pale green eucalypt leaves. Robert and I don't know it as we beam at the camera, but this will be our first and last photo.

I now understand how people can die from their sorrow. I know there are others in Finn Bay suffering too. The town is draped in a communal sympathetic melancholy, knowing that behind closed doors and drawn curtains mothers, fathers, sisters and wives are writhing in their own, private grief. When a telegram arrives, and many do, the community rallies around, but no amount of consoling or support can appease the agony of loss.

Despite the daily struggle of food, petrol and goods rationing, and the terrible reports from Europe, Robert and I tried to keep everyday life ticking over. We thought it was just a matter of bearing the war's challenges and waiting out the conflict until we could resume the life we'd imagined. Animals still got sick for him to attend, and Dunn's Dairy still needed me to tally its accounts. We sometimes went out dancing, Robert endearingly goofy and theatrical in his movements, the frivolity allowing us to forget for a few hours that the world had gone mad. I was so thankful Robert wasn't in harm's way, an enduring limp from child-hood polio preventing and protecting him from enlisting.

But he wasn't, as it turned out, to be spared. Against all odds and imaginings, while men's bodies bled and drowned and burned far from home, Robert was kicked in the head by a bull he was tending on a property less than ten miles from here. A quick, pointless, unremarkable death.

His body now lies in a box beneath turned soil, but Robert's not there. He's here in this room, I know he is, trying to find a way to reach me. He's as real as the wind. He's standing at the basin shaving, pulling funny faces. He's checking his kit bag for anything he might need for a house call before kissing me goodbye. He's kneeling in a paddock to soothe and heal a sick or broken animal. We're both awakening on a Sunday and slipping so easily, so quietly, so knowingly, into making love. Robert is in me, moving rhythmically as his eyes lock with mine and he groans my name. He's laughing as we drive up into the hills of the hinterland, a picnic basket rattling on the back seat as we hit each bump and pothole. He's sitting across the table from me at a local fundraising dinner, silent exchanges of support or humour or lust passing between us. He's flat on his back next to me on the grass in our garden, staring up at drifting clouds, one hand resting under his head while the fingers of his other hand casually, subconsciously, caress the inside of my wrist.

I move my eyes to his birthday present, a wool tweed jacket in an oatmeal colour to complement his eyes. It's draped on the back of a chair by the door, waiting to surprise him. But there'll be no grin of happy astonishment, no embrace of gratitude, no celebration of twenty-six years of life.

'Happy birthday, my dearest darling,' I murmur as I reach back across our bed for him, groping pointlessly at cool sheet and empty air. There's no reply.

Pauline

As soon as she saw him walk towards her, his expression welcoming, Pauline knew the session wasn't going to go at all like she'd expected. For a start, he was a he. Pauline had booked in to see a Kim in a private psychology clinic in Rorook, a safe enough distance, she'd calculated, from Finn Bay. For some reason she had pictured an earth-mother type with long, flowing hair and sensible loose clothes. Instead, she was greeted and then led into one of the counselling rooms by a solidly built man about her height and age, if the grey hair on his temples was any indication. He was wearing red runners, blue jeans and a crisp white shirt. His features reminded her vaguely of an older, male version of Cameron Diaz.

With senses heightened from nervous energy, Pauline took in the room's eclectic contents. A heavy mahogany desk sat below the window, an incongruously modern plastic chair tucked under it. On top lay variously coloured manila folders arranged in neat piles, a black mobile phone to one side. Two plush armchairs, upholstered in a heavy floral pattern, sat against one wall. A black leather two-seater couch was positioned opposite and a light-toned timber coffee table took centre stage, supporting a pewter jug, a water glass and large box of tissues. The last was a bad sign, Pauline surmised wryly as she stood in the centre of the room, waiting for him to close the door behind them.

Invited to sit wherever she wished, Pauline selected one of the armchairs, and Kim settled himself onto the couch. After exchanging pleasantries about the weather he introduced himself properly, explaining his training and background was in individual and couple counselling but with a special interest in middle-age depression.

Despite the awkwardness of being there Pauline immediately warmed to this counsellor. As someone who liked to cut to the chase and focus on solutions, she watched him briskly open his notepad and prise the lid off his pen, and sized him up as being the type averse to wasting time in flowery analyses and long-winded reflections. He would listen to her problems then ask a few poignant, soul-searching questions that would produce the required answers. Firm handshake. Thank you very much. All sorted. Nice to have met you. I'll be on my way now with the means to heal.

In the end she'd only booked the appointment to get Sam off her back. After she'd summoned up the courage to share the GP's diagnosis with her husband, it had seemed that every time she was remotely upset or out of sorts Sam had been adding up the tally, as if collecting evidence of her need to see a professional to properly sort out her head. Perhaps he just didn't want to carry that responsibility himself. Every problem has a scientific solution according to Sam, she'd thought. Typical engineer. But she was sure she'd only need one session, two max, and then she'd be all set to cast off this goddamn despondency and get on with being the Pauline of old.

'So,' began Kim with a relaxed yet direct manner, 'what brings you to counselling?'

That was easy.

'I want to be happy again.'

First question done, tick.

'And what do you feel is making you unhappy?'

That's easy too.

'Well, predominantly I'd say I'm worried and sad about my mother, who's moved into care. But I think it's also that I'm worn out. I run around taking care of everyone and it's exhausting. I know the simple and sensible answer would be to stop doing that, but I feel trapped.'

'Trapped? How so?'

'I can't afford to retire, I can't abandon my mother, or my daughter or her kids, I can't simply walk away from all the everyday things that need doing …' Pauline trailed off, thinking she must sound so whingey. She looked down at her lap, one leg jiggling, and fiddled with her wedding ring, wondering with a hint of embarrassment how she could seriously expect this man to feel any sympathy. He probably saw clients forced to deal with serious issues, such as abuse, bankruptcy or children with incurable diseases. What right did she have to be sitting here, taking up his valuable time?

'Tell me about one of these aspects. Why don't we start with your job?'

Pauline relaxed, crossing one leg over the other and clasping both hands over her knee. She outlined her role as principal, the demands and responsibilities, the hours she worked as well as the aspects she liked the most. She spoke about the targets she was expected to achieve by the end of the current business plan and the many ways in which others – staff, students and parents – depended on her. When she finally stopped talking she was astonished to realise the hour-long session was already more than halfway through. All that Kim had said was the occasional 'Go on' or 'Tell me more about that'. Could she really have been rambling on all that time, she wondered? It had felt good, though, to talk about herself to someone whose job it was to be fully attentive and focused on her.

For the next ten minutes Kim's questions revolved around Pauline's home situation. What did she rate her marriage out of ten? ('Eight. No, an 8.5, I guess.') What three things do you most value about it? ('Companionship, I can rely on him, he makes me laugh.') What would the marriage need in order to increase to a ten? ('That's a tough one … can I have more time to think about that? More "deep and meaningfuls", probably.') How do you feel about looking after your grandchildren for Rachel and her husband? ('It's nice to be needed and keeps me close to Rosie and Luke – they're growing up so fast. I wish I had more time to be with them though.')

For the briefest moment Kim's attention transferred from Pauline to the wall behind her that she assumed held a clock.

'Unfortunately we're nearly out of time,' he confirmed. 'I think we need some more sessions to dig a bit further here. Now, please correct me if I haven't heard you properly, or accurately interpreted what you've said, but I get the impression that despite its many challenges you gain a lot of satisfaction from your job, and that your family and home life is, overall, a source of happiness for you. I can see these create some stress though, and that we have work to do together on managing the high standards you set for yourself. But I get the sense there is something else, Pauline, something much deeper, at the root of your unhappiness.'

Pauline nodded. The session had triggered no bubbling angst or real emotion, no need for those tissues. Even briefly making reference to her mother hadn't set her off in floods of tears.

As if reading her mind, Kim asked, 'You mentioned about your mother. May I ask where she's living?'

Pauline's heart flickered, signalling a blatant warning about the pus that might erupt if the boil of this topic was poked too hard. 'Mum's in Blue Vista, the retirement-slash-nursing home in Finn Bay.'

Kim nodded. Assuming she had no choice, Pauline reluctantly elaborated.

'She's eighty-seven. She's still mobile but only just. One of the staff took her down to the beach a while back and it took her days to recover from the effort. So, you know, she's finding it hard. Her hip gives her a lot of grief.'

Kim's head moved up and down some more.

'She had to be moved into there mostly because her memory wasn't great. That was eleven months ago and, um, we've noticed a definite decline even since then. She seemed happy there at first but she's been a bit down recently, with good and bad days. It's difficult for her. Leaving her house was a real upheaval, understandably, and now she's been diagnosed with dementia ...'

Pauline moved her eyes from Kim to her lap to the tissues, where they remained fixed.

Keep it together.

'Okay, well if it's all right with you, what I would like to focus on in our next session is your mother. You suggested you spend a lot of time with her and at the start of our session you used the word "abandon". Perhaps there's something there that we can explore. How do you feel about that?'

Boom. There it was. Kim uncrossed his legs and leaned forward, quietly adding, 'I can see from your face that that's triggered an emotional response. It's tough to watch someone you love go downhill and feel you're helpless in stopping it.' He pushed the tissue box closer to his client. 'Before we meet again next week, would you be open to keeping a diary concerning your mother? It can be feelings, events, thoughts, pictures, anything really. It will be a useful tool for us to explore this area in the next session.'

Although the appointment left Pauline exhausted and unsure a diary was either useful or wise, on her way back to the car she popped into a newsagency and bought a small, ring-bound notebook. The heat inside her car was intolerable so she wasted no time starting the engine and winding down the windows with an almost manic urgency. After fossicking in the glove box for a pen she opened the notebook to its first, unblemished page, balanced it on her thigh and wrote her first entry:

I've feel like I've abandoned Mum.

It made sense to her that this was at the core of her depression. Worries about money and time and responsibility and middle-age invisibility were just smokescreens to the true issue of the deep, unforgivable shame that she had let her mother down.

Pauline closed her eyes for a moment to let that fact sit, to permit her mind to swill it around and taste it, to allow and accept it into her very being. When she opened her eyes though, almost as if her hand was working ahead of her brain, she wrote another sentence.

But she's also abandoning me.

Shocked at the selfishness of her words, Pauline threw the book and pen onto the passenger seat like they were covered in poison. She leaned back in her seat and, pulling the sun visor down, peered into its mirror. Her face looked the same as before but she felt rubbed raw, as if she'd shed a skin and uncovered a layer that nothing and no-one could heal.

Her mobile rang, startling her. Cursing, she flipped the visor back up and fumbled around in her bag for the phone. The call, she saw, was from Blue Vista. They usually didn't make contact unless there was a problem. She pressed to answer and, with a deep and forceful sense in her gut that she should get back to Finn Bay, wasted no time in tucking the mobile between her face and shoulder and yanking the car into gear.

'Hello? Pauline? It's Donna Charleston. Have I caught you at a bad time?'

'No, no. I've just been doing some Christmas shopping.' Pauline pulled out from the curb, appalled at the ease with which the lie had slid off her tongue.

'Gosh, I haven't even thought about gifts yet. You're very organised.'

The compliment sang for a fraction of a second before Pauline realised the absurdity. 'Not really,' was all she could think to reply.

'I suppose you'll have your family gathered together on the day? Your mum has been mentioning that.'

'Has she? Yes, it will probably be the usual lunch at our place.' Although aware this was all filler chat, a kind of sweetener before the call's real purpose, Pauline played along out of politeness, despite her pulse racing. She liked Donna and was very appreciative of the care she took of Lily. 'What about you? Will you be spending Christmas with your family?' she asked, checking her side mirror with difficulty as she changed lanes to get onto the main arterial to Finn Bay, and thinking how foolish it was to do so with a phone wedged into her neck.

'Um, no, I'm rostered on for a double shift.'

'Oh, that's not much fun for you.'

'Not really. I like being here for Christmas. It's a breeze compared to a whole day with my family.'

Pauline caught a hint of bitterness and discomfort but wanted neither to press further nor go there. It was time to cut to the chase anyway. Cursing herself for not having put her phone on speaker, she planted her foot in readiness for merging into the faster-moving traffic of the highway. 'So, is everything all right?'

'It is now but I'm calling because your mother had a bit of an upsetting thing happen at lunch and I said I'd ring you as I was the one who helped her afterward.'

'Why, what happened?' Seeing another vehicle looming in her rear-vision mirror, Pauline realised she'd absentmindedly taken her foot off the accelerator. She put pressure back on the pedal.

'She's apparently been feeling a bit off for the last few days but didn't tell any of the staff, and then at lunch today she had a little accident.'

'What do you mean? Is she all right? Has she fallen?' Pauline had visions of her mother with a fractured pelvis or wrist.

'No, she's not hurt or anything. She had an incontinence accident, which is common at her age, but unfortunately it happened in the dining room.'

Pauline's hand whipped up to her mouth. 'Did anyone else see this?'

'I'm afraid so. And what made it worse was that, well, it seems she's got another, much worse urinary tract infection, which as you know causes your wee to smell pretty awful. I'm so sorry.'

'It's not your fault, Donna. But ... poor Mum.' Pauline's whole body tightened.

'Well, luckily one of the other residents coughed and cleared his throat to alert the staff and I looked over and was able to quickly wrap Lily up and take her back to her room. The doctor's on her way and will call you once she's seen your mum but I'm sure she'll be looking at putting her on a course of antibiotics, which will kick in quickly and make her a lot more comfortable.'

Pauline's mind played out the whole sorry scene from her mother's perspective, overcoming her with both love and compassion. 'Thank you so much for letting me know. She hadn't mentioned anything to me about a recent UTI or having symptoms. God, she must be mortified.'

'She was quite upset but she'll be okay. Look, I'd better get back to things but I just wanted to keep you in the loop. Lily is fine now so don't worry too much. And you can always call the supervising nurse if you need to know more.'

'Thanks, Donna. You've been great. Thanks for being there for Mum.'

'Oh, and Pauline? I think it might be time to look at your mum wearing incontinence undies. Lots of the women here, and the men for that matter, use them. I know it's a bit degrading initially but it's better than having another accident, now we know she might be prone to them. Maybe that's something you can talk about with her.'

'Of course. Bye, Donna.' Pauline deliberately relaxed her shoulder and the phone fell, clattering between the door and her seat. She inched the car up over the limit, a subtle yet insistent and uneasy feeling nuzzling in the depths of her stomach, a sense that nothing would ever be the same. Where had she been when her mother had urgently needed her?

Whining to myself about feeling abandoned. Get a fucking grip, Pauline.

Donna

Her shift over, Donna collected her things from the nurses' station and walked out through Blue Vista's main doors. The afternoon was a perfect combination of delicate breeze and gentle sun, and she closed her eyes briefly as she inhaled the perfume from the rose beds to either side of the entrance. Checking her phone, she saw there was a single text message – from Vedya, from half an hour earlier.

Meet me at Nobody's after you clock off. No excuses. Have news. V

Thinking it was about the imminent expansion of Wild Side, and deciding she could do with the distraction after what had unfolded today, Donna texted back:

Will do. Leaving work now. Just need to duck home and change first. Xx

Nobody's Inn was quiet, even for a Saturday. As Donna strolled in, Vedya waved excitedly from a barstool, appearing very pleased with herself and patting the seat to her right. 'Hi! Come and plant your arse next to mine. I'm celebrating.'

They embraced, Donna catching a slight odour of dog hair.

'So I see. You look ... different ... you've ... parted your hair down the middle.'

'Thought it was time for a change. What do you reckon? Suit me?'

'Abso-bloody-lutely, Ved. But then you could have straw for hair and it would look good.'

'Yeah, yeah, whatever. Anyway, you can talk. I've had hair envy ever since I met you.'

Donna's astonished look prompted Vedya to continue. 'Don't tell me you don't know how great your hair is. It's so thick and shiny. I bet you have quite the bush *down there*.' She grinned, nodding towards Donna's crotch. 'It must cost you a bomb to keep it under control.'

'Vedya, you're terrible. For your information, I'm neat and trim *down there*, thank you very much. Anyway, what's all this about having news?' Donna was keen to put an end to the subject of her pubic hair and equally keen to have her mind taken off the day's events, still chastising herself for not being more on top of her game. Lily's recent confusion, a passing mention of an aching back, some slight coordination issues reported by Lexie to the supervisor the day before yesterday – Donna had assumed it was a set of symptoms in line with Lily's dementia and general aches and pains. Lily herself had said nothing so no-one had joined the dots until the incident. Donna had pushed a distraught Lily back to her room, gutted by the old woman's despair.

She got the barman's attention and mouthed, 'A Coke, please,' as Vedya settled into the reason she'd summoned her friend.

'Okay, don't judge me – promise? – but … I've met a guy.'

'That's fantastic. Wait, why would I judge you? Who is he? Anyone I know?'

'Hmm, well that's the thing. You're unlikely to know him because, well, he lives in Sydney.'

'Uh-huh. Sounds promising so far.'

'Okay, here's the other thing. We kind of met … online.'

Donna executed an exaggerated blink. 'Oh my god, Ved, are you joking?'

'Don't stress,' said Vedya, rolling her eyes. 'It's actually become a popular way to meet someone. You put up a profile of yourself saying what your interests are, what you're looking for in a partner, your age, that sort of thing, plus a photo. And then if you like the look of someone else's profile you can arrange to meet for a coffee.'

'Ved, weren't you afraid you'd meet up with this guy and he'd be a total wanker?'

'Sure, a bit, but then I figured: what do I have to lose?'

Donna was processing all this. It still seemed a weird way to hook up with someone and not a little risky. 'Only your safety maybe. What if he'd been a weirdo, or an actual psycho?'

'I met him in a public space, not a dodgy hotel room. Give me some credit.'

A group of gabbling older men in golfing gear entered the pub but, thankfully, made their way to a table in the far corner. Donna wasn't in the mood for flirty chitchat, requiring as it did a certain frame of mind, a brightness of spirit. That was far from how she felt this afternoon, her mind still very much wandering. Staying with Lily to help and comfort her through the aftermath of her ordeal, she'd briefly, involuntarily, imagined helping Lily to avoid her father's fate. But, even aside from the prospect of a jail term and the end of her career, the image of actively participating in Lily's death had been so surreal and horrific that she'd just as quickly dismissed it.

Lily's daughter had been out of town and when she'd come in had been jumpy and prickly, not helping Donna's low mood. Berating herself for missing the signs earlier, Donna had popped her head in now and again to check on her charge who, by mid-afternoon, was moaning softly, her face and neck coated in a light sheen. At least by the time Donna clocked off, antibiotics were finally coursing through Lily's system, but Donna's confidence and frame of mind remained at an all-time low and she was finding it hard to concentrate on Vedya's words.

A soft drink now in hand, she took a sip and forced her attention once again to her friend. 'Sorry, I know you wouldn't do anything that stupid. So, you met this bloke, and, what, he's actually nice? Normal? Single? Straight? An earthling?'

Vedya laughed. 'Yes, all of the above. In fact, he's gorgeous. Not in a classic Brad Pitt kind of way but in a dinkum everyday sort of way. He's a chippy; works for himself. Lives with a mate. And we've seen each other four times now, twice here and twice in Sydney.'

'What, so you've flown down there already?'

'Sure, why not? He pays half the fare and it's been fun. His flat's super nice and he even likes to cook.'

'What do your parents think?'

Music suddenly blared at a ridiculous level, making the two of them jump.

'Some idiot forgot to turn down the volume!' yelled Vedya just as the sound level abruptly dropped and her last words resounded through the bar. Donna smirked and Vedya shrugged by way of an apology to the other patrons. 'I haven't introduced them yet. They're away at the moment anyway. They'd probably prefer I married another Indian but I'm sure they'll be cool once they meet him.'

'I don't know, Ved. He could be portraying himself as someone he's not.'

'I know he could be, but I don't reckon he is. I think he's the real deal. His mum and dad even dropped by one of the times I was there and they seemed lovely, and he was, I don't know, what's the word? So genuinely respectful of them. He's really, really nice, Donna. You'd like him. He's going to be in Finn Bay again in about a month so I hope you'll meet him then.'

Donna had run out of arguments. Anyway, it wasn't her place to parent Vedya. 'Well, okay, sure, that would be nice, as long as I don't feel too much of a third wheel.'

Vedya grinned. 'Okay, so that was the other thing I wanted to talk to you about. I think you should register on the same site. Then we can go on a double date.'

Donna opened her mouth to protest but Vedya put up her hands in defence as she forged on. 'Before you huff and puff and shake your head, think about it. One, you only have to make contact with someone who ticks all your boxes. Two, no need to go to parties and bars and negotiate the whole pick-up scene. Three, it costs bugger-all plus the cost of a cup of coffee. And four, if you don't like him you say thanks and see-you-later and never have to face him again. It's so easy, Donna. Admit it, it's kind of tempting ...'

The thought of intimacy, physical or emotional, made Donna's heart skip a beat, and not in a good way. 'But I genuinely don't want to meet anyone. I'm happy as I am.'

'I don't believe that for a second. You just need to find the right partner. Don't be put off by what happened with Douchebag Derek. Please just think about it, okay?'

Donna chewed on her lip, wondering if her friend was right. She was so used to telling herself she'd never go down that road again that she hadn't bothered to stop and really question if it were in fact still true. Her eyes passed over the men sitting nearby. 'Okay, okay. I have to agree it's got a certain degree of merit. I suppose it makes sense to meet someone you already know on paper is a good fit.'

'Well, there you go. I knew it would appeal.' Vedya looked smug. 'So you'll put up a profile?'

'Appeal's too strong a word. But I'll think about it.'

Vedya placed the palms of her hands together and clapped her fingers.

'But, BUT, I'm not making any promises,' Donna went on, one hand up like a stop sign to prevent her friend's enthusiasm from going too far. 'And if I do go ahead I won't be letting you help to write my – what's it called? – profile. You'd have me as a skinny twenty-something astrophysicist with a love of cars and cricket and a sex addiction.'

The two chuckled. It felt cathartic to agree to something so uncharacteristic, and Donna experienced a tiny thrill from even contemplating something risky, something bold. Maybe it was just what she needed to help neutralise the blemish and stink of impotence still shrouding her from Shelley's party, not to mention her cowardice in playing down Lily's worries.

'Donna, I wouldn't do that to you. Anyway, in all serious-ness, there's no point painting a false picture because one meet-up and the cover would be blown. When you write about yourself, be totally honest. Well, perhaps not totally. I wouldn't go mentioning your tendency to buy skin-coloured granny undies.'

'What's wrong with my chastity belts?' Donna quipped, giggling. 'They're very comfortable, I'll have you know, and good under white jeans. But I guess I could manage to wear something a bit sexier if I went on a date. Note the emphasis on *if.*'

'Here's to choices and being daring,' Vedya toasted.

Over the next hour they chatted more about how their respective jobs were going, and Vedya's new boyfriend, as well as friendly gossip about various mutual acquaintances. When Vedya said she had to get going, they walked out into the still-warm afternoon together and by a quarter to five Donna was back in her flat. Three quarters of an hour later her profile was up, including a photo taken of her on a sailboat off the coast the previous summer. The edge of an orange spinnaker billowed in the background, Donna's face beaming with exhilaration as the yacht skimmed over the water. She liked the image. It spoke of a side of her she wanted to voluntarily give free rein to all the time, not only in occasional moments forced upon her through circumstance. A side that was carefree, courageous and unquestioningly happy, not merely content.

An hour later, still floating on her lingering high spirits, she'd received five messages. Only one, from a Xavier, 'ticked the boxes'. The problem was, he lived in Colorado, USA. Still feeling light-headed and bold enough to throw caution to the wind, Donna messaged him back.

TUESDAY 18 DECEMBER 2007

Donna

Having helped her to get comfortably seated, Donna
brushed Lily's long hair, careful to spy any knots before the
brush located them. A piano sonata drifted from the adjacent room, providing a muffled but soothing background.
Last week's ordeal seemed a world away. Lily's infection had
cleared and she hadn't mentioned it or her anguish since.

Coloured sticky notes peppered Lily's room. They'd been
there for the last few days, attached to her bedside table
and strewn across the cupboard door. Yellow squares listed
scheduled visitors (*Rachel on Saturday, Sam on Monday*),
blue was for upcoming activities (*Mon pm – singing, Tues
am – speaker on Ancient Rome*), green provided basic updates
on each family member (*Luke, 2, at creche Mon and Fri, cur-
rently into trains,* Spot *books & elephants. Christos has taken*

up lacrosse) and orange earmarked upcoming medical, dental or podiatry appointments. It was an impressive feat of organisation by anyone's standards.

'It looks like a rainbow in here.' Donna loosened a small tangle from Lily's hair as cautiously as possible. 'I think the colour-coded notes are such a great idea. Your daughter says she plans to keep all your reminders up to date. She's very methodical, isn't she?'

Lily twisted slightly to scan the room. 'Yes, I'd be lost without her.'

'You're very lucky to have Pauline. Lots of the folk in here have no-one.'

'I am indeed. I'm blessed to have you too. But if you don't mind me sticking my nose in, do you have anyone, Donna? I worry about you sometimes.'

'What do you mean?' The brush now moved freely so she gathered Lily's hair into a ponytail.

'Well, it's just that I don't think you've ever talked about your family, and it's really none of my business but I gather you haven't got anyone here in Finn Bay. I was single for most of my life but I had my parents near, and of course Pauline. I hope you don't get too lonely, that's all.'

'You'd think I would, but no.' Donna was chuffed that Lily cared enough to ask. 'To be honest, I like that my family aren't close by, and I have friends here at work and outside work.'

'What about a relationship? Not that it's essential but it's nice to have someone to share things with.'

'It's funny you should mention that, because I've recently met a man.'

Donna liked the thought of sharing this particular news with Lily, perhaps getting some grandmotherly advice, as a part of her worried she'd made the wrong decision going along with Vedya's matchmaking suggestion. The fear of rejection still lurked. Lily's short-term memory wasn't great but Donna sensed she still had plenty of wisdom to share, harvested from a lifetime of experiences.

'Oohh, tell me all. That sounds exciting. What's his name?'

'Xavier. Xavier Jones.' Donna was aware of the pride in her reply.

'Oh, what an exotic name. What does he do? How did you meet?'

The first question was going to be easier to answer than the second. 'He's in marketing, working for a big firm in the US.'

'The United States? How long will he be posted there for?'

'He's not an Aussie working over there, he lives there. He's American.' Donna wound Lily's strands up into the French bun style she loved. 'We've been talking on the computer every day for the past week. We really like each other and have plans to meet up one day, maybe in Hawaii as it's halfway. Then, well, who knows what might happen from there?'

'You haven't actually met? Donna, dear, this all sounds very suspicious. It could be part of a scheme to get a visa to live in Australia. Sorry to sound sceptical or rude, but I think you could be falling into some kind of trap.'

Donna's glow faded with the lack of approval. She walked around Lily's chair to check her handiwork from the front.

Lily must have turned heads, she thought – a stunner as well as a force to be reckoned with. Although, Donna had decided months ago, it seemed Lily was the calmer one when compared to her daughter. Lily shifted and her brow creased. Donna wasn't convinced it was entirely out of worry for her romantic prospects. 'Are you in pain? Do you need to stretch your legs?'

'I'm fine, thanks, just a little sore. Pass me the mirror, will you, dear?'

Donna obliged and watched as Lily inspected the hairdo from several angles.

'I know what I'm doing. He seems really nice, very kind and easy to write to; though he's a terrible speller, mind you. But we have lots in common. I'm surprised by how excited I am about it. And he isn't looking to leave the US, at least not yet. He has children there from a previous marriage.'

'Oh, goodness.'

This time Donna caught an unmistakable wince of pain flaring across Lily's face. 'Can I get you some aspirin? Where does it hurt?'

'No, I'm all right,' Lily said, brushing her off, 'but be careful. This man could be taking advantage of your good nature and, if you don't mind me saying so, your lack of confidence.'

Donna was taken aback. How had Lily picked this up about her? And was there a chance Lily was right? Could Xavier just be using her? Was he even who he said he was?

'I had a few hopeful suitors in my time but at least I was able to eyeball them and use my sixth sense to gauge if they might be worth the effort,' Lily continued. 'You can learn a lot about someone by whether they can look you straight in the eye.'

Donna placed a few more hairpins to properly secure the bun. 'Well, he's sent me a ton of photos and his eyes look sincere.' Satisfied Lily's hairstyle passed muster, Donna reached for the hairspray and sent a mist over her head before standing back. 'There, all done. Not bad if I say so myself.'

'Thank you, Donna. It's lovely.'

As Donna collected up the comb, mirror, remaining pins and can of spray, she took the chance to broach a delicate subject, even as a voice inside her head was questioning the wisdom of doing so. 'Lily, you've always said you wanted to know what's going on with you, to be kept informed and aware.'

'Yes, of course. Why, what's happened?'

'Well, apparently you had a bit of a turn last night. At handover we were told you were humming a lullaby, and the night nurse couldn't get any sense from you. She said you didn't know where you were. Do you remember?'

Lily looked confused and, if Donna wasn't mistaken, a little indignant. Donna immediately regretted having mentioned anything.

'I don't know. Did I? It's possible. Although the only person I know who sings a lullaby is my mother. Was she here?'

In the few seconds it took Donna to form a suitable reply, Lily's face dropped. 'Oh, Donna, what's happening to me? My mind is abandoning me ...'

'Look, I've probably made it out to be worse than it was. I'm sorry. I didn't mean to upset you. That's the last thing I want.'

'You have nothing to be sorry for, Donna. I appreciate your candour. But what else have I done that I don't realise?'

'Nothing. Honestly.'

Lily narrowed her eyes as she delivered a long breath and stared with such intensity and displeasure that Donna didn't know where to look.

'I'm not sure I believe you. But even if you're telling me the truth, it will only be a matter of time before the next episode, then the next.'

Donna braced for what she knew was coming. It was no longer a new topic.

Lily's eyes pleaded. 'I'm not frightened of death. I've had a full and long life. But I need to go on my terms while I still have some control, before this narrow window closes on me and I no longer even know that that's what I want. Will you please help me to die if I get any worse? I don't know who else I could turn to. We've come to know each other well and I'm so fond of you, Donna, and I know you're fond of me. We get each other, so you understand, don't you? Look at all these bloody notes, for Christ's sake,' she lamented, pointing around the room. 'Here, pass me one,' she demanded.

Donna unpeeled a paper square from beside Lily's bed and handed it to her, sighing as she did so. No good could come of this discussion.

'Listen to this: *Rachel is now teaching pottery* ... Before I know it I won't know who Rachel is.' Lily screwed up the paper and hurled it onto the floor, tears welling.

'There's been the odd lapse but mostly you're doing okay.' To hide an expression that might have exposed the sugar-coating, Donna bent down to retrieve the little green square, which had landed under the bed. She was no doctor, or even a registered nurse, but it had occurred to her that Lily might have had a small stroke the night before. Perhaps she'd suffered more than one in the last few months, a more likely cause than dementia alone for her recent deterioration. Donna had seen no documentation to suggest that, but maybe they'd all missed the signs, like they had with the UTI. She pretended the paper was hard to reach to give her thoughts time to gather.

'I think you're probably being optimistic,' said Lily. 'Either way, I'm getting worse, not better. I want to go while I still have some clarity of mind. You need to promise to help me to die. *Please*, Donna.'

Donna straightened back up then sat on the corner of the bed, near the armchair, daring herself to meet Lily's eyes. She sympathised with Lily's situation. She hated the idea of her suffering. She had even, in a moment of craziness after Lily's incontinence accident, pictured injecting her with some sort of lethal cocktail. But at the end of the day she knew she simply couldn't help with such a wish.

'We've talked about this before. It's illegal to assist someone to die, no matter how much they want or need it.' Seeing the anguish on Lily's face, she added: 'I do understand your situation. I really do.' Donna's body felt heavy, like the weight of Lily's world was on her.

'But no-one would have to know it was you.' Lily's words came out in a rush now. 'It would be our little secret, taken to my grave. You could choke me, or give me pills, or an injection. You must have access to that sort of thing.'

Lily's begging was a gut-wrenching show of desperation, but as the images of various euthanasia methods sped through Donna's mind, each was equally unpalatable. She was an interminable distance from feeling the end would justify the means.

'I would go to jail! Please don't ask it of me again. We'll face this together. You're a strong woman. From what I've learned about you, you've always made the best of every situation.'

'That's what I'm trying to do – make the best of my circumstances by taking control.' Lily bent forward and encased Donna's face in her crooked fingers. 'I'm scared.'

Donna flinched involuntarily, taken aback at the intensity of Lily's stare. 'Please don't be. It will all be okay.' She delicately took Lily's hands in her own and rested them back in Lily's lap, achingly aware of the platitude, but she was rattled and didn't know what else to say. An awful hush hung between them. The only thing for it was to change the subject and hope the two of them could move beyond this impasse. 'And you're looking very smart,' she added, standing up and smiling, even though guilt made it almost impossible to do either. 'Do you want to head across to afternoon tea now or should I come back in a few minutes?'

'I think I'll have a tray in here, if it's all the same,' Lily replied, her voice flat.

The rejection smarted but Donna forged on. 'Not a problem. I'll bring one back for you. And thanks for your advice on Xavier. I promise I'll be careful.'

Lily stared at her with a blank expression. 'Who's Xavier?'

'No-one. I'd better go now.' Donna's smile of encouragement and comfort felt inadequate. She smoothed Lily's bed cover where she'd been sitting, before skulking out of the room like the miserable coward she felt herself to be. She felt hogtied by the law and by her own feelings of impotence and fear, and spent the remainder of her shift robotically carrying out her duties while going over and over Lily's words.

Although still flustered, she prayed the matter was closed, that Lily understood that under no circumstances could Donna assist her to end her life. Still, her mind was unable to clear itself from the challenge of one burning question.

If it came to it, would I have the guts to help her?

Pauline

Despite the fresh and challenging emotions surfacing since her first counselling appointment with Kim, on reflection Pauline had to admit she'd found the session a tonic. And although initially hesitant to keep a diary for fear it would give oxygen to her depression, thinking she could cope on her own without such a prop, she'd dutifully kept up the entries.

> *Mum needs to wear a nappy now. I can't imagine how degrading that must be. She gets sullen eg she misplaced a packet of toffees the other day and got so cranky. Turns out she'd put it under her mattress because she didn't trust some of the staff. Would be funny if it weren't so tragic. Ask Kim re paranoia.*

Had to say no to Rach re G'parents Day at kinder as clashed w Mum's specialist appointment. I felt dragged in two directions but it's not Mum's fault.

She's managing to shower and dress, walk in the gardens and make reasonable conversation but everything seems such a momentous effort. Shit shit shit. It's like Mum's life force is bit by bit making an exit.

Received a letter from BV saying they've changed the front code and suggest Mum shouldn't be told the new numbers 'for her own safety'. I feel rejected on her behalf like when I wasn't picked for the netball team at school – excluded and inferior. How awful for her.

Did some more research on vascular dementia. Called the Association. Not a pretty prospect.

Feelings? Helpless, deserted, sad.

Migrating the words from her head onto paper cleared Pauline's thinking and, although it raised challenging emotions, it left her feeling she was at least attempting to do something about her depression. The only problem was that the reprieve was always short-lived, another dejected thought waiting in the wings to sweep in and take centre stage. It was like successfully swatting at a fly only to discover the dozens of others loitering right above it.

'Hi, Pauline, nice to see you again. Please, take a seat,' Kim said as she entered his consulting room. Pauline selected the same chair as ten days before, inhaling deeply to collect herself and shake off the skittishness. The students might already be on holiday but Glenmore College's administration was still in full operation and she was flustered that she'd barely got to the four o'clock appointment in time. The armchair hugged her reassuringly.

'How have things been for you this past week?'

'All right. Busy, as usual. It's been hectic at work but this term is always a killer. The school's officially closed now for Christmas but the holidays will be a chance to get a lot of planning done and generally catch up on things without the students and teaching staff there.'

Kim nodded. 'And on the home front? How are things with Sam?'

Pauline sighed and looked towards the window. 'We had a big argument on, what, Friday night, I think it was, about the kitchen, of all things. I'm desperate to get it renovated over the summer break but he thinks we shouldn't waste our money when there are other things we could better spend it on, like our mortgage.'

'How did that make you feel?'

'Cross,' she began more loudly than she meant to. 'I just wish he'd see how happy it would make me. He can be so ... unemotional.'

'Maybe you could talk with him about it, but couch it in terms of your feelings. You have a lot going on right now with your mother and perhaps you're looking for something material to distract you and bring you a shot of happiness. Maybe he doesn't realise it's more about that, than about the actual kitchen.'

'Yes, perhaps I'm being unfair on him.' She wasn't convinced, but it felt like the right thing to believe anyway.

Kim nodded, his face remaining impassive. By not taking up air space he was allowing and encouraging her, Pauline realised, to keep going, to dig down.

'He's a good person. And mostly he does understand and support me. But I know him. He's not really comfortable talking about feelings.'

Kim crossed his legs and leaned forward a little. 'Some-times, just the process of expressing how we feel, truly feel, to others, can make us feel better in ourselves, and closer to them. It can build a bridge, even if it feels uncomfortable to start with. That goes for both of you.'

'I can – I have been – talking to Sam about some things, of course. It's him that pushed me to see you, for example. I mean, he's aware of my struggle with Mum moving into a home and her health going downhill. But I don't think he'd cope with the true level of shit going on in my head.'

'Can you tell me about one of those deeper things?'

Pauline thought about her diary entries. She swallowed. 'Mum was apparently extra confused last night. I'm having a hard time reconciling the Mum I've always known with the person she's become. I wrote down the word "deserted" this week. Is that selfish of me? It's not as if it's her fault she's got dementia, for heaven's sake. But I … I feel kind of lost without her. The old her. Old as in younger. You know what I mean.'

Kim delivered his understanding with a knowing smile, relaxing back into his seat again. 'Life as you know it has changed. When a parent becomes almost the child, it's a role reversal that some people find very challenging. The cared-for becomes the carer. It's not easy, practically or emotionally. But Pauline, you need to give yourself permission to feel, as you say, a bit lost as you navigate your way into what is unsettling new territory for you as a daughter.'

The remainder of the session found Pauline delving further into her mourning of the Lily that was, and her fear of losing her mother altogether, the time passing as quickly as the last appointment. Part of her felt cleansed from expressing her grief and sadness but she also felt small and selfish from making the situation all about her. Kim had been adamant in insisting her feelings were normal and justified, but it still all seemed so self-absorbed.

After booking in for another appointment in the new year she met Sam as prearranged at the mall, the retail options in Finn Bay being limited in comparison. She was looking forward to immersing herself in the pleasant distraction of Christmas shopping. Although it seemed every other person within the shire was on the same mission, she and Sam managed to find most of the things on their Christmas list, periodically returning to the car park with loads of groceries as well as toys and games for the little ones. Pauline was particularly pleased with a pretty cushion they'd found for Lily. It was in her mother's favourite colours, with a lavender filling that Pauline thought might help her sleep. They'd bought movie passes for Christos and Rachel so all they needed now were some books to fill the kids' Christmas stockings, and they'd be done.

Having decided on three picture books for Luke and two early readers for Rosie, Pauline was close to her shopping tolerance limit, the piped carols on loop in the mall doing her head in. Sam was still mulling over *The Very Hungry*

Caterpillar, skimming through its pages from start to finish and back to the beginning again.

'It's a classic. It's fine. Let's just get it and these others and go home,' she said.

'All right, all right, keep your shirt on. I want to be sure he'll like it.'

'He'll love it, Sam. What child doesn't?' Pauline was finding it difficult to hide her annoyance. 'I'm going to get in the queue, so please hurry up and decide by the time I'm being served?'

Pauline stood in line behind a teen boy and a woman managing a pram overflowing with plastic shopping bags. Pauline supposed there was also a baby in there somewhere but from her angle she couldn't be sure. It brought back memories of the challenges of shopping with Rachel as a youngster, and if she hadn't felt so tired she'd have muttered something understanding and empathetic to the woman in maternal collusion. As she thought about those days, a young couple approached the checkout queue, taking up a position as much beside Pauline as behind her.

She sighed. Her feet ached and she was aware her posture had drooped, a weakness she abhorred in others. The boy moved away from the till quickly; Pauline caught a disappointed expression on his face, presumably after being told a particular book had sold out. The young mum was having trouble finding her purse in an oversized baby bag hanging from the buggy's handles, but this suited Pauline as there was still no sign of Sam.

The woman finally paid and manoeuvred herself and her paraphernalia away from the counter, making room for Pauline to fill the void. To help her out, Pauline shuffled one step to the side to allow the wheels of the pram easier passage, but was blindsided when the young couple pushed their bodies up against the counter in a statement of service expectation and claim. A flabbergasted Pauline stared at their backs, her mouth hanging open, blinking in astonishment at their audacity as well as her own lack of vigilance.

A fierce, uncontrollable rage and heat consumed her. She bellowed in a voice so gravelly, so manic, she didn't feel it could possibly be coming out of her throat, 'Excuse me but it's my turn to be served. Who do you think you are, pushing your way in like that?'

The man and woman turned, and he protectively shot his arm out and in front of his girlfriend. 'Take it easy, lady. We didn't see you.'

'Think I was born yesterday?' Pauline barked with menace. 'Just because I'm older than you, older than everyone here, shouldn't make me invisible. How *dare* you!'

Behind the couple, the shop assistant's mouth hung open as she stared at Pauline with a fascination feebly masked as concern. But Pauline couldn't stop the tirade. She knew exactly what was happening but it was all occurring in a curiously detached way. She felt balanced on the precipice of a breakdown, teetering on its brink, the emotional equivalent of the anticipatory letting-go moments of pleasure before an orgasm. She could see how she must look to the small crowd in the shop. It was the strangest thing, though – she didn't care.

'Getting old is fucking awful,' Pauline snarled. 'You just wait. You'll get old one day, then, then … you'll disappear too.'

Collapsed into her emotions, she became aware of Sam's hands on her waist, calm but firm. 'Please love, that's enough,' his voice urged in her ear.

Hysteria melted into wretchedness as Pauline snapped back into reality, her legs like jelly. She'd been so close to letting her pent-up emotions carry her forward into carefree lunacy. For those few seconds she'd wanted to be taken away by kind-faced ambulance officers in starched uniforms to a hospital bed with nice nurses and nice doctors and everything so utterly *nice* and sterile and white and uncomplicated.

With a muttered apology from Sam to the shop assistant and other patrons, Pauline let herself be steered past the gawking shoppers and out of the store.

In the throng of the mall, Sam directed himself to face her. 'Do you want to talk about what happened in there?' His voice, measured and kind, only added to her shame.

She felt she might fragment into a thousand splinters at any moment. 'I don't think so. Oh, I don't know. Maybe.'

'Do you want me to find you a cup of tea?' Sam's hand hovered protectively over his wife's arm. 'I think there's a cafe around the corner, past Kmart.'

'It was like something took over me,' she replied, ignoring his offer. 'I didn't see it coming. Was that really me in there, Sam? That poor shopgirl,' she groaned. 'And I think she might have been ex-Glenmore ...' Pauline strained her neck to peer back towards the bookstore, fighting a desire to cry.

Sam grasped her by the shoulders, forcing her around to face him again. 'Never mind that. Half the shire are college alumni. But I'm concerned about you. Even when you were going through the worst of your menopause you weren't like this.'

'I'm sorry.'

'Jesus, it's not a case of being sorry. You've got a lot on your plate and it's clearly taking its toll. I should have seen how bad things have got for you. I mean, look how thin you are. I thought it was because you've been overdoing the running but …'

He tilted in towards her, his eyes big, but she hung her head to block him. 'Don't. If you hug me, I'll blubber.'

'Love, you need to look after yourself better, eat better. I can't pretend to understand everything you're going through with Lily, but I see the strain on your face every day. I know we talk about your mum and I hope it helps, but I can only do so much to support you through this.' His arm around her, Sam guided Pauline gently towards the car park. 'I'm glad you've been seeing a counsellor. You do so much for Lily, you know, not just the visits but all the running around. And she is getting worse, no doubt about it. It's a hell of a stress.'

Pauline stopped. People were walking past and around them but the compulsion to get things off her chest outweighed any normal inclination to keep private conversations private. 'I just can't see a way out of this, this intense sadness I'm feeling about her. She will suffer; she is already suffering. And eventually she will die from this nightmare of a disease – and, Sam, it won't be a good death.' Pauline blinked, tears welling. 'Watching her go downhill is like pulling off a bandaid, but really fucking slowly.' A new Christmas carol started up, louder than the one before, the only benefit that it masked her words from anyone within earshot. 'I'm not sure I'll ever get over the sorrow of it all.'

'I don't know what to say. I agree with you,' Sam said, as he continued leading her towards the car park. 'But for now, at least, she's tracking okay.'

Pauline's mouth fell open. She stopped again and turned to look at him, this time forcing a woman behind to veer around them, the sharp corner of a plastic shopping bag cutting into the back of Pauline's leg as she passed.

'Shit!' Pauline exclaimed, bending to rub furiously on the injured spot. 'But that's just it, Sam. For how much longer will that be the case? I don't think you realise how bad she's getting. She's in pain most of the time but hides it to spare us. She's always been so sharp but planning anything seems beyond her now. Her judgement just isn't there like it used to be. And remember when she and I sang and danced to ABBA? She's forgotten. It was such a special moment, and she's bloody forgotten it. And if she can't remember me being there, how close is she to forgetting *me*?'

Pauline let the tears stream. Being strong in front of Sam seemed, all of a sudden, so pointless. She extracted a tissue from her bag, twisting it around and around a finger.

'C'mon, let's sit down for a sec. There's a seat just over there,' Sam said, his tone soft and sympathetic as he took Pauline's hand and slotted his fingers between hers.

'God, I feel so embarrassed.' Pauline rested her head on Sam's shoulder and allowed herself the space to mentally regroup. 'Do you remember when Rach was sixteen and we caught her with cigarettes in her jeans pocket?' she asked after a long pause. 'She swore black and blue it was the first pack she'd ever bought and would be the last.'

'Yeah, she said something like "I'm just experimenting. It's no big deal. I don't even like them".'

'Right. So remember we followed her up to her room? You stood in the doorway, rational as anything, saying it was all right as long as she promised that this would be the end of it?'

'I guess I carried a semblance of empathy. I didn't want to be a hypocrite.'

Pauline grunted then blew her nose. 'But I went absolutely ballistic. Do you remember? I lost all control. I can't blame Rachel for slamming her door in my face. I had to retreat to our room to let my anger settle.'

'Yeah, she only emerged when we couldn't hear you swearing any more. She did apologise though. She was pretty sheepish, if I recall.' Sam gave a chuckle, but Pauline wasn't seeing the humour. She watched a family of six walk past, one of the children carrying an enormous teddy bear with a large gold bell around its neck, jingling in time to the little girl's footsteps.

'That's just it. She hadn't really done anything bad, certainly nothing to warrant that level of vehemence. But it was one event, a long time ago, when I was having those bloody hot flushes and sleeping so badly, and, well, afterwards I never thought I'd blow up like that again. But I have. I've been losing it – on the road, at Glenmore students … and now *that*, back there,' Pauline said, glancing over her shoulder. 'It's as though I'm coming undone.'

Sam massaged the soft, pulpy mound under her thumb. 'You're under strain. You do so much, Pauline; more than most. Look, why don't we get home? You're exhausted.'

'But we didn't get the books.'

'I'll go back for them another day. Let's get out of here.'

They made their way to the car with Sam's arm securely around her shoulder, Pauline happy to acquiesce, or rather not having the strength to argue. With the skin on her face taut from the salt of dried tears, she felt more connected to him than she had for a very long time. But even her husband's sympathy and warm embrace couldn't stop her feeling brittle, like she had fault lines running so deeply through her soul that she could break at any moment, and no-one would be able to put her back together.

Donna

It was well and truly dark when Donna got home, still glum
and racked with guilt. After changing out of her uniform,
she collapsed on the couch and opened her laptop, hoping for an email from Xavier. She was about to type in his
address when she remembered Skype. She'd never used the
software before but had managed, with Xavier's encouragement, to create an account with the intention they'd try it in
the lead-up to Christmas. The idea had panicked her at first,
but then she'd thought through the concept and figured
face-to-face communication via technology couldn't be any
more awkward and daunting than the real thing. She wasn't
entirely ready to meet Xavier in person, but if she couldn't
be strong for Lily at least she could prove herself a bit more
gutsy in her personal life and take it to this next level.

She logged in, her heart thumping. The webcam, a feature she'd previously ignored, felt like an intrusive eye. When she heard the ringtone she quickly patted around her head, pinched her cheeks and licked her lips, cursing herself for not taking these measures before she'd called. For not thinking this through.

Perhaps I should hang up now.

'Well, hey there, gorgeous.' Xavier's face loomed on her screen, larger than life and grinning, though he looked puzzled and a bit dishevelled. A strong light shone from the side, casting a weird shadow on his features.

The first thing striking Donna was his velvety voice. It was absolutely intoxicating.

'Hi. I, um, thought I'd give this Skype thing a go. How are you?' she asked, awkward and apprehensive.

'I'm great. It's three in the morning here, though. But that's sweet. I don't mind. How 'bout you? I thought we were goin' to do this closer to Christmas. You look beautiful, by the way. Even better than your photos.'

Xavier was softer – pastier and more feminine, almost – than his shots had portrayed. Perhaps it was because he'd just been rudely woken.

'Thanks. You look good too,' she lied, her thoughts whizzing. 'This feels a bit weird, doesn't it? I feel like we've started to get to know each other by writing but also like I'm meeting you for the first time now.'

Xavier shrugged, dropping the corners of his mouth. 'I guess it is strange, but here we are. So, at the risk of sounding clichéd, what're you wearing?'

Donna froze. This was becoming all too real, too quickly. She'd happily started a relationship that allowed her to hide behind the curtain of email. Now she was faced with an actual real red-blooded man, and one who wanted to move things along a bit too fast for her liking. Was he already trying to lead her down the cybersex path? She forced a laugh, but Xavier's face remained passive and unnervingly expectant. She wondered if he was leering just a little, and, if he was, whether it was flattering or creepy.

'Look, I think maybe I should have waited until Christmas. I've woken you up. Do you mind if we take a raincheck? Let's call each other in a week. Sorry. Sleep well.'

Although embarrassed at her own rudeness, Donna ended the session before Xavier had a chance to reply, slapping the escape button with gusto. She wilted forward over the computer, putting her head in her hands. 'Well, that didn't go how I thought it would,' she lamented aloud to her four walls. Did his looks bother her? Were they even important? She had come to regard him over the last ten days as a funny, interesting, thoughtful guy. And he wasn't exactly unattractive. Normal and regular looking, really. Just a weeny bit, well, not as much her type as she'd thought. And if she was honest, her reaction to his come-on was as much about her lack of self-esteem and nerve as anything he was doing.

She closed the laptop. What did it matter if Xavier didn't look as appealing as she'd expected? After all, it would be no surprise if he'd thought exactly the same about her.

Lily

The only light comes from my bedside lamp but I still see the pity in her eyes as she helps me into a clean nappy, its plastic edges rustling as she guides them up my legs. She's probably unaware of her belittling expression, but I recognise it. Only Donna manages to carry out the task with poise and humour, leaving me with a shred of dignity the others somehow don't quite pull off.

'When I was your age I didn't exactly plan for this either, you know,' I say, glancing at her badge. *Lexie.* I should know her name. It's not as if I don't recognise her. But sometimes trying to remember things is like attempting to scoop slippery fish out of a muddy pool with bare hands. I make the occasional contact and even hold on for a short time, but then the images, sounds and emotions slip away again and

I'm jerked back to the immediate, the now, which is always such a huge let-down. I've possessed a sharp mind all my life. It's been the cornerstone of my success and my whole self-image. Without it, what am I?

'There. Ready to hop back into bed?' Lexie asks as she helps me wiggle my nightie back down.

I nearly lose my balance, my heart skipping a beat. She steadies me but in the process one of her nails scratches against my skin, nowadays so thin it's almost translucent. I inhale sharply. It's hard to hide pain. It takes effort.

As she assists me into bed all I can think about is how much relief it will be to unshackle myself from this dilapidated carcass. I don't recognise this body as my own any more. It's odd to think it contains the very same bones and muscles that carried me with ease up the hill to the southern lookout, lifted my child onto my shoulders for a better look at the annual Easter parade, or directed my fingers to whip over a typewriter. It's the same body that chased seagulls along the beach as a girl, but I can't see myself down at the shore of my beloved bay again.

'I can't remember: which side were you lying on before?' Lexie asks.

'If you can't remember, I don't feel so bad that I can't.' I dig out a smile. 'But it feels like it must have been my right.'

She positions me, tucks me in. The quiet of the night magnifies the scuffle of her shoes on the carpet as she manoeuvres around the bed and smooths everything over. 'There, does that feel better? You get some more shut-eye now, okay? Buzz me if you need me,' she says, her obligations complete.

It's the middle of the night but I don't want to be alone again, not yet. She's nearly through the door when I blurt out, my cheeks blushing hot, 'Are you looking forward to Christmas?'

She twists on her heel but stays where she is. 'Doesn't everyone? Although putting up the gazillion gold baubles and miles of silver tinsel here is always a challenge.'

She's smiling now, yielding.

'Yes, that must have been quite an undertaking, but they do add cheer to this place.' I'm pitiably grateful for her time and attention.

'I don't mind. Donna and I did most of it and it was kind of fun. Your room is pretty colourful too, with all these sticky notes everywhere,' she says, sweeping her eyes around my room. 'Your daughter did these, I'm told. Such a neat idea.'

She takes a few steps towards me but stops short, as if she can't make up her mind whether or not she's enjoying our talk. She's hedging her bets. She's so young. 'Now, is there anything else you need? Are you comfortable?'

I suppose she wasn't enjoying our chat that much after all.

'I'm fine.' It's easier to lie than begin on the list of ailments that will continue to keep me awake for several more hours. My fingers are like crow's claws, curled in on themselves. I'm still managing – just – to hold cutlery or a pen, use toilet paper, hold playing cards, brush my hair; but how much longer will it be before these tasks are beyond me? I'm find it increasingly difficult to get sufficient enough grip on the back of a chair or a walker handle to hoist myself up or lower myself down, so I can't move about safely these days unless there's someone nearby to help me.

I ought to thank my body for falling apart, I suppose. It's doing its best to win the race to the finish line, to protect me by checking out before my mind does. It knows I've reached my use-by date. It's only the religious zealots who think they know better; who think they should have the final say over *my* body. Bloody stupid, the lot of them. You spend most of your life wishing you had more time but eventually time becomes your enemy, its hold torturous.

'I don't think I've bought presents for anyone, including the little ones. It's so hard to get to the shops,' I add, before she takes the chance to slip out.

'Perhaps that's for the best. If they're anything like my nieces and nephews, they'll be receiving way too much stuff anyway. Are you going to your daughter's on Christmas Day?' The girl is pointing to a blue sticky note just in front of her, on my bureau.

Ah, the customary Christmas lunch at House on the Hill. So much fuss and expectation. 'I presume so. Makes me tired just thinking about it, but it means a lot to the family, especially the littlies.'

'You never know, it will probably turn out to be a wonderful occasion,' she says before smiling and closing the door behind her.

I'm left alone to ponder her statement. Perhaps I will try to be thankful on the day, for their sake and mine. After all, I hope it will be our last Christmas together. My gift will be to make sure the day provides my family with happy memories. You can't put a value on that. I suspect that, as we've always done, we'll sit down to lunch and pull crackers before everyone passes plates and tucks in. And I will savour the time with those I love so dearly.

But as the noise level rises I will also send a silent message to Robert, a man my daughter and granddaughter never met, for all the Christmas celebrations he never experienced, for the children he never fathered, loved or spoiled, and the places he never had the chance to see. Life is a gift, with its difficult but often exciting choices, its thrilling messiness, the randomness of its sorrow and joy. My beloved Bobby missed out on so much.

I can still recall the essence of the times we had together. Its sounds and smells, its texture and taste – and it all felt like happiness.

1940

'I'm in love with you, Lily Ferguson. I adore everything about you, from the way you look to the way you smell.' I search Robert's face for the joke, although I hope he's actually referring to my perfume. But when his eyes twinkle we fall about the front seat, guffawing until our faces ache.

We're parked across and a little way down the street from my parents' house in Haversham Road. Four hours ago Robert picked me up from the dairy to drive us in his Hillman into Rorook, a much larger and busier town than Finn Bay. It's the hub of the local dairy industry as well as, more recently, autobus manufacturing. Its hustle and bustle is why Robert set up his veterinary practice there. It has a movie theatre, and that's where we went this evening, on our first outing together, to forget about the war in Europe and see a comedy called *Let George Do It*. The film had a thrilling speedboat chase across the waters of Sydney Harbour. It had been just wonderful.

'So,' I venture, 'you knew.'

'A gentleman never discusses such things,' he says, trying to keep a straight face.

'You're never going to let me live it down, are you? Can we just pretend it was a cow outside the window?'

'A cow? I don't think so. Cows aren't quite that loud.'

I slap him on the knee, evoking an easy, teasing laugh. Without further thought I lean in to kiss his cheek, but he turns his face and it's his lips I'm now exploring as desire instinctively drives our embrace. When we draw back, we're both breathless and smiling.

'I'm so glad we met, Lily. And that we became friends.' He takes my hand. His touch, warm and reassuring, sends a current zinging right through me. For a moment I remember Billy.

'It's all thanks to Mr Dunn, I suppose,' I say.

'And to you making such a memorable first impression.'

'Let's change the subject, shall we?'

The subject is an incident from two months ago. I'd been working away in my office at Dunn's Dairy, my head down and looking to my left at the costing sheets splayed out on the desk, my fingers flying over the comptometer. The movement of its keys are loud and robust enough to make the floor vibrate, so when I felt someone's touch on my right shoulder, albeit lightly, the surprise made my body react three ways. I jerked back in fright, cricking the side of my neck as I did so. My fingers pulled away from the keys and knocked over a glass of water that I'd carefully placed to the right of the machine, away from the papers. And most excruciatingly, as I stood up I let out a gust of wind that I'd been holding in until I could get to the lavatory on my lunch break.

I'd composed myself as best I could before meeting brown eyes that smiled out from the slightly weathered but not at all unattractive face of a young, fair-haired man dressed in a grey herringbone wool jacket.

'My sincerest apologies for frightening you,' he'd said, mopping up the spilled water with his handkerchief. He was perhaps too guided by manners to let anything register on his face but I suspected he knew what had occurred. He offered a handshake. My face burned.

'My name is Robert Harford. And you are?'

'Lily, as in the flower.' If it was possible, I blushed even more at the silliness of this statement.

'A pleasure to meet you, Lily. Would you be kind enough to point me in the direction of the manager, Mr Dunn?'

I tried to turn my head to point in the direction of my boss's office but a fiery pain clenched my neck. I instinctively rubbed where it was sore in an attempt to loosen the offending muscles.

'You've hurt yourself.'

'I'm fine, thank you,' I said before accompanying him out of my office and down the passageway. I noticed he walked with a limp, one leg not able to stride as far as the other. Mr Dunn was obviously expecting him, so I left them to it. I remained well out of view until I observed them exit the administration building, Mr Dunn chatting away and gesticulating towards the nearby pastures and tin-roofed outbuildings, and (thankfully) escorting the visitor back to his motor vehicle.

Trying to put the incident out of my mind, I spent the next few days praying that Robert Harford, whom I ascertained is a well-respected veterinarian, was actually somehow professionally deficient and would not be contracted to tend to the dairy's animals. When he turned up again a few days later, in gumboots and overalls, I groaned. I knew I wouldn't be able to keep avoiding him so decided to pretend nothing had happened.

Now, feeling the cool night air sneaking its way into his car, I have an irresistible desire to be back in Robert's embrace. Since the day we met, he has become a regular visitor to the dairy, often calling in when one of the cows has trouble with her milk production or if there is a general health issue among the herd. It soon became obvious that something was brewing between us. He would happen to brush his arm against mine if we passed in the corridor, go out of his way to compliment me if I wore my hair up in a different style, and linger in the office after logging his hours in the ledger. 'Definitely all signs,' Ma said one evening. She was right, of course. She usually is.

'Well, if that topic is off limits, what about if you tell me how you came to be working at Dunn's, doing the profit and loss and using that marvellous contraption.'

He's considerate to change the subject. 'Well, let's see. After finishing school I completed a secretarial course – you know, typing, shorthand and bookkeeping, that sort of thing – and with encouragement from my father added on an eight-week comptometry program. I'd always enjoyed numbers and mathematics at school and he thought having skill on a calculating machine would give me an edge when trying to get an office job; which it did.' I can't hide my self-satisfaction.

'Where did you undertake your courses?' he asks, still caressing his fingers over my right hand, which is resting on the small stretch of leather seat between us. A tingle runs its way down to the very core of me.

I clear my throat. 'At a private college on the outskirts of Brisbane.'

I'm not sure Robert really cares where I studied. What I do is certainly not as interesting as his veterinary work. I suspect – hope – he's simply trying to prolong our evening together.

'That's a long way to travel.'

'Yes, which is why for most of those two years I arranged to stay in the city with the Blecks. They're an aunt and uncle of a friend from school. In return for my lodgings, I did most of the household tasks, like sweeping and mopping, doing the dishes and tending to their garden. I wasn't asked to do any washing or ironing, thank goodness.'

Robert's eyes are fixed on me. 'What were they like, the Blecks? I hope they took good care of you.' He's stroking the skin between my fingers and I can barely think for the intimacy of it.

I swallow. 'Mr Bleck – how can I put this nicely? – is a rotund and rather sweaty man, but he was nice enough to me. I liked him better than his wife, anyway. The arrangement suited her because I think she fancied herself as a bit of a society woman and the idea of manual exertion didn't complement her self-importance. In fact I'm sure she felt a tiny thrill every time she was able to casually drop the word "housekeeper" into tete-a-tetes with her friends.' Robert smiles, encouraging me to continue the story. 'Anyway, after I completed my course and returned home to the bay, I'm not sure if she replaced me or had to pick up the reins. By then the Depression had been affecting everyone for years so I suspect she was forced to rent out the spare room for money, not labour. Oh gosh, I've been rambling. Sorry for such a long answer. I'm sure you didn't want all that detail.' My cheeks must be the colour of my hair by now.

'I'm interested in anything and everything about you, my darling.'

My insides melt. Am I really Robert's darling? I daren't allow myself to think so.

'Do you like the comptometry work?'

'I'm learning so much more about business than if I was just typing, and being quick on the machine means the data is compiled faster, which Mr Dunn likes. And it pays more than typing.'

'Is it hard to use? It seems quite an acquired skill.'

'Are you sure you're interested in this?' I push with curiosity. 'I mean, it appeals to me but surely your work with animals would be far more fascinating to talk about.'

'Lily, I want to get to know you: what you think, what you like and don't like, what makes you tick. I think you're an amazing girl.'

For a moment I'm lost for words. This feels surreal, like it's happening to me but shouldn't be, for some reason. Romance like this isn't for ordinary people like me. I try to remember Robert's original question but all I can focus on is how close his body is to mine.

'It takes a bit of getting used to, but it's actually fun. You need a good understanding of how to use it, of course, but also its capabilities. I suppose you also need quite a bit of finger strength.'

'Well, from what I can see you have the respect of everyone at Dunn's.'

'Thank you, Robert. I'm just happy to be bringing in a wage to help out Ma and Pa. And being a woman who's respected among the sales staff and managers gives me a kick, if I'm honest. But what I probably like best is that it's exposed me to other areas like sales and accounting, agriculture, animal husbandry, even farm machinery. It's opened my mind up to the wider world of business and I confess ... I've developed a real interest in it.'

My stomach clenches as I half expect to be judged for my ambitions, but to my relief Robert seems impressed. Conversation flows on, easily and about all sorts of things, from the progress of the war effort in Europe to the benefits of one type of hen over another for optimum egg production. 'I can't believe we're talking about bull semen,' I say at one point when we get to the economics of trialling the potentially profit-making practice of artificial insemination.

'So, Lily Ferguson, would you like to step out with me again?' A cross between a smile and a look of hopeful anticipation inhabits his face.

We lock eyes and I nod before reluctantly saying, 'But I suppose it's time I got to bed and let you start your drive back to Rorook.'

As he escorts me across Haversham Road and along the footpath to Ma and Pa's house, I hook my arm into his, ostensibly for warmth and balance. Walking like this, I'm aware of the subtle pull of his unusual gait. One day I'll ask him how he got it.

A car drives towards us, its headlights intrusive. As it gets closer Robert drapes his arm around my shoulders, steering me until our backs are to the beam. There's an unspoken ease of movement and understanding between us as though we have been, and will be, like this forever. Outside my gate we kiss again, this time lingering and deep, the message clear, the craving so intense it threatens to crush me.

CHRISTMAS DAY 2007

Donna

Jolted awake, Donna lifted her head and reached for her mobile on the low stool that acted as her bedside table. Lying back down, she balanced the device on the side of her cheek.

'Hey. Merry Christmas.' A rich voice melted down the phone line.

'Xavier? Goodness! What time is it there?' Donna sat up and rubbed her eyes, but they resisted focusing.

'Mid-morning, the day before Christmas. It's six in the mornin' there, right? I thought I'd call to catch ya before work and before I have to hit the road.'

Donna blinked hard but the time on her clock radio remained fuzzy. 'Ah, I think it's five, but that's okay. I guess you could say it's karma for me waking you last week.'

They'd reverted to emails since the awkward attempt at Skype, and Donna had increasingly appreciated that, in many ways, written communication allowed and even encouraged a greater degree of connection than face-to-face contact. But that didn't mean she wasn't thrilled he'd called. A tiny shot of excitement bolted through her, a schoolgirl flush.

'Oh, sorry. So, what are your plans for Christmas? I think you mentioned doin' two shifts back to back?' His tone was warm, soothing and sexy.

'Yep, I'll be stuffed.'

'I'd wager you Aussies can't possibly eat as much as we do at Christmas.'

She laughed. 'I meant stuffed as in tired, not stuffed full, but yes I'll probably be both. We put on a huge lunch for the residents and I'm bound to overdo the Christmas pudding.'

'You'll need a stiff drink after such a long day. Or ten.'

Although it still struck her as odd to be forming a connection with a man over twelve thousand kilometres away whom she was yet to meet in the flesh, the more they had corresponded this last week, the more they'd seemed to gel, and the more her self-worth had blossomed. And if they were to have any chance longer term, there was no room for secrets. Besides, she wanted the freedom that can only come with honesty.

'I don't drink very much these days. I … I had a problem with alcohol in my past and really don't want to go there again.' Once the confession was out Donna felt only relief.

'Gee, that's no good. Full on, was it, the drinking? AA and all that?'

'Pretty bad at the time, yeah. Stuffed up a relationship, actually. Although one could argue it was a symptom rather than a cause …'

'Shit. Well, good for you that you don't fall back into temptation, baby.' There was an awkward pause before he added, 'So, I'm gonna be pretty much uncontactable for the next couple of days.'

'Oh. No worries. Maybe when you get back we should start phoning each other as well as emailing,' she suggested after some small talk. 'Maybe even try Skype again.'

'Sure. Look, it's been real nice talkin' with ya. You have a real sweet voice. Sorry I woke ya.'

'Not a problem. Merry Christmas.'

'Seasons greetings, Donna. Bye.'

Donna frowned at Xavier's earlier-than-expected exit but quickly concluded it had stemmed from his embarrassment at disturbing her so early, and reflected a care and consideration. Unable to fall back asleep, she decided to cut her losses and just get to Blue Vista early.

Upon arriving, her good mood was boosted even further. The gifts purchased and wrapped by management over the last few days were now massed under the Christmas tree, which was beautifully adorned with fairy lights and a range of baubles and trinkets made by the residents themselves in recent craft classes. After breakfast she joined them as they were treated to carols, and it struck Donna, as they listened to the exquisite voices of a local men's choir, that the residents were her true family.

The double shift was passing quickly. At every opportunity Donna took pleasure in quietly going over and over her

call with Xavier, a thrill jetting through her at recalling the
word 'baby'. Her thoughts were marred only by a twinge
of disquiet when she got stuck trying to remember exactly
where he'd said he was going to be for the next few days.
Something, she thought, about visiting his aunt in a small
town in Iowa or Ohio or some such place. In fact, as the day
went on, Xavier's plans and explanations seemed more and
more nebulous.

Pauline

Pauline was particularly looking forward to seeing her
mother that day. Being with family seemed to inject Lily
with a renewed vitality, if nothing else did. Normally,
Pauline would have asked Sam to do the pick-up, but this
year she felt a strong compulsion to be the one to bring her
mother home for Christmas.

Lily was sitting on the single chair in her room when
Pauline arrived. She hoped her mother hadn't been waiting there long, with nothing to do but watch the door with
inescapable patience, listening for approaching footsteps to
herald that someone cared. Her mother's purple cardigan,
fleur-de-lis shirt and cobalt blue pants created a jolly effect
in the room. Pauline bent down to kiss her on the forehead,

inhaling the scent of face powder and the slightly fusty, unpleasant smell of old age.

'Hello, Mum. Merry Christmas.'

'Merry Christmas, darling. I thought Sam was coming to fetch me.'

'He was, but you've got me instead,' she said, smiling. 'You look very smart. Are you ready to go?'

'I think so.'

Pauline noticed one of her mother's stocking socks had bunched around her ankle. She crouched down to ease it up over Lily's calf, but let go when her mother cried out in pain.

'Did that hurt you? Gosh, I hardly used any force.' On lifting Lily's pant leg Pauline saw, to her distress, a splatter of angry marks peppering her lower leg. 'How on earth did you get these bruises? Have you knocked against something?'

'Not that I remember. I think it's just what happens when you get to my age.'

'And these shoes – they look way too tight, Mum.'

'Oh, don't fuss. They're fine. My feet swell, that's all.'

'Anything else you're hiding from me?' Pauline searched her mother's face for the truth.

'I'm just *old*, Pauline,' she said, as though resigned to the fact and slightly irritated that she had to point out the obvious. 'Aches and pains come with the territory.'

Pauline stretched up to lean her head against her mother's. Lily sighed and cupped a hand around her daughter's chin, holding it with practised affection, and something in Pauline's chest tightened. In this quiet, beautiful, confusing moment, who was consoling whom? The ancient and familiar sense of comfort from her mother's touch and nearness, so rich and entrenched in her view of Lily as protector and guide, was at such odds with the fragile, age-ravaged woman beside her. Pauline's breathing slowed.

Lily's walking frame was already in position by the door, a handbag propped safely in its basket. Pauline helped her mother up and they made their way along the corridors towards reception, their pace relaxed. Carer, child, protector, dependant – what did it matter? It was just mother and daughter, as it always had been, with their tightly shared past and their implicit, unquestioned understanding of each other.

As they passed through reception, Donna looked up and gave a little wave from the front desk where she was rearranging red and white carnations in a green vase. 'Have a lovely day, Lily. I'll see you when you get back. I'm on a double today.'

In no time at all they'd arrived at House on the Hill. Sam bounded out to greet them, sporting an elf apron and Santa hat and making a big fuss of his mother-in-law. He helped Lily out of the car, steadying her by the elbow and bending down slightly to chat as they made their way into the house. Pauline picked up her mother's bag and followed them in, where she was greeted by an overexcited Rosie, covered head to toe in tinsel and jumping up and down while pulling on her grandmother's blouse.

'Can we please open our presents now? Pleeeease?'

Resistance was futile.

Sam milked the whole Santa thing for all it was worth ('Hoho, who's this one for? Let me see – Rosie! Hmm, it's making a bit of a rattle when I shake it ... what could it be? ... Okay, okay, keep your shirt on, Rosie-Posie. Here you go ... Mind you don't drop it now ...'). Ten minutes later,

wrapping paper was strewn across the floor like a cyclone
had swept through the room. Rachel and Pauline cleared
up, Sam retreated to the kitchen to check on the state of the
roast potatoes and Christos took Luke outside to attempt to
teach him how to throw his new Frisbee. Lily remained on
the couch and played Snap with a delighted Rosie. The ratio
seemed to be five wins to one in Rosie's favour by the time
lunch was ready.

Sam assisted Lily to her usual place at the head of the
table, which Pauline had decorated with a green tablecloth
and slender red candles propped in her mother's antique silver candlesticks. After crackers were tugged, and thanks and
praise given, the food was passed around with much flour-
ish and fanfare. Lily looked pensive at first but then seemed
to emerge from her own thoughts. The children managed to
remain unusually polite and calm despite the earlier con-
sumption of several candy canes. Rachel and Christos were
in particularly sunny spirits, either a reason for, or as a result
of, their children's good behaviour. Although Pauline had
been sure her mother's hearing would be compromised by
a noisy room, Lily appeared for the most part to follow the
thread of conversation and even contributed the occasional
comment of her own. Only once did she seem a little confused, asking Sam if he would be driving her back to King
Street after lunch.

Once the Christmas pudding was served, Pauline sat
back and allowed herself a minute to take in the scene. As
she cast her eyes around the table she listened to the chatter, observed the passing of cream and brandy sauce, and
grinned at the laughter and joy as Christos entertained
everyone by somehow managing to hang a dessertspoon off

the end of his nose. As Lily watched the antics, the edges of her mouth lifted a little but then she seemed to give up. Pauline studied her mother's pale, pinched face, registering the fatigue and physical toll the celebrations had taken. It was clear that only through supreme emotional and physical effort was her mum making sure they'd all look back on this day with the happiest of memories, not ones tarnished by ill health or regrets.

Lily turned her gaze to Pauline. Their eyes met squarely and held, and it wasn't until a spoon clanged to the floor and Rosie squealed with glee that Lily blinked, the connection severed. Pauline felt as if so much had been conveyed to her in those few seconds, things she didn't want to hear. She held her breath, taken aback at a resentment and anger rising to the surface from within. She had a strong desire to shake her mother for the very idea of wanting to leave her daughter, and her family. Of giving up on life.

'Lily, you look like you're starting to wilt,' Sam said with perfect timing. 'Just let me know when you want to call it a day.'

Lily lightly waved him away. 'I'd prefer to stay a bit longer, if that's all the same.'

Pauline let herself breathe again and she and Christos set about clearing the table. It wasn't until Rachel rounded up the children almost two hours later that Lily finally made noises about wanting to get back. Sam hunted around the room for his mother-in-law's bag and gifts, which must have been moved in all the tidying, while Pauline assisted Lily to stand and get her balance. They embraced.

'It's been such a nice day, Mum. I hope you've enjoyed it. I hope there'll be many more just like it.'

'I've had a lovely time,' Lily replied as they broke away. 'But I'd like nothing more than to float away tonight on the memories of such a wonderful day, and never wake up.'

Sam stopped what he was doing and darted a look in his wife's direction.

Pauline's insides flipped. 'Please don't talk like that. I can't bear to think of a Christmas without you, Mum, or anything without you,' she croaked. Sam moved closer, ready to rescue.

Lily's mouth set tight as she looked, head tilted, from Pauline to Sam and back again, her eyes narrowed and determined. She sighed, long and pointedly. 'Sometimes if you love someone you need to support them in their wishes, no matter how hard that might seem.'

The three of them said nothing more as Lily was helped to the car. After waving goodbye, Pauline returned inside and washed and put away the dishes. With Sam still not back she did another tidy of the living room, staying on the move enough to keep her mind clear. When he finally returned Sam seemed uncharacteristically preoccupied, plonking himself on the sofa. Pauline shuffled up against him, resting her aching feet on the coffee table.

'How did Mum seem when you left her?' she ventured.

Sam yawned. 'Sorry. Big day, eh? Er, she was subdued. Tired. She didn't say much.' He picked up the remote, brought the television to life and began channel surfing.

Unable to shake her mother's words, Pauline readjusted herself to face her husband. Although he seemed disinclined to talk, she asked, 'Sammy, do you ever think about your own old age?'

Sam replied without taking his eyes off the screen, his finger still pressing buttons. 'I must admit I don't, but that's probably a defence mechanism. I'll face it when I have to and not before. You're obviously thinking about it, though.'

Pauline frowned. 'I don't fear death, just the concept of never being with loved ones again. Ever. The absolute finality is the bit I can't get my head around.' Sickened at the thought, she leaned further into Sam. 'So I could never choose death over life. Ever.'

Having determined the television offered nothing of worth, Sam flicked it off and turned to her. 'It's inevitable though, isn't it? We can't all live and be together forever, much as we'd like to. We usually don't have a choice in the matter.' He stretched his arms above his head as he yawned again. 'Why don't you treat yourself to a bath, love? It's been a big day. I just want to take the empty bottles out to the bin, then I'll come up too.'

Pauline followed Sam's advice and mustered the energy to stand, before kissing him on the lips. As she headed towards the stairs she thought about his words, and by the time her hand rested on the banister she'd recognised what had been viciously gnawing away at her, probably birthed at the first signs of her mother's memory decline almost two years ago. It was a recognition that everything Pauline was, everything her life had rested itself upon with confidence and reassurance, was bound up with her mother's fortitude and mental strength, her almost-invincibility. Without these, it was as if the whole lot – all that Pauline had known to be dependable and true about her mother and therefore herself – could tumble at any moment.

She looked back towards her husband. 'I know life's not a bed of roses for Mum and I'm sure others might see her wish to die as showing some sort of incredible courage, but to me it just lacks backbone. It's not the Mum I know. She can choose life or she can choose death. So since when has she been a quitter?'

Sam stood and, making his way to the kitchen, muttered under his breath so that she barely heard him, 'It's not quitting, love, it's taking control.'

Lily

All I want is to die. But today, instead of dying, I went to
Christmas lunch at House on the Hill.

It's early but I'm in bed, drained, my stomach uncomfortably full of food. I lie on my back, the sheet drawn
up and over my chin, a soothing habit from childhood.
Donna is fiddling around in my bathroom, tidying things
up and humming to herself. Closing my eyes, I try to take
myself back through the day before its details escape me.
It was a happy occasion and I enjoyed the gentle chaos.
I played a card game with my great-granddaughter but my
reflexes were a liability. Sam was dressed as Santa, and he
and Pauline were busy-busy-busy. The brandy fumes from
the Christmas pudding made everyone laugh when it was
brought to the table. Luke and Rosie sat near me, so well

behaved. She wore a red dress. Such sweet children. There was plenty of chatter, at times quite loud. But what did we talk about? I can't recall the details now. Come on. Think, you ridiculous old woman! I screw my eyes up tighter but my mind is a blank.

My eyes open as Donna appears from the bathroom, declaring, 'Righto. Time for sleep, I think. You must be exhausted.'

Exhausted? Just tired of living, more like it.

A flash of memory drops in for a visit. It's my little brother, Davey. At the tender age of twenty-three he volunteered for service in the Korean War. He was a deep-thinking, beautiful, peaceful young man and managed, thank god or fate, to dodge enemy bullets and bombs, but several of his mates weren't so lucky and I know the guilt stayed with him. I'd just had Pauline so I found his decision difficult but I had to respect that he wanted to make a fresh start over in Perth — about as far away as he could get from here. He carved out a happy enough life as a furniture maker, and I think there was something about creating new and lovely things that helped him cope with the loss and trauma. He eventually fell in love with a caring man called Evan but when, in Davey's late fifties, that relationship ended, he blessedly decided to leave the west and return to Finn Bay.

I can still see him casting his rod from the rocks at the end of the beach, his favourite fishing hat not only protecting him from the sun but also serving to shield his eyes from the view of passers-by. He would tip the brim as a gesture of amiability but continue to stare out to sea, making it clear he valued his solitude. I'd recently retired by then, but

I never interrupted him, content to sit on the sand nearby or walk on and leave him to his fish and his thoughts. We spent many an evening enjoying a wine together though, and when he passed away ten years after coming home I felt utterly abandoned by everyone I'd loved – first Robert, then Pa and Ma and finally my brother.

But I'm ready to see them again. It's as if they're all reaching out and beckoning me. They're tantalisingly near.

'I'm afraid of enduring what life holds, not of dying. I just want to go with dignity. Is that too much to expect?' Donna closes her eyes and bows her head but I push on, undeterred. 'I can't ask Pauline, but I can ask you. You have ways; you must have ways. When I'm past being able to see how decrepit my mind has become, I won't know to keep asking you for help. Can't you see that this is my very dilemma? I'll be at the mercy of what this disease will do to me.'

Every muscle in my back and arms and hands clenches, hard as stone. 'I need to take charge. Please, Donna, help me to go out on my terms, while I still have a choice of my own.' My begging hangs between us like the woeful thing it is. I'm worn out from my efforts. I look at her. She has lifted her head but is shaking it, her mouth set in a tight grimace.

My face crumples. Blinking back tears, I seize her arm, clasping the flesh as fiercely as my sorry, bent fingers allow. 'I love Pauline – I love all the family – but life now offers very little else.' My hand holds fast, desperation providing unexpected strength. 'I don't want to go through the misery my father endured,' I cry out, 'and I don't want Pauline to have to witness it!'

My grip releases without warning. It's the oddest sensation.

'You know I can't help,' I vaguely hear Donna reply. 'We've talked about this countless times before and I don't know what more to say. Please don't ask me again, Lily. I mean it.' She leans forward and takes my hands in hers, her motherly tenderness a peace offering. But my neck feels thick with pressure, my head throbbing like it's being used as a bag for boxing practice. I feel foggy, heavy, confused, my left cheek heavy as a sack of wet sand.

'Oh my god, Lily, are you okay?'

It's as if I'm hearing under water. Who is this woman touching me on the arm and gawking at me? I try to move away from her but my whole left side feels like it's not there. How can that be?

'Go 'way.' My own voice sounds odd. I'm having trouble getting words out.

This person is looking agitated; is getting too close. She's turning me on my side.

I try again to resist. 'Thon't touch me. Get out of my house. Ro-ert. Ro-ert!' My right hand moves but the left one remains limp by my side. I don't understand what's happening.

The woman covers me with a blanket then backs away as if in surrender. She picks up the phone and talks urgently, but I'm not catching what she's saying. She's speaking more slowly, speaking to me now, a whisper I can barely make out. 'It's okay, Lily. I think you're having a stroke but it's going to be all right. It'll all be okay.'

Where is Robert? I'm so tired, so very tired.

1938

The houses in our street are mostly timber workers' cottages, each with a low fence, front verandah, rusty red tin roof, and just four rooms. They're not much to write home about, but Pa says we should be grateful to have a roof over our heads. I used to complain about the toilet out back, but it's only outside if you count the fact that you see sky for a few seconds on your way from the kitchen door. Despite our humble home, Ma's on a spring-clean warpath. I'm back home on a break from my secretarial and bookkeeping studies and, on her instructions, in my bedroom sorting through trinkets and childhood bits and bobs.

I gasp as I spy Billy's postcard, on top of a pile of letters and notes stashed in an old biscuit tin. The picture on the front of the card shows a new-looking building, with *Greetings from the Waterloo Hotel* printed across the middle of the photograph. In almost a year I've never shown this to anyone, I suppose because I feel a little embarrassed about it. I turn it over and read the imperfect but legible scrawl.

> *Dear Lillie,*
> *I think about you every day. Melbourne is cold but all right. Mother has a good job with the bank. One day I will ask you to marry me. Would you say yes?*
> *Billy*

I can still recall every detail, every emotion and sensation of last Christmas Eve as if it was yesterday. At seventeen, so practically a grown-up, I'd started planning my future because Pa said I had to stop thinking of it as a series of predetermined, neatly orchestrated adventures waiting to happen to me; that I had to work hard and create goals for myself. So I'd decided I would become a secretary and then get a job in Finn Bay so I could stay close to my parents and my little brother Davey. I'd even thought in a vague way about possible husbands, but I certainly hadn't planned on kissing a boy!

For years the annual Haversham Road street party has brought much-needed cheer, especially to our men who fought in the Great War. Pa says they saw things that no-one should have to see. As far back as I can remember, the turnout has been first-rate, although for a few years now some families have made excuses, the Depression's effects still lingering over Haversham Road and beyond. The celebration last year was typically full of cheer, inspired by a gloriously warm night on the back of a hot, blue-sky day. I remember because I'd gone for a swim in the bay with Davey in the afternoon and we'd both got burned, his pale skin as cursed as mine.

My brother did his best to help Pa carry our kitchen table out to the middle of the street and place it next to several others already positioned. Ma and I laid it with our best tablecloth before bringing out the cakes, meatloaf, devilled eggs, jelly and a bowl of punch we had prepared together throughout that day. Each family produced fare according to their financial capability, and when we saw that the Flemings' table was a bit on the sparse side we told them we had too much to fit on ours. By the time several other neighbours had done the same, I don't think Mrs Fleming knew how her kids were going to eat everything or how she could ever repay the generosity. We weren't being generous, we were just being good neighbours, and Mr Fleming was still only getting the odd bits of work so no-one expected anything in return.

The adults chatted and drank, pretending to keep an eye on things but knowing that if any child got into trouble or mischief someone would no doubt step in to take care of the situation. That's what this community is like: we all look out for each other. As the sun set and the night sky appeared, the men got the bonfire going in the vacant lot four doors down from our house, watching it build into a satisfying blaze. The children were instructed to keep their games of hopscotch and skipping rope on the roadway well away from the flames, and when one boy produced a toy bow and arrow and pointed it at the others, the sound of delighted squeals from the littlest ones filled the air.

Not long after, a jelly fight started up. Red and yellow coloured the darkening air between several boys until one of their mothers put an end to it with a stern warning, but not before I got caught in the crossfire. And it was as I was trying to get the blobs out of my hair that I noticed Billy, a cousin of the Heath boys from five doors up, looking at me as he leaned against the base of a streetlight. There was something about the way his focus was fixed on me that made me return his stare. Under the lamp's glow, I was struck by the blondness of his hair and I no longer saw the awkward, skinny and annoying boy from years past. Instead, I found myself focusing on sinewy but distinct muscle, height and confidence. When had this miraculous transformation happened?

I felt compelled to go over to him but as I approached I wondered if in fact it was the bits of gelatine in my hair he

was looking at, and whether at any moment he'd switch
back into silly young Billy. But no jokes or ridicule were
forthcoming. I stopped just a foot in front of him where
he'd retreated into the shadows, the blue of his eyes cutting through the dim. We became two invisible people in
a mass of preoccupied revellers, the laughter and chatter of
the crowd shrinking into an irrelevant background buzz.

Without saying a word he reached forward and pulled
me in to him. Bending down, he held my face, cocked his
head to one side and inched closer, in what felt like slow
motion, until I felt until his lips press against mine. Rather
than freezing with shock and self-consciousness, my body
took me by surprise by relaxing into his. My hips, as if with
a mind of their own, pushed forward, my arms reaching up
and around his warm, smooth neck. As he gently forced my
lips apart, his tongue probed its way into my mouth and I
returned its caresses as he drew me even closer, into the heat
of his body. Oh, it felt divine!

The prospect of a kiss that night, with Billy of all people,
had been the furthest thing from my mind, and it wasn't
how I'd predicted a kiss would be. It was way, way better. I thought I knew, from *Gone With the Wind* and other
romantic novels circulating among my girlfriends, how a
proper kiss would feel: a skittish, fluttering sensation as
a boy's hands pull you towards him in a manly yet tender fashion. But the passionate nature of our embrace, the
unexpected wetness of his mouth and hardness in his pants,
caused a pulsing wave of pleasure that caught me by surprise. It was disturbing and delightful, bringing guilt and
glee in equal measures as I found myself driving back into
him with passion, a thirst demanding to be quenched.

We were jolted apart when a sudden desperate mix of a shout and a scream crashed through the hum. The source of the commotion was Mrs Lonergan, who had caught her young Michael about to light a cracker and probably lose a finger or his face in the process. Lord knows where he found one, but he should have known better than to think of making a sound that would scare the living daylights out of our shell-shocked veterans. From our secret idyll in the semi-dark, Billy and I held hands as we observed the situation resolve before turning to face each other again. We still hadn't spoken when he produced the sweetest yet most lust-saturated grin and, with gentleness but purpose, let his fingers slide from mine.

'You have the softest, smoothest skin. You're so beautiful,' he said. Then he turned and walked off, just like that.

A faint breeze carried the salty smell of sea towards me as I stood and watched Billy swagger away. I wondered in a fluster if I should follow, but my stomach was in my throat and my legs felt like two immovable objects not even connected to the rest of my body. At the end of Haversham Road he didn't look back before disappearing around the corner. I stood rooted to the spot, my hands hanging stupidly where he'd left them, not knowing what to do. My mind raced, trying to guess what the kiss meant, and wondering why he'd left me so abruptly and absolutely. Was it because he wanted to savour our moment, capture its purity without the risk of contamination? Or had he just carried out the most convincing seduction, one meaning nothing to him other than a victory and bragging fodder with his friends? Was he just like the egotistical cads in some of those novels, enjoying the sadistic thrill of leaving the heroine to wallow in her romantic foolery?

The rest of the evening passed in a blur, and after a restless night and a simple round of presents the next morning I helped Ma wash and tidy the mess we'd left in the kitchen, then followed her out to the back garden. It was another sunny day and I could hear Pa in the back shed humming a Christmas hymn. Davey was in the living room gluing together the pieces of a new toy aeroplane, the perfect gift for a ten-year-old obsessed with all things he could construct or take apart.

Ma had begun plucking fruit from our plum tree, placing them carefully into a bowl.

A nervous flurry in my chest, I reached up and did the same, adding to her pile. 'Ma, have you spoken with Mrs Heath recently?'

'No, Lilykins. Why do you ask?'

'Oh, no particular reason. Just wondering how the Heath boys are,' I ventured.

The bowl was filling quickly, the crop fat and purple and juicy-looking. Ma scrutinised me for a moment and seemed about to say something before changing her mind.

'Ma?' I prompted.

'Go and grab me another bowl, will you?' she asked distractedly.

I raced in and brought two back outside. We filled up both before I dared to broach the subject again, nervously asking, 'So, the Heath brothers …?'

'They're doing fine, as far as I know. The older one managed to get himself a job at the whaling station though I'm not sure for how much longer that will be. There's talk of it being closed down.' Ma started to head back inside. I picked up one of the bowls and followed suit, desperate to keep the topic open.

'It's just I thought it strange that their cousin was there last night when his own family doesn't live in our street,' I said, taking the risk that Ma would have no idea why I was bringing Billy into conversation.

I watched as she filled the sink with water and started transferring the plums. 'Do you mean Billy? He and his two sisters and mother are moving down south today, on an early train, I believe. They've been bunking in with his mother's brother since last Sunday.'

My heart plummeted.

'Gossip has it that it's to get away from her old man,' Ma continued. 'He's always been a ruffian and a drunk but your father says the brute's been taking his troubles out on her recently, so I suppose she's had enough. I'd be doing the same in her situation. No wife should have to put up with a man striking her.'

'That's awful.' I tried to imagine living in a household like that but it was too foreign, and anyway my thoughts were racing.

'Too right it is. The Depression has hit hard, Lily, but there's no excuse for a man to beat his wife. He's bound for jail as far as I'm concerned and he'll be getting what's coming to him. Funny sort of woman, if you ask me. But she's probably under a lot of stress. The things she was overheard saying at the post office; caused quite a stir ...'

Ma kept talking as she bobbed and rubbed the plums but all I heard was 'moving down south'. I don't think she even noticed when I left the kitchen. I lay on my bed, facing away from the door in case Ma followed me and saw my blubbing. I was being an idiot, I knew. After all, I didn't even know Billy that well, so how could I imagine I'd miss him? The truth, as I realised much later, was that it wasn't the person I longed for, it was the sensation of his touch and how he'd made me feel. I wanted that feeling again.

I moped about all day, pining. Davey convinced me to play tiddlywinks with him but afterwards I felt listless and unmotivated to do anything other than the chores required of me around the house and running an errand for Ma on my bicycle.

For days after that I imagined and prayed for a letter from Billy, telling me he felt the same yearning. But, thrilling as the encounter was at the time, when I received this postcard a few weeks later, I found myself touched but not excited, feeling foolish and self-conscious by then about the whole episode. The physical memory had faded and I'd come to brush it off as a misguided lapse in judgement. I realised that Billy's newfound height and physique had tricked me. He was an unconscious fraud, walking around in a man's body when he was just a boy of sixteen.

It didn't help that the scallywag Michael Lonergan had seen us in each other's arms that night. On Boxing Day he'd detonated out of his front gate while I was walking past, nearly skittling me. Rebounding, he'd grinned like a Cheshire cat then chanted 'Bill-ee and Lill-ee, Bill-ee and Lill-ee'. I spun around, grabbed him by the collar and stated calmly and icily in his ear: 'You repeat that anywhere, to anyone, Mickey Lonergan, and I'll tell your old man that I've seen you helping yourself to Freddo Frogs from Mrs Jones' store'. As Mr Lonergan is an amateur boxer with a nose like a saddle and not much of a sense of humour, I was pretty sure Michael would be keeping his mouth firmly shut. But his rhyme echoed around and around in my head, and it wasn't long before all I could think of was Sill-ee Lill-ee, the ridiculous phrase helping to well and truly demote the incident from a wistful reminiscence to a dumb mistake. The postcard merely represented a sweet postscript to my first kiss – I felt nothing. It was as if Billy had become an apparition. I began my studies soon after that, and heard a rumour a few months ago that he's planning on signing up for the Royal Australian Navy at a training base in Flinders, wherever that is.

I look again at the card. It is, I suppose, a love letter in its own adorable way. A proposal, even. I should probably throw it out. It was, after all, just one kiss and I'm sorry, Billy, I wouldn't have married you. But my first, fleeting experience of romance will always stay with me.

Donna

Donna began her last rounds of South Wing, checking on any last-minute needs and wishing those still awake a final 'Happy Christmas'. She wondered if it had been pure luck she'd been right there when Lily had her stroke, or whether in fact it had been their conversation that had brought the whole thing on.

At around eight o'clock, after Lily had drawn a reluctant Donna into yet another difficult and, this time, highly charged discussion about assisted dying, her face had suddenly drooped noticeably on one side, reminding Donna of two slightly misaligned sides of a face in a Picasso. With accompanying confusion, the vulnerability and fear in Lily's eyes had conjured the image of a wild animal caught in a trap, not understanding what's happening but knowing instinctively it's in grave danger.

Donna's mind had frantically darted this way and that as she tried to recall then carry out the appropriate first aid. She'd done her best to reassure Lily then rung through to the nurses' station. The next hour had seen a flurry of activity, with an ambulance arriving and Lily's daughter being contacted. Donna would like to have gone to the hospital but knew it wasn't her place and instead went home after her rounds, emotionally and physically spent.

Still awake at two am, she called work to get an update. Molly answered after the first ring. 'Hi, Donna. Can't sleep? I guess you're wanting news on Mrs Harford.'

'Have you heard anything?' she asked, chewing on her lower lip.

'It was a minor stroke,' Molly confirmed. 'They're going to keep her at Rorook Mercy General for a few days, then we'll need to arrange for a hospital bed to be put in her room here.'

Donna sighed. 'She'll hate being so confined but I guess there'll be a residual weakness along her left side so we can't take any chances.'

'I suppose so, yeah. But with physio and speech therapy she should hopefully recover pretty well. We'll just have to wait and see, I guess. Bloody lucky it wasn't a larger stroke.'

Donna nodded to herself, trying to see the positives when all she could think about was how unfair this latest blow was for Lily. 'I might drop around to see her after she's discharged. Will you let me know when that happens?'

"Course. But aren't you supposed to be on leave for the next week?'

Donna yawned. 'It's no trouble.'

'Oh, and Donna? We've all been told we'll need to keep an extra close eye on Mrs Harford after she gets back. Apparently the tests showed it probably wasn't her first stroke, and the specialist said it possibly won't be her last.'

SATURDAY 29 DECEMBER 2007

Pauline

Pauline had taken the call on her mobile just after falling into bed on Christmas night. Her mother was on her way to the Mercy General in Rorook, the charge nurse at Blue Vista said, having had a suspected stroke. Further tests would be carried out but if a stroke was confirmed it might be a slow and difficult recovery, she'd warned. She could quite possibly have more, the woman had said with sympathy.

When Pauline and Sam first arrived in Emergency they'd had to wait for several hours while Lily was examined and treated and trolleyed away, before eventually being directed to a room in one of the wards. They'd found her fast asleep but were able to glean from the duty nurse that she'd already shown small signs of improvement and would hopefully fully recover, but, as the nurse explained, only time would tell to what extent.

Drained, they'd returned home in the early hours of Boxing Day, Pauline highly anxious, knowing that this turn of events could plummet her mother's already sunken mood, exacerbate her memory issues and greatly hinder her quality of life. It might also make her more determined to give up. The following days merged into one exhausting hotpot of emotions, journeys between home and Rorook Mercy General, and a flurry of research into all things stroke-related, including what would be involved in her mother's rehabilitation and the likelihood of further episodes. Pauline wanted to be fully informed, armed with all of the necessary tools to combat the consequences of this latest blow. To not lose this latest battle.

After four nights in hospital, Lily was due to return to the care home today. At the kitchen bench, Pauline leaned her chin on her hands, her eyes grainy from fatigue. She'd appeared downstairs just as Sam was cracking eggs into a pan sizzling with butter.

'Good morning, or should I say afternoon?' he quipped.

'I can't believe I've slept in so long.' Pauline spoke through her yawn.

'You look a bit bleary-eyed, love.'

'I didn't sleep well. I was tossing and turning all night thinking about Mum.'

'I know. Me too. Would a coffee help?'

Pauline nodded, absently fingering through a newspaper on the bench, the words in its headlines failing to register.

'I'm making eggs,' Sam continued. 'Would you like some?'

Pauline had no appetite and felt a bit dizzy, her heart racing. Even the aroma from the coffee pot was making her nauseous.

Sam looked at his watch. 'Lily's due back about now so we could go and see her in a bit if you like, eh? Perhaps cheer her up with a bunch of flowers?'

Pauline bristled. 'She's going to need more than a bunch of flowers. I want to get in there as soon as possible, talk to the staff, make sure a physio has been organised, that they're on top of her new meds—'

'Pauline,' Sam interrupted, 'you've already gone in there twice in the last three days. I'm sure they've got it all covered. The stroke was only mild and she's going to recover okay.'

A wave of heat rippled through Pauline's cheeks, her nerve endings burning hot. She tossed the newspaper aside and leaned forward. 'Jesus, Sam, didn't you hear the specialist? This could happen again any time, and worse!'

Sam held the spatula up as if calling for a ceasefire. 'Hold on, why are you getting angry at me? I'm just trying to help.'

Seeing the frustration and sadness etched on her husband's face, Pauline realised he was only trying to be upbeat for her sake. 'I'm sorry.' She sagged her forearms onto the bench, her elbows sliding out. Her head was throbbing and her stomach rolling. 'Seeing Mum in hospital, so miserable, I just feel so helpless.'

'We've all felt helpless. There's only so much that modern medicine can do. Her body's slowly checking out.'

'But she can't just give up! Her wanting to die goes against everything we know about her, everything she's instilled in me about being strong.' Pauline had an overwhelming urge to go back to bed but felt sure she wouldn't make it to the stairs before either throwing up or blacking out.

Sam raised his brow and held it there, almost as if daring Pauline to challenge her own words. As realisation dawned, Pauline clenched her fists so hard they ached. Her nails dug into the flesh of her palms as every inch of her skin exploded into pins and needles. 'It's not just her, is it?' she almost whispered as she searched Sam's face for help. 'I'm as weak as her because I can't imagine losing her.'

Sam walked around the bench. 'There's nothing weak about you, Pauline Walters,' he said, stroking her hair. 'You're just as strong as Lily; you're made of the same stuff.' He leaned back, looking at her with concern. 'Love, are you all right? You've gone really pale. Shit, your face is sweaty. You're not having heart failure or anything, are you?' Sam's voice was thick with worry.

'No, I don't think so. I think I might be having some sort of panic attack though.' Pauline's legs wobbled as she began to gulp in air like a landlocked fish.

'Try to take some deep breaths. Or maybe I should call triple zero in case …' Sam started to reach for his phone.

'No,' Pauline gasped. 'No more hospitals. I'm fine. Honestly. I just need to lie down. Can you help me?' She grabbed Sam's shoulder and tried to focus on getting her heart rate back down as he accompanied her to the lounge room. After more persuasion and assurance he settled her on the couch, but for the next hour returned to check on her every fifteen minutes, insisting each time on taking her pulse and asking her over and over if she was okay. Only once he seemed convinced that her anxiety had subsided did he announce he was going to duck over to check on Lily and that Pauline should stay put and try to get some more rest. Within half a minute she was fast asleep again, her body as spent as if she'd just run a marathon.

Donna

While on leave and as a distraction in the days following Lily's admission to hospital, Donna had started gasping and heaving her way through twenty laps of the local outdoor pool each morning. Not used to sporting pursuits, she was dog-tired but already feeling like a new and improved version of herself. She had also set herself the task of cleaning her apartment from top to bottom, even using an old toothbrush to painstakingly scrub the grout between her bathroom floor tiles. Once the flat was spotless, she'd tossed out any clothes and shoes she hadn't worn for more than two years, finding the whole process quite therapeutic.

This flurry of activity was, however, accompanied by an emotional tug of war between contented daydreams of Xavier and worrying about the after-effects of Lily's stroke. Would it make her charge even more determined in her quest to die? Donna now had a colourful bruise on her upper arm, a testament to Lily's desperation.

After learning that morning that Lily was about to be discharged from hospital, Donna planned to drop into Blue Vista later in the day to see her. Then that night or tomorrow she'd Skype with Xavier. She figured he would be back from Iowa or wherever by now.

Noting the absence of anything fresh in her fridge, she made a toasted cheese sandwich and sat down to list some resolutions for the New Year.

- *Keep enjoying Xavier. Don't overthink it.*
- *Keep flat tidy*
- *Tone up/get fit*
- *See friends more often*
- *Learn Spanish*
- *Keep fridge better stocked*

Determining that resolutions were much more likely to be kept if she narrowed the list down to just three non-negotiable and important ones, Donna took a fresh piece of notepaper and began again.

- *Enjoy Xavier*
- *Keep fit*

Her laptop pinged and her heart did a little jig under her ribs when she saw Xavier's name appear next to the email notification.

Hey Donna, its me. Didn't get away in the end because guess what the boss called up on Christmas day and ive been offered a posting to Belgiam.

It's a promotion! Huge office there. Pay hike like you wouldn't believe. Couple of others going too incl Lisa and Gus. We start in 2 weeks. So i was thinking that what with the upheaval and evrything and the fact its even further from you that we should probably stop seeing each other.

Anyway, good luck with everything. Happy NY and all that. Xav

Donna stared at her screen where the open message sat, mocking her. She seethed, a white-hot rage engulfing her at her own idiocy, naivety and schoolgirl romanticism. She was pretty sure he'd mentioned a Lisa a few times. Was that telling her something? Had he decided to cut ties after her confession about the drinking? Did it even matter why?

What a colossal wanker. Didn't even have the balls to pick up a phone. And he's known all this for FOUR days?

She read the email once more then pressed delete – five times. Just to be sure he was gone, from her computer and her life. What a waste of her time and emotional effort! She'd fooled herself into believing she'd been getting to know Xavier, that she was safe to be vulnerable with him, when in reality he was as unknown and unreachable as a distant star. Even his touch had only existed in her imagination.

Even more, she was pissed off that she'd been spinelessly cossetting herself in an online liaison, with its convenient limits and its tidiness, instead of risking a real relationship, too afraid someone would immediately see her plain body and plain face and plain personality and run for the hills. But in the end she'd been dumped anyway, and why not? What was there to love about Donna Charleston? A glorified, unworthy bum-wiper who, when life punched her in the guts or threw a scary curveball, shied or even ran away. Who also, through her weakness and cowardice, had quite possibly caused an amazing human being to be so terrified at the prospect of further decline that she had a stroke, and might never be the same again.

The third and final resolution came into Donna's head and she scribbled it down, surprising herself by giving it shape and serious consideration. A heartbeat later she frantically and violently scrawled it out again until not a single letter was discernible. She replaced it with something less specific and much more benign.

- *Just <u>be brave</u>*

Lily

Now it's been settled I feel such enormous comfort. A sense of calm and freedom swathes me. I'm light as a feather and I want to sing for the relief of it. 'Lily, you look positively perky,' Betty commented when she popped in just now to welcome me back after the ambulance returned me from Rorook.

My face feels odd but I've at least regained some movement in my left arm. They've set me up in this special hospital-like bed. It's got movable bars on each side to stop me from falling out should I have another 'turn' but is a bit like being incarcerated. It reminds me of Pa, though he was actually strapped to his bed – a wretched sight if ever there was one.

But enough of negative thoughts. My fate is happily sealed, and when I go my only regret will be parting from

Pauline. My girl, who was once a tiny swaddled baby, my inquisitive little toddler, my feisty teenager, a determined young woman making her own way in the world, and now a principal, mother and grandmother. I'm the only other person on god's earth who has the power to see all of her. She's doing it tough at the moment and it upsets me I've been a burden to her, but not, thanks to the champion of my cause, for much longer.

Ah, I can hear the tea trolley coming, its squeaky wheels in need of oil. I could do with an afternoon cuppa.

'Hi, Mrs H.'

I try to read the girl's badge but it's obscured by her long, silvery hair. 'Hello, young lady. Doing the rounds today?' The heat rises in my face.

'Yes, my turn,' she replies and I catch a look at the name as she fortuitously flicks her hair back. 'What can I get you this afternoon?' she asks, black-lined eyes alert and amiable.

'Tea, thank you, Molly, and those biscuits look tasty.' I should know what they're called, but I can't remember. 'What are they again?' I ask.

'Chocolate Royals, Mrs H,' Molly replies as she goes about placing two on a small plate, along with a paper napkin. 'How are you feeling? You seem more sprightly. You're lucky. I hear it was only a small blockage. You're talking normally again, which is a great sign.'

'Yes, I'm feeling much better, thank you. And happier.'

'That's good to hear. I saw Donna on her way out earlier. Seems she made a special visit just to see you. She isn't actually due back at work until after the new year.'

I'm passed my biscuits. 'Yes. Bless that girl ...'

'And your son-in-law was here just after lunch. In fact lots of people have dropped in to welcome you back, eh? You've been super-popular today. Now, did you say you'd prefer coffee or tea?'

'Tea, please.' Sam, dear Sam. He said Pauline was having a rest but didn't say any more, I don't think. My stay in hospital must have been very stressful for everyone.

'You're fortunate to have such a supportive network,' Molly says as she pours my drink. 'Here, let me prop you up a bit.'

She rearranges and pummels the pillows. Sitting up straighter, I can see the view better. 'Would you be able to open the doors?'

'I don't have a key, but.'

'It's all right. I know about the one you had hidden above the doors.'

Molly feigns innocence.

'Pauline moved it into the top of the bureau,' I continue. 'But even with it there, there's no chance of me running away, not from this jail-bed,' I quip.

After opening the drawer, Molly rummages around, even pulling a few items out before turning to me, a frown poking out from under her fringe.

'Sorry, but I can't find it. Look, I probably shouldn't be opening your doors anyway. If the charge nurse found out I'd be in heaps of trouble.' She moves back to her trolley. 'I'll be back a little later to check on you and escort you to the dining room.'

After she leaves I'm disappointed but sip my tea, lie back on the cushions and draw in as much oxygen as I can muster. I think about how blessed I am to have people around me who care so much – Pauline and Sammy, the staff and residents here, my granddaughter and her fella, the doctors – and what more potent demonstration of love is there than the pact that's been made. I never truly believed someone would agree to do something so courageous for me, but life and people can surprise you.

I see death as the unpeeling of the layers of time, like a game of pass the parcel, until all that is left will be my soul, full of the energy, optimism, joy, potential and potency that still exists somewhere deep inside me. Yes, when I die, when I'm released from this old body, I'm going to run like the wind, just like I did as a girl, bursting with the promise of freedom, full of hope.

1932

My thighs are hard and strong, running errands on my bicycle as I do for Ma and Pa, and getting to and from school, and riding around the streets with my friends. Ma used the word 'sculpted' to describe my legs recently. I'm not sure exactly what that means but she was smiling and not in a teasing way so I suppose it was meant as a nice thing.

After two hours diving into the waves and making castles and trenches in the sand with Davey, my skin is starting to go blotchy from the sun. I jab my fingers into my forearm then release them, watching white return to pink. Yes, sunburned all right. Why did I have to be born with such fair skin and freckles? My hair, salty wet, keeps getting stuck across my face. It has started to really blow along the beach, a sure sign my parents are about to declare the outing over. It's nearly dinnertime anyway. The dry, finer sand grains are flicked up, stinging my legs like a thousand tiny pinpricks, making my baby brother cry as they lodge in his long eyelashes. He should have been born a girl with eyelashes like those, and with the way he cries so easily.

Something about the wind is making me unsettled, like I want to swap places with it and be the wind, flying and bumping into things, making everything move with my force. My legs start to run, away from my howling brother. I cartwheel, and chase seagulls along the shoreline, leaving Ma and Pa to deal with Davey.

As I get further from my family, Pa's calls for my return fade almost to nothing, no competition against the sound of air rushing past and into my ears. I slow down to a jog, then a walk, before stopping about a hundred yards away. I turn to look back at my father. I can't make it out from this distance, of course, but I can picture the little valley in the middle of his forehead. Ma calls it his 'worry crease' and I know it's because of money. She says that because Pa has Scottish blood, he's always kept his earnings under their mattress. This is a very good thing because the Depression has ruined the banks, she says. I don't really understand all that but I know we haven't suffered as badly as many others have. Pa's hardware store is doing all right. Because people can't afford to buy anything new they have to fix whatever has broken or stopped working around their homes, and rely on Ferguson's to buy the small tools or bits and pieces needed. He's explained to me that the main reason we're able to put food on the table though, is because he stocked up on radios for a good wholesale price and they have been selling well. Ma says they're our 'bread and butter'.

The sea is churning, all fidgety like me. I feel wicked and although I know I'll be in big trouble when I go back, I think it will be worth it. I wonder how long I can get away with standing here, being this naughty. I have a confession, you know. On more than one evening, after I'm supposed to be in bed, I've sat instead in the hallway to find out how things really are. Grown-ups have a bad habit of giving children a nicer version of what's happening in the world and in our lives, to protect us. More than once I've overheard Pa and Ma talking quietly at the kitchen table and it's usually the same discussion leading to the same debate. Pa has taken mercy on a regular customer, allowing him some credit (I think that means he's allowed to owe money to the shop), but Pa's suppliers don't offer the same favour to him, so he gets squeezed into a bit of a money pickle. Just last week I heard him say: 'Jean, what do you expect me to do? His wife's expecting another bairn!' and Ma sighed and accused him of being a sentimental old fool. I'm sure she loves him for being such a kind person but it does mean we occasionally have to go without a proper meal, and it seems there's never enough money when we want to buy something special. I'd like a brand-new bicycle, for example, but that's not ever going to happen.

I think about what to do next. Ma's hoisted up Davey, who's small enough at four to be held in her strong arms, safely above the sand grains that are now positively swirling. Ma isn't much taller than me but she's red-haired and strong and feisty and everyone looks up to her. She sews for other people, usually for money but sometimes for nothing because, although she hates to admit it, she's a sucker like Pa. Another thing I've found out by listening when

I shouldn't is that before Davey came along she lost two babies. It makes me sad thinking I could have had sisters. But not once has Ma cried or acted sorry for herself, at least not in front of me, so I suppose I don't really have a right to.

There seems such a big space of beach between me and my parents, full of grumpy wind and crazy salt spray. I feel alone, which is bad, but I also feel free, which is good. I know I'm safe because when I look at Ma and Pa I see shelter and warmth and comfort. Pa's shouts have now been joined by my mother's and that could mean trouble with a capital T so I start to jog back, this time the wind pushing me along like tumbleweed in the Wild West. I'm pretty sure I'm going to get smacked. But as I get close Pa takes his camera from around his neck and brings it up to his face, pointing it at me, telling Davey and Ma to gather in. I grin with relief and stick my hands on my hips, just like I'm sure Greta Garbo would do. Pa clicks the shutter.

'The wind's really gusting now, Ken,' Ma says. 'Let's head home. Come on, Lilykins, help your father and me. And it'll be straight into the bath for you two.'

I gather up the towels and Davey's bucket and spade, and we begin the short walk to Haversham Road. Nothing is said about my disobedience, even after we get home and strip off to get clean. It's not until the bathwater has become uncomfortably cold, and Davey and I are waiting for Ma to fetch us some clean towels, that I feel I can't stand it any longer. I have to know.

'Ma, why didn't you get angry with me for running away on the beach?'

She drops the towel over my shoulders and rubs my back with it. 'You're a good girl most of the time, lovey. You mind your p's and q's and always do your chores and your schoolwork. You were being defiant when your father called but then we thought it might be nice for you to get some distance.'

What does defiant mean, I wonder? And does Ma mean distance in a how far apart way or in an independence way? I must be looking at her like I don't know because she adds, 'You're nearly a young lady, Lilykins. We thought you'd like to feel a bit grown up for a few minutes.'

Independence, then, and it's the strangest thing: I do feel more grown up than I did when I woke up this morning.

I go to bed early to read. Davey is already asleep and I listen to his snuffly breathing. The wind rattles our bedroom window, trying to sneak its way in through the cracks of the house. What is it about wind? I still feel restless, like I want to burst. I toss my book onto the floor and the thud causes Davey to turn over. It's a childish story anyway.

I can't wait for time to pass and for me to be a grown-up. My future self is there, all laid out ahead and just out of reach, like one of the mouth-watering fruits that Ma grows, waiting patiently to be plucked. I just need to hurry up and get to it.

Pauline

Awake but still dozy, Pauline felt the bed wobble. She rolled over to see Sam lying on his back on top of the covers, looking sideways at her. The evening sky cast an orange-pink glow into the bedroom.

'What's the time?' she asked, her voice croaky.

'Nearly eight.'

'I've been asleep all this time?' Pauline's body was like lead but her head felt as inconsequential as a feather.

'Yep, like a rock. I'd have woken you earlier but figured you must need the rest.'

'I was having a dream just then. I was due to take a lesson and was running late but I couldn't find the classroom, and there was water everywhere so I kept slipping, terrified that I'd never get there in time,' Pauline said, still groggy. 'I realised I needed to go to the toilet, as in right there and then, but the only toilet was in the corner of the room with just a flimsy curtain around it and I was trying to make sure the students couldn't see me but of course they could ... sorry, too much information.'

'That's okay. Vent if you like.'

'Ugh, why do I have these kinds of dreams?'

'Because you carry so much shit in your head all day?' Sam fumbled for her hand, clasping it softly. 'It's bound to have a field day when your brain relaxes. Maybe it's nature's way of facing and solving problems subconsciously, so when you wake you've sorted things out somehow. I don't know. I'm no psychoanalyst.'

'I don't want to be such a mess, Sammy. You must think I'm a nutcase.'

'None of us is perfect. Far from it.' Sam paused, looking pensive. 'I love you. You know that, right?'

Pauline saw the depth of worry she'd put behind Sam's eyes in recent months. He brought her hand up to his lips and kissed it before rolling his body toward hers, his erection evident. At first she felt irritated he could possibly be in the mood when she was so clearly not, but then decided that maybe a screw was just what she needed to help bring her back to earth from the weird disconnected bubble she found herself in.

She sat up, pulling her nightie up and over her head as she did so. And as Sam looked at her with relief and wonder, she wordlessly straddled her husband. The sex was surprisingly passionate, Pauline aware of acting more robotically, more assertively or even selfishly, than ever before, like some sassy squatter had taken up residence in her body. They made love until well after the room had wilted into darkness.

Afterwards, sweaty and still tingling, Pauline began to talk, confessing the true level of her frailty. Relief drenched her as she spoke of her guilt, and the depth of love for her disintegrating mother. She expressed again her inability to imagine her life without Lily, her inability to say good-bye, and her determination to keep her mother around as long as possible, even in the face of this latest setback. And without interruption Sam listened, embracing his wife with tenderness while she bared her soul.

Then she cried, gulping and sobbing in spasms of sorrow while her husband continued to hold her yielding and gently shuddering body.

NEW YEAR'S DAY 2008

Donna

For a moment Donna had no idea where she was. As sleep receded and consciousness rose to the surface to replace it, she realised she still had her dress on from the night before, uncomfortably gathered up under her back. She looked at her alarm clock – it was after six-thirty – and groaned before dropping back heavily onto her mattress. Cushioned as her pillow was, her head throbbed. When the room rolled, it dawned on her that she was incredibly hungover; in fact, possibly still quite drunk.

The large, almost empty water bottle on the bedside table reassured her she'd at least had the sense to drink some water before passing out. She gulped a few mouthfuls and immediately her stomach heaved. She made it to the bathroom just in time, as a mush of liquid and unidentifiable semi-solids gushed up her throat and into the toilet bowl, each convulsion accompanied by a moan of disgust but also bringing some relief. She used the toilet seat as leverage and pushed herself back up to a standing position. Her legs felt weak and shaky and her abdominal muscles hurt, but at least the queasiness had temporarily passed.

Wanting to rid her mouth of its acrid taste she brushed her teeth, looking sideways as she did so at the tall and narrow mirror propped next to the shower. She had bought it to help make a cramped bathroom look more spacious. Returning her vacant stare, the ragged reflection appalled her. Puffy eyes, smudged eyeliner and pallid skin with, if she wasn't mistaken, an actual tinge of green.

The image was in such complete contrast to the evening before, when Donna had been off to see in midnight with three of her aged-care graduate buddies who'd driven east from Brisbane to experience New Year's Finn Bay–style. Nobody's Inn always put on a good shebang and, at fifty dollars a head plus drinks at bar prices, it was as good an option as any, so the girls had arrived a bit after nine o'clock ready to party and take Donna's mind off Xavier. Getting ready, Donna had felt reckless, almost rebellious, determined to prove to herself she was worthy and lovable and, goddam it, not over the hill at thirty-nine. Her reflection last night had therefore been gloating, boasting a closely fitted red and deeply V-necked dress, strappy silver heels, matching dangly earrings and a heavy dose of mascara. It had proceeded to apply some gloss and smack its lips together as if to further make the point.

The evening had been fun to begin with. She remembered that much. There was a decent crowd, including

Vedya, who'd turned up for a while with a couple of her own mates, and the finger food was passable, and the DJ hadn't let them down, playing everything from Santana to INXS. The tables had been stacked to one side to create a temporary dance floor where the seven of them gyrated between re-congregating to talk, laugh and, in some cases, flirt with locals.

It wasn't until about two hours in that everything started to sour. After seeing Vedya off, Donna had just returned inside when one of her girlfriends elbowed her in the ribs, saying, 'Check out the talent that's just walked in. Know any of them?'

Donna followed the line of sight. Five men had settled themselves strategically at the bar and were unashamedly sizing up the room. Her eyes swung to the tallest and her face froze. It was Derek, her Derek, looking straight back at her.

What the hell is he doing here?

She'd heard he'd moved down to Melbourne after their divorce. She assumed she'd probably never see him again. A deluge of thoughts burst through her mind in a tangled, criss-crossing mess.

Christ, do I want to talk to him? Or do I want to avoid him? What would be achieved by us speaking anyway? But I want him to see I've survived without him and that I still look okay. Hot, even. Do I look hot, though? I'm a lot older than when he last saw me. Who am I kidding? Wait a minute, what do I care whether he thinks I'm attractive? Look at him, he's got a receding fucking hairline. Hah. You're being an idiot, Donna. IDIOT. It would be a kind of closure. And it would be weird not to. We were once in love, for heaven's sake. We have a history. Big breath. Stomach in. Boobs out. Head up. It'll be fine. Could even be nice.

It hadn't turned out to be at all nice. Ignoring her friends' questions, Donna had woven her way through the revellers towards the bar, her heart beating furiously. The DJ had taken a break and the volume of voices had risen to fill the gap. When a woman shrieked with laughter it caused Donna to flinch, making her aware of how on edge she was. Her ex-husband had turned his back to her and was paying for a drink as the pretty young thing of a barmaid tossed her head back and laughed at something Derek had said. They had only been married for a few years but in that time Donna had come to know his greatest fears, proudest achievements, favourite holiday moments, even the names of each of his childhood pets. She knew how every inch of his body felt, smelled and tasted. But she now felt like a stranger.

She was arm's length away now. She sucked in a breath and tapped on his shoulder. Donna knew he'd seen her when he'd first walked in, but he took his time turning around. The belittlement was excruciating. She looked better – certainly more sober – than when they'd parted ways eight years ago, but not so different that he'd have mistaken her for someone else.

'Wow. Donna. What are you doing in Finn Bay?'

His measured and cautious tone threw her, slicing her attempts at confidence into a thousand shreds.

'Hi, Derek. How are you?' she'd said as airily as she could. To her horror, though, it came out sounding ridiculously flirtatious.

He turned to his friends. 'Er, guys, this is my ex.'

What, I don't have a name now? You dick.

Blood pounded in Donna's ears, all other sounds fading to a muffled buzz.

'I thought you lived in Melbourne,' she said.

'I did, but I'm back in Brizzie now.'

'Oh?' Donna could feel the interaction sliding into hideous small-talk.

'Yeah, I work with these guys at CheetR Tech. Mike here just bought himself a coastal weekender and invited us to stay,' he added, casting his arm around in a lazy, all-inclusive imitation of an introduction, eyes still purposely averted from her.

And that was it. Derek's eyes glanced left and right the way she knew they did when he was flustered. He couldn't have made it clearer that he wanted her to go away. He wanted his past to stay right where it was.

Her skin bristled but she smiled again, this time with her lips tight. She felt her face flush with embarrassment and anger. Mustering every cell in her body to rise above this, she spoke as calmly and warmly as she could.

'Well, lovely to meet you all. Have a good night. Good to see you, Derek.' She wrangled her face into a smile and added, 'Happy New Year and all that.'

Muttering 'tosser' under her breath, she turned and walked away as steadily and sexily as she could, her mind whirring as she replayed the scene. She didn't know what she'd expected but had always imagined that if she and Derek ever saw each other again there would at least be a semblance of affection, a nod to the good times. Clearly this was a fantasy.

'Who was *that*?'

'Do you know them?'

'The one with the beard is C-U-T-E!'

Making up a story that the men were waiting for their wives and girlfriends to show up and that she vaguely knew one of them from years ago, Donna managed to deflect questions and at the first opportunity had excused herself to head outside for fresh air and solitude. She was disappointed to find several people milling around, mostly smokers. Some sat at the picnic-style tables near the pub's entrance while others stood in scattered groups. The music resumed, muffled by brick and glass, and the peculiar shadows cast by streetlights and the plumes of smoke created a quiet, phantom version of the party going on inside. It seemed fitting. Donna had felt equally insubstantial as she thought about all the setbacks she'd endured in the past two months. Lily. Rick. Xavier. Derek. Four brutal kicks to the gut.

Craving invisibility, she'd walked away and around the corner to the side of the inn. Even from here a sliver of the bay was visible in the distance, moonlight glinting off a flat sea. Normally she'd be uncomfortable in such a lonely, obscured spot, but right then she enjoyed the seclusion. She leaned against the building, the bricks rough against her back, and cried in quiet hiccups.

A side exit burst open to her left, spilling light and music as a kitchen worker carried a large plastic crate towards an industrial bin by the back fence. Donna was jolted into action, remembering the companion waiting inside, the one she'd turned to when her marriage had thrown its nasty left hooks.

Heading back in, she'd made a beeline to the far side of the bar where she would be obscured from her group's view. She'd ordered a vodka on the rocks and hadn't looked in Derek's direction as her fingers enveloped the smooth, cool glass and her arm pivoted upwards in an all-too-well-remembered action. Her lips fell apart as she tipped her head back and she swirled the first mouthful, washing it around her teeth and tongue before swallowing, the drink burning as it travelled down her gullet in one hit. Her shame was horrendous, sitting like a stone in her gut, but she'd closed her eyes and allowed the rush. With her blood pumping fast, and her sorrow washing away, she'd ordered the next glass.

Now, as she faced her disappointing reflection in the unforgiving light of day, a stab of self-pity ran through her, making her knees weaken. She could recall being at the bar for quite a while, but nothing more after that. Did Derek, did her friends, witness her speedy slide into leglessness? She ran the cold tap, splashing water onto her splotchy face in the hope it would jog her memory for subsequent, and hopefully more enjoyable, parts of the evening such as a midnight countdown. She drew a blank. The remainder of the night was lost and how she'd got home was a complete mystery. The only additional image she could muster was more of a physical recollection, of her face being scratched. Had a friend or bouncer been forced to drag her away from the bar for making an idiot of herself? She removed her eye make-up and took a closer look in the mirror, seeing the mark on her cheek. Maybe her face had made unfortunate contact with someone's ring on the dance floor. Or maybe she'd in fact walked home and had staggered into the path of a low branch.

Donna gave up the fruitless fossicking through her memory bank. She dried her face, deciding that with a pounding headache and a mouth like the Nullarbor it might be better to return to bed. Lying down, she closed her eyes, still feeling woozy. It was no good. She sat up again, slowly this time, then plodded to the kitchen for a cup of coffee. While waiting for the kettle to boil she sat at the kitchen table and took three deliberate breaths. To blot out any thoughts – negative or otherwise – she forced herself to meditate by concentrating on as many of the five senses as she could, zeroing in on the hard, wooden chair beneath and behind her and the cool passage of air as she inhaled and exhaled. She acknowledged the taste in her mouth, pungent as it was. She focused, too, on sounds: the kettle gurgling and, in the background, the running of water in pipes from the flat above.

She had just picked up the distant noise of a truck changing gear and was feeling herself begin to relax when the sound of her phone receiving a text message rammed its way in. Miffed at the intrusion, she opened it up.

> *Hey Donna, I'm so sorry to tell you this but Lily Harford passed away last night. Call me if you need, I know you guys were close. Molly xx*

As she stared at the message, Donna's tears stung the scratch on her cheek. Almost immediately she felt a bead of sweat form on her upper lip and her hand shot up to the wound. Her brow furrowed and her toes curled as she shrank away from a terrifying thought, one that she tried to shoo away but it just wouldn't do as it was told. Like a mosquito in the night, it kept buzzing and hovering. A fear clutched her, lapping at the edges of panic.

She poured hot water over some coffee granules and gulped a mouthful, scorching her tongue and throat in the process, before dashing to her bedroom to change. Gathering up her bag and keys she headed out the door, the bang as it closed echoing up the building's concrete stairwell. Knowing she was breaking all sorts of laws, she still drove, speeding up the headland to reach Blue Vista in a dangerously fast time.

Sweaty and sticky, she walked into reception. Everything seemed normal and quiet, as expected for half past seven in the morning, but it was all so at odds with her internal torment. Molly looked at her curiously, almost sympathetically. Donna's thoughts, muddled as they were by remnants of liquor, were on one thing – to get to Room 18 as quickly as possible – but she didn't want to appear unhinged. Trying not to breathe on her colleague, she muttered, 'Hi, Molly. Thanks for texting me,' just as Carol, the nursing supervisor and a relatively new member of staff, appeared from out of the office.

'Ah, Donna, you're here. Did someone get onto you already? Poor Lexie found Mrs Harford during her rounds about half an hour ago.'

Donna's stomach dropped at hearing the news again.

'We're not broadcasting anything yet,' Carol explained, 'but the doctor has just been in to confirm her passing. He's writing his notes in my office. So I'm about to call Mrs Harford's daughter to give her the sad news.'

Donna tried to gather her thoughts but her mind was buzzing and she wondered if she might vomit again. Barely managing to get the words out, she asked, 'Do you mind if I see Lily, just quickly?'

'That should be fine. I hear you were particularly fond of her. But mind the fact that the Walters will be here very soon, so best if you make it quick.'

Donna nodded and made her way to South Wing's corridor. The only signs of activity were the receding sounds from the kitchen where the residents' breakfasts were being prepared. It seemed incongruous to Donna that everything was proceeding in Blue Vista as usual. It was a new day, the first of a new year, pulsing with promise and possibility for all the occupants and staff, most not yet privy to the news that Lily had never woken up to see or feel the sun, and never would again.

Reaching the far end of the corridor, her breath shallow, Donna pushed on Lily's door. Someone had opened the garden-view window, making the room's day curtains sway this way and that like jellyfish tentacles gently pulsating in water. Lily was flat on her back, her legs straight out under the sheet, her arms down by her sides. Tentatively, Donna approached the bed, still irrationally hoping there had been, somehow, a mistake.

Gingerly she picked up a cold, stiffened hand. The tips of Lily's fingers were darkened – a deep purple matching the colour of her lips. Lily Harford's spirit was no longer here, only a corpse. The real Lily, the essence of Lily, had shed her body, like a growing snake sheds its skin. She'd left it behind as something useful for a funeral service, to be offered up to fire or worms, and Donna had no longing to bend down and kiss or hold this discarded shell. Lily was gone and at peace.

But Donna's own peace was destroyed, for it seemed quite within the realm of possibility to her that Lily was dead because, in a state of false, inebriated bravery, Donna had gone to Blue Vista in the early hours and, worn down by an old woman's pleas, carried out Lily's most fervent wish. She thought about the times Lily had said she was tired, in pain, scared of what lay ahead if she continued on her downward slide. Of all those times she had begged for help and Donna had only managed to provide tepid responses of sympathy, moral support and understanding, placating and pleasing Lily the same way she tried to please everyone. In the face of Lily's deepest anguish, then, had Donna found the alcohol-fuelled strength to go through with her request?

She hugged herself and began rocking back and forth as she quietly moaned, 'Oh, Lily, I'm so, so sorry.'

Pauline

Vigorously, almost viciously, scrubbing her skin with soap, Pauline stood under the hard stream of water, trying to loosen the knots in her shoulders and quell her agitation. The shower was a salve, its cocooning warmth and the hum of splashing water an antidote to the anxiety and tension that had been tormenting her in an inescapable choke-hold. She noticed a tiny space open in her chest, something approximating breath, even relief.

Over the last three days she'd experienced the sensation of mentally floating, a quiet unravelling. She'd watched herself move through the usual, required motions: seeing her mother, going to the supermarket, returning a book to the library. Sam had skirted around her, visiting Lily when she couldn't, offering to cook dinner and run errands, but withdrawing a little himself as well.

By last night Pauline had been operating on full auto-pilot, her brain completely and peacefully disengaged from her body, calmly observing everything happening around her with a kind of bemused detachment. And although it was New Year's Day, before dawn she'd peeled her body away from the heat of her husband's comatose one. Although she'd felt detached from him, from every-thing in the last few days, a tiny speck of yearning within her had wished he would wake and pull her back towards him; would reel her in, would stop her. But, accustomed as he was to his wife's routine, he'd simply grunted in his sleep and turned over. With the sheet barely covering him, Pauline had briefly and lightly caressed Sam's freakishly unblemished back, as smooth and hairless as a baby's. She'd absently allowed an erotic thought to swoop in to the depths of her belly, before carrying through with her resolve and pulling on her running gear.

By the time she'd returned, the house was imbued with the first inklings of morning light from a waking sky, but Pauline had lain stiffly on the couch, not wanting the shower to wake Sam on a public holiday when it was still so early. She'd stared at the living-room ceiling until after seven-fifteen before returning upstairs and to the bathroom.

After her long shower, Pauline grudgingly turned off the taps and let the drips fall from her body before stepping out onto the bath mat. Just as she reached for her towel she heard her mobile's ringtone. Sam didn't seem to be in any hurry to pick up the call. She figured he must be particu-larly tired but after several more rings she heard his voice, gruff and sleepy.

'Hello?' Then, shortly after, more muted: 'Jesus ... When? ... I see ... Pauline's in the shower ... No, no, we'll get there as soon as we can ... Thank you ...Yeah, that would be helpful ... Okay ... Yeah, okay. Thanks ...'

Pauline was standing naked in front of the mirror, trying to recognise herself, when Sam appeared in the doorway, the solid frame of his reflection dwarfing hers. She shifted her focus across and up from her own wiry body to his face, streaked with pain and concern. For an instant she felt a familiar sense of sanctuary, a brief rush of connection and comfort and security, that everything would be okay, for she knew what the call must have been about. But the solace vanished as quickly as it had arrived, and she was alone again in her anguish.

Sam stared at her, looking like he was close to tears. It was as if there were words he wanted to say but he was stuck trying to get them in order.

'Who was that?' Pauline thought she sounded too casual. Her heart thumped against her ribs and her ears pulsed deafeningly with each surge of blood. Her mouth felt dry, her chest tight. Time had stopped and the two of them were hovering, poised in a moment after which they both knew nothing would be the same.

Not able to remain in such suspension any longer, she needed to move, to do something normal, proceed with her mundane morning ritual. Maybe all of this would go away; it was too awful to possibly fit in with the familiar and harmless pattern of the everyday. Like a plane headed for a sunny holiday destination instead going into a nosedive.

Sam stepped forward and in front of her. He lifted Pauline's chin, forcing her to meet his eyes, crowned with a deep frown. 'I, er, I have some bad news. Your mum ... Lily ... she's passed away.'

He appeared to be bracing for his wife's reaction. As she watched him tense his body, every muscle in Pauline's body was on high alert and for a few seconds her pent-up emotion threatened to spew out as a ridiculous laugh. She found herself recoiling a little from his funky morning breath. She wanted to tell him he stank. She wanted to be cruel.

'She was found about seven, about half an hour ago, in her bed. They're not sure how long she'd been ... how much earlier ... probably died in her sleep, they said. Maybe another, bigger stroke like we were warned about. The doctor is there now.' Sam's shoulders slumped. His hands looked like they didn't know what to do with themselves. 'Love? Are you okay? Did you hear what I just said?'

Pauline nodded. She wanted to scream, move outward, release, but her body did the opposite. It shrivelled, doubling her over. Abruptly she was retching, a violent purging so powerful that she cried out as her stomach contracted and splattered its disgusting contents over the tiles. The reek was immediate and her mouth and nostrils burned.

When it seemed there wasn't a drop more to expel, with Sam's help she straightened up. She was cold and shaky and her nakedness only heightened her frailty. She couldn't move. It felt like those scenes in horror movies where a secondary and disposable character, with an attack imminent and nowhere to hide, idiotically stays rooted to the spot, bracing for the rip of claws and teeth.

Then she felt nothing. Her brain closed down again, the familiar mantle of detachment pouring itself over her in magnificent self-protection, but this time denser than ever. She was soothingly separated from Sam, from the repulsive mess at her feet, from reality. She vaguely searched her mind for something, anything, because she knew she should be reacting. There should be words, but she was drifting in a bizarre, involuntary stupor.

'We should get over there, don't you think? Are you going to be okay to do that? Pauline?' Sam moved into action and guided his shivering wife towards her closet, helping her into a dress and lightweight cardigan before throwing on his own clothes. After escorting her downstairs he bundled her into his car. In a haze, Pauline stared straight ahead to the road but she could see, at the edges of her vision, her husband regularly steal worried glances across towards her.

Slowly, she turned to take in his profile. His cheeks were devoid of colour.

He looks terrible. Perhaps he's in shock.

Other than a handful of vehicles in the staff bays, the car park of Blue Vista was empty. As they walked across the bitumen, the fragrance of frangipani mixed with the earthy aroma of the soil in which they took root was a pleasant change from the remnant stench of vomit that lingered in Pauline's nose. The silence seemed loud and heavy, inter-rupted only by their footsteps and an occasional honeyeater, calling its machine-gun staccato from the grove of grevilleas abutting the main entrance.

The four-digit code tapped in, Pauline stepped into the foyer, Sam close by her side, his palm on the small of her back. For a moment she stood there as the entry closed behind them, the sensation one of a prison gate shutting them in. She had to remind herself that, unlike many of the residents here, she could escape whenever she desired. She wanted to now, and it took every bit of willpower to not make a run for it.

A woman she'd met only once or twice before greeted them. She was on the large side for her height, with round glasses and a no-nonsense cropped haircut. For a moment Pauline thought absently that it might be soothing to simply collapse into her bosom.

'Hello, Mr and Mrs Walters. You might not remember but I'm Carol. I'm the nursing supervisor on duty today.'

'Yes, of course. Hello.' Sam shook the woman's hand, uncharacteristically taking charge of the formalities.

'I'm so sorry for your loss,' Carol proceeded with solemnity just as Donna, dressed in jeans and a T-shirt, appeared around the corner from the corridor leading to South Wing. Pauline observed that the nursing assistant's usually relaxed face appeared decidedly haggard as she offered her condolences.

'Thank you, both. Er, should we go to Lily's room?' Sam asked, though his words came to Pauline as if from a huge distance. 'What's the procedure in this situation?'

'When you're ready, and only if you want to, of course you can see her,' Carol replied. 'Some people say that can be extremely helpful in accepting a loss. But for others it's not something they want. It's totally up to you. Every family is different. Either way, I'm sure you understand there'll be a few things to talk about so that we can start on making all the necessary arrangements. Blue Vista can notify the funeral home. Or if you prefer you can take care of that yourself. We'll fit in with you; whatever you want ...'

Carol's rambling irritated Pauline, albeit in a kind of theoretical way. She wanted to put her hands over her ears and drown out the words. To make this all go away. She looked around reception, almost as if scoping for somewhere to hide, and noticed Donna staring into the distance, nervously biting her lower lip while repeatedly jabbing her chin with her thumb.

'Pauline, are you all right? Do you want to sit down?' Carol indicated to the visitor chairs in reception.

Pauline knew she must look how she felt – drawn and ashen – but shook her head in the tiniest movement.

How do I do this, process it?

'Thanks, Carol. We can talk more about arrangements a bit later,' said Sam. Then, turning to Pauline, his expression pinched, his shoulders still heavily slouched, he added, 'Do you feel up to seeing her? We don't have to. It's your call.'

Pauline nodded, in as small a gesture as before. The enormity of everything threatened to overwhelm her. She forced a wan smile, out of politeness and duty, but it took all her reserve, her lips dragging dry against her teeth.

As Sam took Pauline's hand in his, Donna blurted, 'I'm so, so sorry,' her face taut with an anguish that unsettled Pauline.

Pauline's voice finally found itself, though when the words came they were oddly composed and mechanical. 'Nothing to be sorry for, Donna. These things happen.'

For a moment Donna appeared to waver between stepping forward and hugging Pauline and remaining at a distance more in line with professional protocol. The agony on her face was palpable though, and caused Pauline to step back into her skin so abruptly she felt like she'd been woken from a dream. She couldn't help but take in the torment on Donna's face, and without the protective fog of shock grief hit her like a bullet to the body. She clutched onto her husband's arm, her knees buckling.

'Come on, love, lean on me,' she heard, as she and Sam moved in the direction of Room 18 on an agonising walk towards a scene neither of them wanted to face.

WEDNESDAY 9 JANUARY 2008

Betty

It was a beautiful service, Betty thought as she removed her best shoes, her feet glad of escape. She would miss Lily Harford. After all, she'd known a little of her fellow inmate since their tennis days and, in cohabiting, had come to greatly admire the woman. Lily had not been one to boast; Betty could tell she was too classy for that. But from their chats, Betty had made her own deductions. Yes, especially after today's service, she was left with the impression of a life lived fully by a woman with a great deal to offer and a ton of pluck.

Betty picked up a silver-framed photo from her bureau, the picture of her sons taken on her last birthday in a swish restaurant overlooking Sydney Harbour. They had flown their mother down there especially for the occasion, putting her up in a hotel room (apparently none having enough space in their own homes, even though they seemed plenty large enough last time she'd looked) and pooling resources to buy her a cashmere cardigan and matching scarf. She was yet to wear either, the climate of Finn Bay not exactly calling for wool. She hadn't seen any of her boys in the four months since. She sighed, placed the frame back in pride of place and returned to ruminating over Lily's funeral.

Lily's daughter had worn a black sleeveless dress appropriate for the sweltering conditions, her hair up in a loose bun. She'd looked sallow and fragile but was supported by her husband who, Betty noted, never left her side. She had given a stirring eulogy although she'd seemed, understandably, to be in somewhat of a haze. Betty hoped, but doubted, her own progeny would be just as bereft when she passed away.

The daughter's words had the congregation chuckling in some places and quietly weeping in others. It was a moving and clever tribute, telling, Betty concluded, of an indisputable closeness between mother and daughter. Instead of hymns or Bible readings, a granddaughter, dressed way too casually for Betty's liking, had recited a moving piece from a Rodgers and Hammerstein musical. Betty rather liked the whole event and intended to keep the Order of Service. It might provide her family with some inspiration when the time came for her own farewell. She had already collected a number of ideas over the years, keeping them in a folder labelled *Because I Like Having the Final Word*.

A montage of screen-projected photos had followed, some refreshingly unposed, others clearly taken at more formal occasions such as the daughter's wedding. One particularly beautiful, almost haunting picture stuck now in Betty's mind. It was a grainy black-and-white shot of a young girl on the beach with a little boy and, Betty assumed, their mother. The girl's hair was flying in all directions, her hands sitting with sassiness on her hips. Something in her face told you she was on the cusp of growing up yet the cheekiness of childhood was still evident. It was hard to reconcile that smiling, fresh-faced girl with the Lily of Blue Vista. Oh, the ravages of time ...

There were plenty of photos of Lily with her daughter, many of them also taken on a beach, presumably here in Finn Bay. For all Betty's whingeing over the years about her dear departed Arthur's failings, she couldn't conceive of having tackled parenthood on her own. A black-and-white wedding photo had shown a stunning, beaming young Lily with a very attractive, kind-looking man. Lily on a tennis court bashfully holding up a trophy; a middle-aged Lily looking triumphant on the ridge of the Grand Canyon; Lily pulling a face in a lime-coloured Arabian Nights costume. Picture after picture, a lifetime summarised in five-second moments.

Towards the end of the service the heat and humidity had built up oppressively in the chapel. Where the stained glass had been bright and colourful at the start of the funeral, the light coming in through the high windows had become noticeably more subdued, casting a gloomy light over the congregation. Betty could hear the trill of cicadas outside. As well as praying for Lily's soul, Betty prayed for the clouds to expunge their contents.

Finally, it had been time for Lily to be carried out in a carnation-adorned coffin, the mourners filing after her pew by pew. Betty had sat patiently waiting her turn, and in preparation tucked the Order of Service into her bag. When Donna passed the end of her row, consoled by a dark-skinned and very pretty young woman, Betty had wondered if the two might be 'special friends', as she liked to call them. She'd also noticed Frank Dartnell making his way down the aisle, and as he passed Betty's pew she was shocked to see he had glistening wet cheeks and was making no effort to hide them.

Although he was elderly and could therefore hardly be described as robust, it was still somehow disconcerting for Betty to witness a grown man show emotion in public. Arthur, bless his departed soul, would never have done such a thing. But perhaps that explained a lot, about him and their offspring. She'd waited until it was her turn to exit and, spying some wiggle room, managed to weave her way closer to Frank. Without a word, she came up behind him and linked her arm through his, escorting him the rest of the way down the aisle and out of St Stephen's and its stuffy air. He hadn't resisted. Betty wondered if he would ever want to be *her* 'special friend'.

The crowd had begun to gather on and below the steps when the first refreshing drops of rain came, large and purposeful. Soon the hearse would be departing for the crematorium in Rorook, hopefully before the gathered grey clouds released their full load. It was rumoured that Lily's wish was for her ashes, in time, to be scattered by her family out in the waters of Finn Bay. Betty thought this a melancholy and lonely resting place, but then again she had never particularly liked the ocean or the beach. The sand just got into every nook and cranny.

As she'd gently manoeuvred Frank away from and to the side of the crowd, Betty glanced upwards. She hadn't known how much time it would be before they and everyone would get a soaking. She'd hunted around in her bag for a spare tissue, Frank accepting it with a nod of gratitude. Although it was out of character, Betty had said nothing, just waited for him to regain his composure. She figured if and when he wanted to talk, he would. Otherwise she would just stay with him until he was ready to rejoin the other funeral-goers. Or until it poured, whichever happened first. But after a few minutes of silence he had turned and stared down at her with a profound sadness, making her feel awkward and self-conscious. He certainly had the kind of blue eyes that could make a girl melt.

'Betty, do you ever wonder what your life might have been like if you'd made just one different decision?'

'Of course, Frank. I think everyone does that. Our lives can turn on a dime, as they say.' She was curious to see where this was heading.

'Please, call me William. Frank is just a nickname. From Sinatra ...'

'Oh, of course.' His blue eyes really were very nice. And here he was, offering the honour of revealing his proper name, just to her. Perhaps he did like her. In that way. She blushed a little.

'All right. William. If you insist. Is there a particular decision you've made or path you've taken that you regret?'

He had sighed before turning his face away, looking into the distance as if she wasn't even there. Only when a drop of rain bounced off his nose did he seem to return, wiping away the residual water as he said, 'I've had a good life and never regretted anything, Betty. Just wondered about forks in the road, that's all.'

Betty had decided it was too hot and the sky too threatening for such vague and philosophical chitchat. Her face powder was at risk of either melting or being washed off if they stayed out in the elements much longer.

'We should think about getting to the minibus,' she'd said after several more raindrops bounced off the path at their feet.

They'd wandered back towards the congregation of mourners, arms linked.

'Lily Ferguson always was a looker.'

Betty was taken aback. 'Ferguson? Was that her maiden name? Yes,' she conceded, aware of a flick of jealousy and how ridiculous and unworthy this was of her when Lily was the one lying in a casket, able to feel neither heat nor rain. 'I had no idea how pretty she was. Those photos were really something. She must have made the boys stand up and take notice in her day.'

'I think you might be right, Betty. As a lass she certainly caught my eye, anyway. Now, let's get out of here before we get drenched.'

AUTUMN 2014

Pauline

The knocking was so delicate that Pauline ignored it at first, assuming it was Sam outside with a hammer, or perhaps rummaging around in the garage working on some or other project. Retirement suited him, suited them both. She'd put all the cake ingredients into the food mixer and was about to switch it on when a much louder rapping demanded her attention. With apron on and hands still floury, she swung open the front door.

'Hi Donna! What a surprise.' Pauline gave her a welcoming smile.

'Hello, Pauline. I'm sorry to appear out of the blue like this ...'

Pauline thought her visitor looked well and seemed more self-assured; *composed* was the word coming to mind. 'Don't be silly. Gosh, it must be at least five years? Wow, come in, come in. You look fantastic. I love your new pixie cut.' Pauline pointed to Donna's hair before brushing her hands on her apron. 'Excuse my mess. I'm just making a cake for Sam's birthday.'

'Oh, I'm sorry. Is this a bad time? I can come back another day if it's easier.'

'No, no. It's not his birthday until tomorrow.' Pauline beckoned her visitor in. 'I'm just trying to be a bit organised and make the cake this afternoon so I have one less thing to worry about tomorrow when Rachel and co are here.'

'Okay, if you're sure.' Donna followed Pauline into the living room. 'You look great too, by the way. The last time I saw you, you were so thin, if you don't mind me saying.'

'Not at all. I wasn't, as you can appreciate, in a good place back then and it took me a while to regain the weight. I've probably gone too much the other way in the last year, mind you.' Pauline smiled as she patted her waistline. 'I go for a run every few days and play golf with my friend Janet, but at my age it's hard to keep the spread at bay.'

Donna nodded towards the adjacent kitchen. 'You've renovated?'

Pauline followed Donna's eyes. 'Yes, a few years ago. All thanks to Mum's estate. I think she would've liked what we've done, don't you?'

'Yes, it looks wonderful.'

'So, it's lovely to see you.' Although curious to know why Donna had dropped by, Pauline pointed to the couch. 'Please, sit down. I heard you left Blue Vista.'

'Yes, soon after your mum died, actually.'

Pauline took a seat on a lounge chair by the couch. 'So, where are you working now?'

'In a small nursing home in Belmont, but just part-time while I gradually gain my full nursing qualification. I've rented a house there, too.'

'Wow, that's great. And not too far from here,' Pauline replied, noticing Donna fidgeting with a ring. 'And is that an engagement ring I see?'

'Yep. Getting back in the saddle, as they say.'

'I didn't know you'd been married before.'

'No, well, it was better forgotten …'

Pauline clasped her own hands together. 'Now, can I get you a cup of tea or coffee? Or would you prefer something cold?' She stood up as Donna delved into her handbag. 'No, that's kind of you but I think you've waited long enough for this.'

Pauline stopped. A small lemon-coloured envelope was being extended to her. She stared at Donna, puzzled.

'Oh? What is it?'

Donna stretched forward and delivered the paper into Pauline's care. 'It's for you, from your mother. She gave it to me the afternoon she came back to Blue Vista from hospital after her first diagnosed stroke. She asked me to pass it to you but was very clear that she wanted me to hold off for at least five years. Made me promise not to even tell you it existed.' Donna paused but when Pauline said nothing, her eyes alternating between the envelope and the flush that had snaked up Donna's neck, she went on. 'It seemed odd, all a bit mysterious really, and I've felt bad withholding it from you all this time. But I felt I had to honour her wish. I hope you understand.' Donna shifted in her seat and bit her lip.

Pauline dropped back down in the chair, her stomach fluttering as a current of emotions swept through her. She'd become almost used to a world without her mother but at the thought she was about to receive a communication from her, the familiar, dreadful sensations of grief and sorrow poured back in. At the same time, there was a slight thrill and excitement at the prospect of reading her mum's words. Would they seem as fresh and real as if she was here with Pauline now?

'I'll leave you to it, then,' said Donna, making as if to get up and go.

'No, please don't. You were a big part of Mum's life at the end, so please stay while I read it.'

Donna nodded. 'Okay, if you're sure …' Pauline felt under scrutiny as she slid a fingernail under the edge and gradually peeled back the flap to reveal two matching pale-yellow sheets of paper, folded neatly in half.

She recognised the stationery now. It had been one of the few items her mother had brought to Blue Vista from King Street. Unfolding the pages, the first thing that struck her was the struggle evident in the handwriting, and the memory of her mother's physical difficulties hit her with a sting. Without hesitation she began reading out loud.

My Darling Daughter,

I hope that you and Sam are both happy – in yourselves and with each other. He's a good man, although I know he has sometimes disappointed you. He only wants what's best for you though, as I do. Sometimes I think I was too hard on you growing up. I wish I told you that it's all right to make mistakes and not always feel you have to do the right thing.

Feeling no shame, Pauline let the tears cascade as she continued to speak her mother's words.

I've had a mild stroke, as you know, but I'm feeling more peaceful than I have for many months and am writing while my mind is having a clear moment. I will be asking Donna to give this letter to you, but not straight away so you'll have had time to heal from my passing before you read what I'm about to tell you. Plus, there's another reason.

It's no secret that I wish to die before this dementia gets much worse and I'm so sorry for asking you in hospital to help me. I felt I'd run out of options, but I saw the misery on your face and I shouldn't have put you in that awful position. The risks and repercussions are too much to ask of you, or of Donna. So I'm very grateful that someone else has agreed to come to my aid.

Pauline blinked and paused for a moment, her mind going at full throttle.

When I first came here I had no idea who Frank actually was, but I would often find him looking at me, or helping me, and there was something about him that seemed familiar. I just couldn't put my finger on it.

Pauline rifled through her memory for a Frank. 'He was the tall gentleman who kept to himself, the one with the missing fingers? Really blue eyes?'

Donna nodded and Pauline, though still reeling, dived back into the warm embrace of her mother's letter.

But yesterday morning, after I was brought back from Rorook, he visited me in my room and that's when he told me who he really is. Frank is a nickname but his real name is William, and it turns out that as a girl I knew him – as Billy. Well, you could have knocked me over with a feather but I took in those blue eyes and remembered him all right. He was my first kiss! Anyway, we talked and talked. After the War, where he lost some fingers but otherwise came out unscathed, he married and moved to Far North Qld but sometime after his wife died (I can't remember now how long ago he told me that was) he came back here to Finn Bay. When I arrived at Blue Vista he knew who I was immediately but when I didn't recognise him he chose not to say anything, perhaps from embarrassment.

He has chronic heart failure, Pauline. He's been told the disease will kill him within a year or two. So we've made a pact that he'll help me to die on my own terms, so that I can have a better death than his poor wife endured. I don't know when, or how, but for me the sooner the better. I don't want to go on like this, destined the way of my father. Please understand. It's what I WANT. Frank says he has nothing to lose and has no doubts I'm still of sound enough mind to make this decision. I trust that by the time you read this he will also have passed away, the dear man, for no good will come of him facing retribution.

I will always love you, my darling girl. Be strong. Know you will always be with me, and I hope I will always be with you.

Mum (Lilian Grace Harford, nee Ferguson)

30th December 2007

PS: I'm sorry I can't write more neatly but what can you do, with my silly old hands?

Pauline touched the long-dry ink of her mother's wonky signature, the structure and nuances familiar but the overall effect severely compromised by arthritis. Numb, she sniffed noisily and looked across to her guest for a clue as to how this would unfold. Donna looked, to Pauline's surprise, relieved.

Donna took a moment to meet Pauline's eyes. 'Pauline, are you okay? This must be shocking news for you to process, when all this time you were led to believe your mum died from a stroke.'

Pauline remained silent, her mind darting like a moth in bright light.

'You know,' Donna continued, a hesitation clear in her voice, 'I suppose now's as good a time as any to confess – and I know you'll think this is nuts – but I've always carried the thought that *I* might have actually acted on your mum's wishes.'

Pauline looked in surprise and bewilderment as Donna went on.

'Lord knows she implored me enough times to help her. So when I got very, very drunk on that New Year's Eve, to the point where I didn't remember anything much when

I woke up, I panicked. I can't tell you how relieved I am; not that she didn't have a stroke, but that I wasn't involved. I've spent many nights over the years stupidly letting my imagination get the better of me.' Donna appeared to be searching Pauline's face for a reaction.

'I remember how rattled you looked that morning,' Pauline said. 'You must have been beside yourself. I don't know what to say. But I'm glad you can now get some peace.'

'Thank you. But now I'm worried about *you*. This has obviously been a lot to take in. But you know, thinking it through, I just can't imagine Frank actually going through with it. In fact, I'm sure your mum must have died of another stroke before he had a chance. I know it's normal for residents to wander at all hours, often confused and agitated about where they are, but someone would *surely* have noticed his stress after doing something like that and it would have prompted them to ask questions. And although no toxicology report was ordered, if he had given her an overdose of pills, for example, she would probably have vomited at least some of them back up, raising suspicion.'

Pauline opened her mouth to speak but didn't remotely know the right words. Her chest pounded. 'Is he still alive?'

'No, he passed away two-and-a-bit years ago.'

Pauline nodded, lost in her own world. 'Can I tell you something in return?' she asked before thinking, suddenly unsure how far she could – should – go. She knew it was possibly her safest chance to tell the whole story, but every cell in her body was shrieking that it would be a very bad road to take. Anyway, what good would come from burdening poor Donna any further, when she'd been through enough troubles of her own?

'I was glad she'd died,' she confessed, a slight giddiness rocking her. 'That sounds horrible, doesn't it? But the strain of seeing her downward slide ... I was terrified of how it was all going to turn out for her. Dementia is so cruel. I know how my poor grandfather suffered from it. After Mum's stroke, when she was in hospital and begged *me* to kill her, I didn't tell anyone, even though it undid me.'

Donna stood up, walked over to Pauline and put an arm around her. 'I remember thinking that morning, when you and Sam came in, that it was like you were there but weren't there, if that makes sense. You were probably trying to work out how you felt. Your reaction was very normal, though, and nothing to be ashamed of.'

Pauline stared ahead to the silver-framed wedding photo of her mother and the man called Robert whom Pauline never met, sitting on Lily's old sideboard. 'After she died I was grieving, but also battling my own demons because I was bereft but also relieved the whole sorry situation was over. It's taken a lot of therapy to get past that. But I still miss Mum. Every day something reminds me of her. This letter, it's like she's here, reaching out to me. It's so nice to hear from her again, to have her in this room.'

An awkwardness hung, the kind that comes after someone's bared their soul perhaps a little more than they meant to and wants to navigate the conversation towards safer waters.

As if to lighten the atmosphere, Donna said, 'To so bravely offer to help your mum, Frank obviously really cared about her. The two of them must have really enjoyed having a pash.'

Donna grinned, and in a contained and muted way a pleasant hysteria filled Pauline. There was so much to digest, but she looked with surprise at her visitor and a giggle erupted from her throat. Caught in a strange emulsion of laughter and crying, she exclaimed, 'Oh Donna, don't make me picture that!'

'I didn't mean pashing in their late eighties, I meant as teenagers!' Donna added, joining in the laughter and, when they finally seemed to have depleted the joke, holding her ribs and declaring: 'Oh Lordy, I haven't cackled that hard for ages. My cheeks are sore.'

A silence fell, Pauline relieved by the therapy of laughter. Donna spoke first. 'I should get going, let you make sense of all of this.' She stood and walked to the front door before hugging Pauline once more, this time with both arms.

After seeing Donna out, Pauline returned to the couch where she picked up the notepaper from where she'd left it and read over her mother's words again, and again, then a fourth time. She tore away the last paragraph, to put with Lily's jewellery and other items most dear to her, before sliding the rest of the note back into its lemon envelope and carrying it to the fireplace.

In the distance she could hear Sam attempting to start the lawnmower and took momentary comfort from the sound of such an ordinary and innocent activity. She picked up a matchbox from the turquoise ceramic dish that sat on the mantelpiece, and as she did so her eye was drawn to the silver of another item in the bowl, a key. She was immediately transported back to before dawn on that New Year's morning when, holding it and trembling from head to toe with the enormity of her deed, her hands rank with the smell of lavender, she'd slipped back out through the glass double doors and onto the dew-soaked lawns beyond South Wing, locking the latch behind her.

Pauline's eyes pooled with tears but still, all these years on, she refused to feel remorse. Frank, bless his soul, had clearly possessed the courage to agree to fulfill her mother's bid to die, and others who also adored Lily had contemplated the same thing. And given time and opportunity any one of them might have gone through with it. But it felt right to Pauline that, as it turned out, the merciful gift of death had come from her, an act echoing and entwined with the wishes, intentions and burdens of all who loved Lily but ultimately powered by a daughter's fierce love and respect for her mother.

In the last two years of her life Lily's body had fallen victim to old age and her mind had begun to absent itself. The latter in particular had pitched Pauline's identity and internal world upside down, made a mockery of all she had known, had aspired to, had held as true and reliable. For if her mother, her rock, was vulnerable, weak, destructible – how could Pauline's world possibly make any sense? So when, in hospital, Lily had begged her daughter to help her die, Pauline had instinctively shaken her head with dismay as if that was the only response she could possibly give to such a selfish and weak abandonment. But by New Year's just a few days later, Pauline was to discover with detached recognition that her mind had since been moving, without conscious consent, on a quiet trajectory of its own, delivering mother and daughter towards salvation. For Pauline had come to see her mother's request for what it was: a monumental act of courage and grit in complete accordance with the way Lily had always lived life and which no illness, memory loss or passage of time could touch.

Pauline blinked the images of that morning away as she took a match from the box and struck it, letting its flare lick at the edges of the envelope, her arm outstretched into the hearth. Blue flame flared to orange as Lily's words turned to ashes. Pauline let go and watched as they fluttered down into the grate, black butterflies carrying their tragic, tender secret.

ACKNOWLEDGEMENTS

My sincere gratitude goes to:

Sarah Fitzsimmons – my daughter's sharp insights and creative talent made an incalculable contribution to the manuscript and I will be forever grateful.

Peggy Frew and Kathryn Fox, successful and busy authors who nevertheless generously gave me their time, encouragement and words of wisdom.

Andrew Lane for his advice on business and accounting practices, particularly of the past; Elisabeth Lenders who helped me understand some of the responsibilities, joys and challenges experienced by school principals; and Penny Purvis, Deborah Ballment and Jennifer Keating for sharing invaluable insights into working as a nurse in aged care.

Katia Ariel whose positive professional appraisal of an early draft lent me cautious optimism that I was on the right track to become a published author.

Literary agent Alex Adsett – thank you for representing me so expertly and cheerfully.

The entire team at HarperCollins, working like a well-oiled machine to ensure the surreal journey from pitch to publication was a seamless delight for a first-time author. In particular, I am indebted to commissioning editor Nicola Robinson for believing in me and turning a writer's dream into reality; and to Annabel Blay whose editing skills are nothing short of superb.

My family and friends for their love and unwavering support throughout this writing ride, and in particular my brother Christopher for his inspirational contribution to the book's ending.

BOOK GROUP DISCUSSION QUESTIONS

1. The title of the book, *Lily Harford's Last Request,* refers to Lily's wish to die on her own terms. Having witnessed her father suffer at the hands of dementia, she is desperate to avoid a similar fate.

   a) Was hers a fair request to ask of others?

   b) What other 'requests' of people did Lily make during her lifetime?

2. In the prologue, Lily refers to a pact.

   a) At that point did you believe Lily's wish had in fact been fulfilled?

   b) As the story unfolded, with whom did you think the pact had been made?

3. The book entwines the perspectives of Lily, Pauline and Donna. What effect does this have?

4. To which character in the book do you most relate and why?

5. Pauline is facing some commonly experienced issues for women in their mid-fifties – invisibility, job stress and fatigue, the work-life juggle as a parent and grandparent, stress over finances as retirement looms, and anxiety over an ageing parent. How do you view her various responses to these challenges?

6. What was the effect of having Lily's flashbacks in reverse chronology?

7. How would you describe Pauline and Lily's relationship?

8. Neither Donna's upbringing nor her marriage was easy, leaving her emotionally damaged. In what ways does her relationship with Lily make her a stronger person?

9. Discuss your reaction to the book's ending.

10. *Lily Harford's Last Request* is scaffolded on the heavy topic of assisted dying and there are many moments of angst and sadness in the main characters' lives. Yet there is also a lightness to the story. In what moments did you feel uplifted?

talk about it

Let's talk about books.

Join the conversation:

 facebook.com/harlequinaustralia

 @harlequinaus

 @harlequinaus

harpercollins.com.au/hq

If you love reading and want to know about our
authors and titles, then let's talk about it.